THE GHOST HORSE

THE GHOST HORSE

A Western Duo

LES SAVAGE, JR.

Five Star • Waterville, Maine

First Edition
First Printing: August 2004

Published in 2004 in conjunction with Golden West Literary Agency.

Set in 11 pt. Plantin by Ramona Watson.

Printed in the United States on permanent paper.

Library of Congress Cataloging-in-Publication Data

Savage, Les.
    [Ghost of Jean Lafitte]
    The ghost horse : a western duo / by Les Savage, Jr.—
1st ed.
       p. cm.
    Contents: The ghost of Jean Lafitte—The ghost horse.
    ISBN 1-59414-002-2 (hc : alk. paper)
    1. Western stories.   I. Savage, Les. Ghost horse.
II. Title.
PS3569.A826G47 2004
  813'.54—dc22   2004047081

THE GHOST HORSE

Table of Contents

The Ghost of Jean LaFitte 9

The Ghost Horse 85

The Ghost of Jean Lafitte

I

They wouldn't take him alive. Ernie Denvers had decided that even before the bay horse had gone down beneath him. Whatever else happened, they wouldn't take him alive. He stood there beside the dying animal, nauseated by the foul odor of rotten mud that rose from the bayou to his left, surrounded by the hollow booming of frogs from the pipe-stem canebrake at his back. So this was Texas. A helluva place. Why hadn't he chosen Wyoming, or Kansas? No. He had to pick Texas. East Texas at that.

His dust-grimed face became alert at the faint sound that rode the wind down his back trail. Them? He turned with a curse, breaking through the first canes. Who else? They had been on his tail all last night and all today. They wouldn't give up now.

Ernie Denvers might have stood five feet six, fighting his way through the clattering brake, but there was something ineffably potent about his square, compact body that precluded any appearance of smallness. A three days' beard made a blue-stubbled shadow over his adamant chin, and his eyes burned, red-rimmed and feverish, beneath the straight black line of his heavy brow. He had no chaps, and the canes scraped his dust-grayed Levi's with an incessant, maddening clatter that knotted his nerves up inside him like snubbed dally ropes. Well, why not? A man that had been

9

chased as long as he. Why not? They wouldn't get him alive, that's all. They wouldn't.

He whirled around to the sudden crash of pipe-stem canes at his side, and his reaction was automatic. The girl stood there, looking at him for a moment, and then a strange, wild smile caught at one corner of the fullest lips he had ever seen, and her eyes dropped to the big Artillery Colt in his hand. "You get it out pretty quick," she said.

Her hair was black and lustrous as the water in the bayous, hanging, thick and tangled, about the shoulders of a flannel shirt that was as old and tattered as the denim pants she wore. Her dirty Hyer boots were run over at the heels as if she did more walking than riding. She cocked her small head to the faint sound through the thicket behind them, and her black eyes flashed excitedly. "You're running from Giddings?"

"Giddings?" he said.

"Navarra was expecting you tonight," she said. "Uncle Cæsar sent me out to meet you. He thought you might have trouble with Giddings, but he didn't expect you to come this way."

"I didn't choose the way," he said warily.

"I understand." Her laugh bubbled up from inside, like there was a lot of it down there, and then she caught his arm. "I'll show you the way. We can reach the house before Giddings does. Navarra will take care of the rest."

He pulled back for a moment, but her hand on his arm was insistent, and she was already turning to brush aside the pipe stems. What was the difference? He didn't know why this was, but it looked better than what he'd been seeing. Nor could he guess how long they ran through the canes. It was all the same. Rattling pipe stems beating against his face and salt grass whipping across his legs and the booming frogs never still. She stopped abruptly, and he couldn't help being brought up against her and was surprised at the clean, sweet smell of her hair. It seemed out of place, somehow, in all the other odors of putrescent mud and decaying vegetation that rose humidly from the bayou they had reached. She took his hand again and led him across the shaky bank through a grove of gnarled cypress trees, festooned with streamers of Spanish moss that slapped wetly across his shoulders. Then the first of the breeze struck him, carrying the faint tang of salt air, and in a few more moments he was surprised to find the mud turning to sand beneath his feet. Had he been that near the coast?

"Dagger Point," said the girl, gesturing toward the row of breakers gleaming dully from the darkness ahead. "It's neap tide now, and we can wade across to Matagorda Island. Take off your boots."

Shrugging, he slipped off dirty Justins, rolled up his Levi's on lean, hairy calves. Again he had no measure of time or distance. The water was never more than knee high, except for the rollers that foamed up over his waist. But he jumped these, and farther out they ceased, and he was wading through quiet water. When the breakers began again, they were going the other way, and finally Denvers and the girl were standing on the wet sand of that shore. She led him over dunes bearded with thick sea grass, and then through the higher bunch grass of the coastal prairie, and finally he saw the house, surrounded by a brooding cypress grove. It was old Colonial, with the tall columns along its front porch peeling white paint that must have been put on thirty years before. Its shuttered windows stared blankly from warped weather boarding, and the porch floor popped dismally to their boots, and the huge, oaken front door swung in on creaking hinges to a dim, musty reception hall.

Denvers wiped sweating hands across his Levi's. All right. She took him into what he thought was the parlor, high-ceilinged and heavily carpeted, filled with the same nameless sense of belonging to the past. There was a pair of Chippendale sofas facing each other in front of the fireplace, the harateen covering on their camel backs frayed and shiny, the *cabriolé* legs bearing scars that looked as if they might have come from spurs. The man stood beside a Pembroke table to one side of the hearth. The first thing Denvers saw was the thick streak of white through his jet black hair, then his face, heavy-boned and heavily fleshed with an indefinable dissolution. The thick lids of his eyes were turned a shadowed blue by the network of tiny veins patterning them and only added to the leashed violence slumbering in the eyes themselves. His shoulders filled out the tailored cut of his long, black coat well enough, and Denvers couldn't see where he packed any gun. The spurs on his polished cavalry boots made a small tinkling sound as he shifted away from the table.

"He was way south of Dagger Point, Navarra," said the girl. "I heard him in the canes. Giddings was right behind him."

So this was Navarra, thought Denvers, and watched the man come forward, wondering how such a heavy *hombre* could move with such apparent ease. Navarra bent slightly to peer at Denvers, and for a moment Denvers saw the anger rise in his eyes, enlarging the black pupils, and then the heavy, bluish lids narrowed like a veil and whatever the man felt was hidden.

"This isn't Prieto," Navarra told the girl, and his voice held the same slumberous violence as his eyes. "What's the idea, Esther?"

The girl's small hand rose in a confused gesture. "You said he'd be there and might have trouble with Giddings. What else . . . ?"

Navarra turned to Denvers impatiently. "You have a name, I suppose?"

"Denvers," said Ernie.

"You want me to keel him, Sinton?" Denvers hadn't heard the Mexican enter the room. He was barefooted, standing over by a serpentine chest of drawers. He had a pair of longhorn *mustachios* that flapped against a dirty white shirt, and his eyes glittered like a sidewinder's from beneath a huge straw sombrero. "I got my gets-the-guts all sharpened up." He grinned evilly, running his brown finger down the blade of a *saca de tripas* he held. "Nobody hears me keel 'im. Nobody knows."

"Shut up, Carnicero," said Sinton Navarra, and then his head rose to the sound of snorting horses outside, and Denvers's move toward the door was automatic because he knew who had come.

"No, *señor,*" said Carnicero, moving in front of him with the knife. "I think you better stay, eh?"

"Out of my way," said Denvers.

"He can pull a gun pretty fast," said the girl.

"I can stick him before he gets it out." Carnicero grinned.

"Go and let them in, Esther," Navarra told the girl.

Denvers heard her move behind him and took a jump to one side, hauling at his big Artillery Colt. The Mexican threw himself at Denvers, heavy body hitting him before Denvers had his gun out.

"Carnicero!" shouted Navarra.

Denvers had to let go his gun, jerking up both hands to grab the Mexican's knife arm as it came down. With one hand on Carnicero's wrist and the other at his elbow, Denvers straightened the arm, using it as a lever to heave the Mexican backward against the wall.

"I have a gun pointed at your back, Mister Denvers." Navarra's heavy voice stopped Ernie Denvers. "If you will, forget whatever ideas you have about your own gun, and back carefully toward the chair on the right-hand side of the fireplace, and sit down?"

The girl slipped out to the reception hall, and Denvers could hear the front door creak open as he backed stiffly toward the wing chair, squatting, dirty and tattered, in the shadows beyond the pair of couches. He knew the surprise must have shown on his face when he saw the gun Navarra held.

"A singular weapon, is it not?" Navarra smiled sardonically. "French, Mister Denvers. A Le Page pin-fire, seven millimeters, twenty shots. A man is a veritable arsenal with one of these. Don't you think it's ingenious? The cylinder, as you see, has two rows of chambers, one set within the other, each row containing ten chambers. The inner set fires through the lower barrel, the outer set through the upper, and. . . ."

He stopped talking with a sudden, enigmatic smile and slipped the gun beneath his coat up by the shoulder. Denvers stiffened in the chair, not knowing whether he meant to rise or what, and then let his weight back down because he saw the futility of that. Sheriff Giddings must have stood six feet four, and he came into the room with an arrogant swagger that pushed his heavy belly against his crossed gun belts and that caused the batwings on his *chaparejos* to flap with a soft, leathery sound every time he took a step. The red strings of a Bull Durham sack dangled across the dirty star pinned on his buckskin ducking jacket.

14

"Good evening, Sheriff," said Navarra easily.

"Not so good, Navarra," said Giddings, stopping in the middle of the rug and hooking hammy thumbs into his gun belts to stand there, swaybacked and self-conscious, as he swept the room with eyes that were meant to be hard. They settled on Denvers, and then met Denvers's glance. It was the sheriff's patent intent to force Denvers to drop his gaze, but Denvers stared, wide-eyed and waiting, at Giddings's pale blue eyes, and finally Giddings's own gaze shifted uncertainly, and, clearing his throat with a hoarse, blustering sound, he looked jerkily toward Navarra. "No. As I say, not a very good evening. Jale Hardwycke was murdered last night."

"Oh." Sinton Navarra's velvety tone rose at the end of the word, and he pursed sensuous lips. "Too bad. What brings you here?"

"We caught the killers red-handed last night on the old Karankawa Trail out of Refugio. Couple of saddle bums. Starting them back toward town when they put up a ruckus. We killed one. The other got away. Trailed him as far as Indian Bog. I'm not going back without him, Navarra."

"Very commendable," said Navarra. "I still don't see how we figure in it."

The sheriff's two deputies shifted uneasily in the doorway. One of them was short and squatty as a razorback hog, his cartridge belt shoved down by a beer-keg belly, his wool shirt covered with mud and horse droppings and other filth. Denvers's hands tightened slowly on the chair arms. He even knew that deputy's name. Ollie Minster. He was the one who had killed Bud Richie. Remembering that moment brought back Denvers's rage so strongly that it blotted out the whole room like a roaring, black curtain sweeping across his vision, and he could hear his own breathing grow

15

heavy and harsh in the sudden, strained silence.

"You got a new man, haven't you?" said Giddings, looking at Denvers.

"So Hardwycke was killed," said Navarra, and his slumberous eyes passed across Denvers, and then he was watching Giddings. "Wart hogs go rooting around the outside of a bush, Sheriff, after their feed, when they could go straight in and save a lot of time."

Giddings flushed. "I ain't beating around any bushes. I'll have that man in the wing chair, Navarra."

"I'm glad you came to the point, Sheriff," said the other. "What makes you think this man is your murderer? You say you found them last night? It was singularly dark, as I remember, without a moon. Could you positively identify him?"

"I'd know the jaspers anywhere," growled Giddings. "Two of 'em. Acted all right at first. Even gave us names. Ernie Denvers and Bud Richie. Then, when we started figuring them in the murder, they got cagey."

"Names don't mean much," said Navarra. "Faces?"

Giddings jerked his head from side to side in a vague, evasive way, finally shrugging his arrogant shoulders. "Like you say, it was dark. Scuffling around and such, I didn't get much look at their faces. But this is him, I tell you. Denvers. Same height, same build."

Navarra's smile was sardonic. "Esther's about the same height as our friend in the chair."

"This *hombre* wasn't Texan," said Giddings. "He didn't talk Texas, and he didn't dress Texas. No leather leggings, no ducking jacket. His hat was flat-topped, and his pants was denim. . . ."

"Esther wears denims," said Navarra.

Giddings bent forward sharply. "You trying to say that Esther . . . ?"

"Don't be obtuse." The contempt gave Navarra's words a hissing intonation. "How could Esther have been there? I'm only trying to point out that you aren't really sure of anything concerning this man Denvers. It could have been Esther, from all the descriptions you give, or a hundred other men in the vicinity. I don't talk Texas. Everybody in this state doesn't wear a center-creased Stetson and leather leggin's. You could find a dozen men tonight that look like this man in the dark. In fact, Jale Hardwycke and I are about the same height and build. Could you have told us apart last night? How do you know it was Hardwycke who was killed?"

"Don't be a fool!" shouted Giddings apoplectically. "I know Jale Hardwycke when I see him. He'd been to Refugio and taken twelve hundred dollars cash out of the bank. We found his wallet with the money in it on this Bud Richie."

Denvers caught the sudden flicker of Navarra's eyes before his thick, bluish lids closed across whatever had been there. "Oh, the wallet. You have it now, then."

Giddings jerked his head from side to side, then blustered: "No, dammit. I found Hardwycke's wallet on this Bud Richie and put it in my saddlebags as evidence. Then the ruckus started, and Richie got in the way of Ollie's bullet, and the Denvers jasper got away on my horse. Now, don't try to block me, Navarra. I'm taking this man."

"Did you see your horse outside?" said Navarra.

Giddings's voice was rising. "I said don't try to block me. I know you ain't fool enough to leave the animal showing. This is the only place he could have come."

"You're throwing your rope on the wrong steer, Giddings," said Navarra, moving in front of Denvers. "This man's been here since Tuesday."

"Has he?" said Giddings. "We'll find out soon enough.

He'll have Hardwycke's wallet. I'm searching him."

"He's my guest, Sheriff," said Navarra, and his voice was velvety. "I wouldn't allow you to search him any more than I'd allow you to search me."

Blood flooded up Giddings's thick neck. "You and Cæsar Sheridan think you're safe from the law, hiding out here on Matagorda Island, but you're under my jurisdiction just as much as any man in Refugio."

"Am I?" said Navarra sardonically. "I'm surprised you even came this far, Sheriff. The last lawman to reach Indian Bog was found dead. I'd be more careful if I were you."

"I'll get you for that one, too, Navarra."

"Do you think I perpetrate every crime that happens within a hundred miles of Matagorda?" asked Navarra. "These things were going on a long time before I came, Giddings, and will continue long after I'm gone. I think I'm the least worry you have when you're around Indian Bog, and I think you know that. Do you think you could get back across the channel with this man? Do you think you can get back alone?"

"Damn you, Navarra!" Giddings almost screamed it and took one lurching step toward Navarra with his hands held out. Then he stopped. A small vein had begun to pulse faintly across Navarra's temple, and Denvers could see his eyes. They were like the eyes of an enraged cat. The pupils were dilated until they showed, black and feline, between the heavy, blue-shadowed lids, flickering with an odd, ebullient light. Giddings stood there on his tiptoes, looking into those eyes, and his lower lip sagged slightly, and he began to pull his hands back toward himself in a strange, dazed way.

"I keel 'im, Sinton?" said Carnicero.

"I'm glad you didn't touch me, Giddings," said Navarra,

running a pale, veined hand over that white streak through his hair. "Don't ever touch me. Don't ever lay your hands on me. It would be most unfortunate for you. Now, I'll ask you to go. You can't take this man from my house without a warrant. You can't even enter my house without a warrant, as a matter of fact."

Giddings's breathing had the driven, grating sound of a blown horse. He stood there for another instant, staring at Navarra. Finally he spoke, and his voice shook with his frustrated anger. "I'm coming back, Navarra. I'm coming back with enough warrants to send you and this whole household to hell! You've thrown your last dally on Matagorda!"

He whirled and stamped, swaybacked, out of the room, shaking the floor with each step, shoving his deputies ahead of him with a hoarse curse. His spurs clattered down the hall, the door slammed hard, and the squeak of saddle leather came faintly through the heavy red velvet curtaining the front windows.

Denvers was on his feet by then. "Why protect me like that?"

"Perhaps because of a singular dislike for our Sheriff Giddings," said Navarra, a soft ebullition in his smile. He held out his hand, a huge jade ring glinting on one finger. "And now, Denvers, the wallet. . . ."

The man coming through the door stopped him, voice filling the room like the roar of a rutting bull. "I saw Sheriff Giddings leaving, Navarra. Did he try to cause your man any trouble?"

"Prieto didn't come yet, Cæsar," said Navarra.

The other glanced at Denvers. "Who's this, then?"

"I was waiting on the mainland for Prieto, like you told me, Uncle Cæsar," said the girl. "I guess I brought the wrong one."

19

"Yes," said Navarra ironically. "Mister Denvers, would you meet Cæsar Sheridan, Esther's uncle, the owner of this . . . ah . . . house, the ruler of Matagorda Island, the king of. . . ."

"Tie up your duffel, tie up your duffel," said Cæsar Sheridan, waving one beefy hand disgustedly. He was a short man with enormously broad shoulders and a huge belly. His broad black belt pulled in tightly till a roll of fat slopped over it beneath his red wool shirt. He moved on into the room with short, quick steps, putting his boots down as if he wanted to poke their spiked heels through the floor. His face was puffy and discolored, purplish jowls patterned by a network of veins, eyes bloodshot and bleary above their dark bags. His lusty, violent approach to life was in every movement, and his thick lips curled back off broken teeth when he spoke, jerking his close-cropped head toward Navarra. "What was Giddings here for, then?"

Navarra's slumberous eyes slid to Denvers. "Giddings was hunting the murderer of Jale Hardwycke."

Cæsar Sheridan looked at Denvers. "You kill Hardwycke?"

Denvers moved a hand helplessly. "I. . . ."

"Giddings must have been pretty sure to come this far," insinuated Navarra.

Sheridan threw back his scarred head and let out a laugh that made the crystal chandeliers tinkle above their heads. "Good for you, Denvers, good for you. I always hated that Hardwycke's guts. He thought all the land in Texas belonged to him just because he dealt in real estate. Always claiming we had no legal title to Matagorda. You must be pretty good with a gun if you got him. Or did you do it dry-gulch style? Never mind, never mind. I don't care how you did it. Any man who finished

Hardwycke's beans is good enough for me."

"It would be dangerous for him to go back to the mainland now," said Navarra softly.

"Dangerous?" roared Cæsar Sheridan. "Hell, it would be suicide. Hardwycke was a big man on the coast. I'll bet they've got a dozen posses out, combing the Gulf. How about signing on here, Denvers? I need a man with a gun like that."

Denvers looked toward Navarra. "You were saying something about the wallet?"

"Wallet?" said Navarra. "What wallet?"

II

The sand of Dagger Point shifted restlessly under a mournful wind sweeping in off the Gulf of Mexico, and somewhere above the hoary crest of a grassed-over dune a sea fowl squawked plaintively at the night. Denvers had a time getting his paint mare into the first foamy breakers piling up on the shore, but finally she was splashing knee deep after Cæsar Sheridan's fat bay. Carnicero shoved up beside Denvers on a shaggy old mule, forking a ratty Mexican-tree saddle.

"Why did Navarra start to ask me about the wallet last night?" said Denvers.

"How do I know?" said Carnicero. "You better not ask too many questions. You better be glad Sheridan let you stay on Matagorda."

"Who is Sheridan?" said Denvers. "He owns that house on the island? It was when he came in that Navarra seemed to forget about the wallet. He passed it off like it didn't matter. Did it?"

"You keep prying and I keel you."

"That seems to be your only pastime," said Denvers. "Carnicero means butcher, doesn't it?"

"Why else should they name me that?" said the Mexican. "It is my life. I was born with a *saca de tripas* in my hand. They pinned my swaddling clothes together with stilettos. I ate my *frijoles* with a Bowie knife from the time I was strong enough to lift it. When they gave me my first machete, I was so happy I went right out and killed my grandmother. You should see what I can do with a blade, *señor*. I could cut your ear off so deftly you wouldn't know it was gone till your hat began to slip down on that side of your head. Colonel James Bowie himself could not slice a man into as many strips with one knife as I. . . ."

"Will you stop that gab," said Cæsar Sheridan angrily. He halted his bay in the shallows breaking on the mainland shore, turning to Denvers. "Neap tide's in the channel now. About this time of year it lasts from midnight till dawn, and a man can wade across on foot at the shallow spots like Dagger Point. You saw how it was. Water didn't get above your stirrups. If you get separated from us on the mainland, just be sure you get back here before daylight. Miss neap tide and you're stuck on the mainland most of the day. Nobody can swim that channel when the water's in. There's a riptide that'll pull the strongest swimmer under. I've never seen a horse that could make it." He paused, looking ahead. "I guess this is Prieto."

The dim shadow emerged from the gloom shrouding the desolate beach, resolving itself into a horsebacker. As he drew closer, the faded denim ducking jacket became visible, hanging slackly from the stooped shoulders of a tall man, and the *conchas* winked dully from the batwings of old bullhide chaps. Prieto had come in the night before, angry at not having been met on the mainland, and his voice was still acrimonious as he spoke. "Bunch of coasters grazing about two miles inland. Your man, Judah, made sure Sheriff Giddings was in Refugio."

Prieto fell in beside Sheridan, giving Denvers a close glance. Denvers caught a glimpse of the gaunt, acrid face with its bitter eyes and tight mouth. Denvers had gotten the impression last night that Prieto was new to Matagorda, and that he belonged to Navarra more than to Sheridan. Denvers wondered why Prieto should be over here tonight. Navarra wasn't.

They lined out of the water to cross the pale sand, and soon the salt grass was swishing at Denvers's *tapaderos*. Post oaks began to loom up out of the night, and they forded a bayou with the rotten mud sucking at the horses' fetlocks and the croaking of bullfrogs all around them. They were riding through a veritable swamp now, the rising moon casting a ghoulish light down through the moss-festooned trees. A bull alligator bellowed somewhere out in the pipe-stem cane, and Denvers slapped continually at the mosquitoes that fogged the air around him. They finally reached a solid bit of ground where a giant mulatto was holding a train of Mexican rat mules.

"They still watering, Judah?" asked Prieto.

The mulatto nodded a bullet head set on a neck like a bull's, and the thick muscles across his bare chest caught the light wetly as he hitched at his white cotton pants. Sheridan slipped a Sharps carbine from his saddle boot, turning to Denvers.

"There's a bunch of coasters grazing and watering in that cypress grove farther on. We're downwind of them. We'll be able to get right close before they spot us. Drop as many as you can before they get out of the trees."

"*Drop* as many?" queried Denvers. "What kind of roundup is this?"

"It's the way we work," said Sheridan. "Any complaints?"

Denvers shrugged, loosing his big Artillery Colt in its worn holster. Sheridan booted his bay, leaning forward in the saddle, and worked through the cypresses. Following him with the others, Denvers finally made out the first coaster grazing in the tall salt grass, a big brindle steer with withers as sharp as a Barlow knife and horns that gleamed like scimitars. The others were farther on, wallowing in the bayou that ran through the cypresses, feeding in the knee-high grass. Suddenly the brindle raised its head, turning toward the men.

"Let's go!" whooped Cæsar Sheridan and flopped his *tapaderos* out wide to bring them back in against the bay with a solid, fleshy thump. The horse shot out of the trees, and Sheridan's rifle was already bellowing. The brindle let out a scream of mortal pain, whirling to stumble a few steps away from Sheridan, then sinking down into the muck. Denvers charged through the salt grass after Judah and Prieto, throwing down on the first beef he neared, a big, speckled heifer that got tangled up in the Spanish moss of a cypress when it tried to run. Denvers put two .44 slugs into it before the beast went down, and then pulled up his paint and charged after another cow, guns thundering all around him, men bellowing as loudly as the cattle. Carnicero was on Denvers's flank, quartering into a big dun steer with a lobo stripe down its back. He got within ten feet of the animal, an ancient Navy pistol held above his head to throw down.

"Shoot dat steer!" roared Judah, emptying a pair of six-shooters in wild volleys at the cattle, laughing uproariously every time a beef squalled and went down. "What's the matter with you, Butcher? Waiting foah him to come up and take the gun away from you? Shoot dat steer!"

But Carnicero galloped on past the dun without firing, shouting something over his shoulder, and whirled to chase after a big black farther on. Denvers's paint stumbled in the muck, and the Spanish moss tore him backwards in the saddle. Struggling in the festoons of wet, green growth, he whirled his paint out from among the cypresses, breaking into the open with streamers of moss flung out behind him like dripping pennons. Suddenly Carnicero's mule stumbled and went down, and the Mexican went over his head, landing, sprawled, in the muck farther on. Judah came charging from the cypresses at one side, splashing into the bayou after a huge steer with blood streaming down its black hide. The giant mulatto had emptied his guns at it, but the beast was still going headlong. It tried to gain the trees again, bellowing frenziedly, but Judah quartered it, once more forcing the steer out into the shallow bayou. Squealing in rage and pain, it floundered straight toward Carnicero.

The Mexican got to his knees, mud dripping off his white pants, and brought up his old Navy. He drew a bead on the charging steer. Denvers thought all sound had stopped as he waited for the explosion of the Navy. Then he saw the strange fear cross Carnicero's face.

"I can't!" he shouted in a cracked voice. "I can't shoot. Judah, get that crazy *cimarrón* before he runs me down."

"What's the matter?" roared Judah. "I can't get him. My guns are empty. Shoot him, you damn' fool!"

The beast had gained momentum now and was bearing down on Carnicero, mud and water showering up back of its churning legs. Denvers spurred his paint into a floundering run through the bayou, slipping off solid land into the rotten muck with a loud, popping sound, viscid mud shooting up into his face. He threw down on the steer, and the Colt jumped in his hand with a hollow click. Empty!

Carnicero was stumbling backward, knee deep in the muddy water, shouting in terror. Denvers dropped his empty Artillery into its holster and tore the lashing off his dally, turning his horse so he would run in between Carnicero and the steer. But there were only a few feet left, and Denvers was about as far away from the two of them as the steer was from Carnicero. He knew he would never be able to cut in front of the steer before it reached the Mexican. He was close enough to see the terror in Carnicero's face. The steer loomed above the man, huge and black. Denvers had his loop swinging, and he leaned forward as he tossed. While the rope was still in the air, he jerked viciously to one side on the reins, thrusting his weight that way as the paint whirled, and, when the loop settled about those great horns, the horse was going full speed in the opposite direction from the steer. Denvers snubbed his rawhide dally on the slick horn, and the violent impact almost pulled his chunky paint off her feet, cinches cracking loudly with the strain, saddle jumping beneath Denvers.

He heard the steer let out a tremendous, raucous bawl, and then he was off the paint, leaving it to stand there with forehoofs braced to keep the rope taut on the steer. At least they bred ropers in this god-forsaken swampland. The beef was on its back in the bayou, hoofs flailing, great horns sending up spouts of foul mud as it tossed its head wildly from side to side. Denvers stumbled toward the huge beef through the muck, jacking empties from his Artillery and thumbing in fresh ones. He waited till the tossing head was turned his way, and, as the steer lurched to get on its feet, he put a bullet between its bloodshot eyes. The beast suddenly stopped thrashing, and the rope went slack, and the tremendous black body sank back into the mud. Only then did Denvers see how closely Carnicero was standing to the carcass. The Mexican hadn't moved from where he had been when the rope snubbed the steer, and he could have reached out and touched the animal's wicked, curving horn. Carnicero opened his mouth, letting out a shaky laugh, lips working around his words for a moment before he could make any sound. Finally he swallowed, stuttering.

"*Barba del diablo,* if that *ladino* had come one more foot, I would have been hanging on those horns instead of your rope. Where did you learn to swing a dally like that, Denvers?" The blood had come back into his dark face by now, and the grin faded, and he began to pout like a sullen child. "*Pues,* just because you save my life, don't think I won't keel you the first chance I get."

Denvers laughed. "Why didn't you shoot that steer when you had the chance? It was point-blank. You couldn't have missed."

Carnicero's eyes lowered uncomfortably, and he wiped his nose, sniffling. "*Dios. Sacramento.* I got my powder wet in the mud, that's all. What else? I got my powder wet. *Sí.*"

Denvers took the Navy from his lax hand, spun the cylinder, then looked up at Carnicero, frowning. "What do you mean you got your powder wet? It didn't even touch the bog. This whole gun's as dry as the top of my hat."

III

They had hauled the carcasses up onto dry land, and Judah dismounted after the last beef had been dragged in. Taking a long skinning knife from his belt, he started to slice a beef's hide down to its leg.

"You going to jerk the meat right here?" said Denvers.

"Jerk the meat?" Judah laughed. "Jerk the meat, he says. Denvers, that meat ain't worth curing even. It's the hides. I guess you ain't been working this part of the country, eh? Two and a half cents a pound for beef in Kansas City. For what it costs to drive cows up there, you could make more profit on dirt. Cows ain't worth raising for their beef any more. Hides and tallow is all we take now. Where you come from, anyhow?"

"New Mexico," said Denvers.

"No wonder you don't know," said Judah. "You're right in the middle of the Skinning War, boy. Ain't you heard? A man in Refugio says that last year Texas shipped out three million dollars' worth of hides. How many hides is that, Butcher?"

"More than you'll ever be able to count," muttered Carnicero. "That ain't all. My cousin, he can read, and he saw in the *Galveston News* that a hundred million pounds of tallow was shipped out in Eighteen Seventy-Four. They don't have branding season any more in Texas. It's skinning season. Hides-and-tallow 'punchers we are now. Not cowpunchers."

"Quit blowing your air and get to work with that skinning blade, Butcher," said Cæsar Sheridan.

"I tell you what," said Carnicero. "I'll haul them in, and you skin them."

"We've hauled them all in," growled Sheridan.

"There might be some we missed out there in the bayou."

"You get to work, dammit!" roared Sheridan.

"I hate to stain the blade of my knife with a cow's blood," pouted Carnicero.

"Maybe you never stained your blade with any blood." Prieto laughed.

"And maybe I keel you."

"Start skinning those hides!" shouted Sheridan, rising up from a carcass with his beefy hands dripping blood and tripe. "Or do you want me to take your hide across the bay with the cows'?"

Mumbling incoherently, Carnicero moved toward the black steer Denvers had thrown. He took out his gets-the-guts, regarding the long, slim blade with a mournful expression, then looked down at the steer. Denvers saw that his dark cheeks were wet.

"What's the matter with you?" yelled Sheridan.

"I can't," choked Carnicero, and then began to cry like a baby. "*Madre de Dios,* I can't bear to think of cutting up this *pobrecito.* Such a pretty *bulto* he was, all black and young and strong. How would you like it if someone came along and shot you and took off your pretty *negro* hide? He never did anything to you. He never did anything to me. And now you want me to desecrate such a beautiful, wild creature by cutting him up."

Cæsar Sheridan threw back his scarred, close-cropped head and sent the Spanish moss to fluttering with that thunderous laugh. Then he moved over to Carnicero in his quick, catty way, and shoved the Mexican toward the horse. "Go on, you old fool, haul them in if you like. I'll bet you never used that knife for anything more than eating *frijoles* with. 'Keel 'im'? You make me laugh. What happens when you come to using the knife on a man?"

"Oh, men are different," said Carnicero, his tears giving way to laughter with a sudden, child-like naïveté. "*Si,* I slit their throats like this"—he drew his *saca de tripas* across his neck, chuckling—"I cut out their entrails with my gets-the-guts like this. I. . . . ." He stopped with his *saca de tripas* pressed against his belly, and he was staring past Sheridan at something in the trees. Denvers followed the Mexican's glance. All he caught was a shadowy motion through the cypresses, but Carnicero's voice was shaking with terror. *"Madre de Dios. ¡Espiritu de Lafitte!"*

Sheridan whirled to look. "Lafitte's ghost? Where?"

Cringing, the Mexican raised a shaking hand to point toward the trees. "You saw him. Right there, Cæsar. Cocked hat and satin knee pants and gold buttons and all. You saw him. Cross yourselves, *compadres*. You are cursed unless you do. You will die like Arno Sheridan."

Cæsar Sheridan grabbed Carnicero by the arm, jerking him toward the trees. "No ghost killed my brother. You're showing me this thing, once and for all. I'm tired of hearing these stories. Whatever put that sword through my brother was human, and I'm proving it. Did you see, Judah?"

The mulatto was bent forward, whites of his eyes gleaming from his black face, lower lip slack and wet. "Lawd, Cæsar, I saw somethin'. Don't go in there."

Still hauling Carnicero toward the trees, Cæsar bent to scoop up his Sharps with a free hand. "There isn't any ghost, I tell you. If you saw something, it's human, and I'm getting it this time or my name isn't Cæsar Sheridan. Come on, you puking dogie, show me."

"No. *Dios*, no!" Carnicero tried to pull back. "You can't catch a ghost, Cæsar. I saw it. Cocked hat and satin knee pants and . . . !"

Cæsar hauled him over the hummock of ground between the two cypresses, and they dropped into the lowland beyond, disappearing in the grove. Denvers started to follow, but Prieto caught his arm. "Never mind. It won't do any good."

"Yeah," muttered Judah thickly. "How can you catch a ghost?"

"What are you talking about?" said Denvers. "This ghost."

"Lafitte's ghost," said Judah, looking over his shoulder. "You know, Jean Lafitte, the pirate? Who do you think built that house on Matagorda Island? It's where his mulatto mistress killed him. As long as there's a woman in that house, Lafitte's spirit is doomed to roam this coast. I've seen him before, over on the island. He'll kill us all, sooner or later, Denvers. You're crazy to stay on Matagorda. I'm crazy. I don't think I'll go back."

He whirled toward the cypresses, but it was only Carnicero, white pants dripping mud up to the knees as he came back through the trees. "Cæsar caught sight of it again, and he was after it like a bull with a fly in his nose. I thought I'd come back."

"That was good work," said Prieto.

"But I really see the *espiritu*," said Carnicero huskily. "Right there between the trees. Lafitte's . . . !"

"I know, I know." Prieto waved a sinewy hand. "It was a good job. It got Sheridan away neat as a white Stetson."

"But I really saw the ghost!"

"Shut up," said Prieto. "We aren't talking about Lafitte's ghost. Sheridan's gone now, and we aren't talking about Lafitte's ghost."

A sudden grin flashed Judah's white teeth across his black face, and the thick muscles over his bare chest rippled as he flexed his arms, stepping toward Denvers. "That's right, Prieto. We better get it done before Cæsar gets back."

Denvers noticed for the first time how the top of Prieto's holster was patterned with a myriad of faint scars that might have come from the man's fingernails raking the leather over and over again, and he suddenly understood that Prieto hadn't come with them tonight for the cows. For this? For what? With that same childish shift of emotion, the fear had left Carnicero now, and he was grinning at Denvers, caressing his *saca de tripas*. All of them, then. Denvers felt his throat close on his breath and sweat broke out on his forehead. "Get what done?"

"Hardwycke's wallet," said Prieto. His holster made a soft, leathery sound against his bullhide chaps as he took a step toward Denvers, and the thin line of his mouth was as acrid and bitter as his voice. "We want it, Denvers."

"Seems a lot of folks want that wallet," said Denvers, trying to watch them all at once. "What's in it, Prieto? Twelve hundred dollars couldn't be so interesting. Something more?"

The salt grass swished eerily beneath Judah's advancing bare feet. "You don't need to worry what's in it, Denvers. You givin' it to us or we takin' it?"

Denvers understood fully now how it was, and he felt the spasmodic twitch of his hand curling above his gun. Three of them? He didn't think so. One, maybe, or even two, but not three. Not coming in from every side this way. Even if a man could pull his gun fast enough.

"I guess we're taking it," said Prieto.

The grass was wet beneath Denvers's feet, and a sudden shift of wind swept a streamer of Spanish moss between him and Prieto, and then swept it out again. Their faces were turned ghastly by the moon, leering at him as each of them continued to move in, the lines of their bodies growing tense.

"Good." Judah chuckled. "Better this way, anyhow."

From the corner of his eyes Denvers caught the ripple of Judah's heavy black chest. *All right, damn you.* Carnicero was easing his knife down, and Denvers had seen that kind of thrust before, used by all *saca-de-tripas* men to rip a man's guts out. *All right.*

"I keel 'im?"

"You'll kill nobody!" shouted Cæsar Sheridan, plunging up out of the bayou on the other side, slapping the mud from his leggings with the barrel of his Sharps. "What's going on here?"

Prieto turned with a palpable spasm, forcing a weak smile. "Nothing, Cæsar, nothing. Get him?"

"What do you think?" said Cæsar disgustedly. He looked narrowly from Prieto to Denvers, and then the others. "Why didn't you come?"

"Nobody could catch a ghost," said Carnicero sullenly.

"Ghost?" Cæsar Sheridan looked out into the somber depths of the cypress grove, shot through with pale, eerie moonlight. Somewhere a cat screamed, like a woman in mortal pain. Cæsar moved his enormous shoulders, as if shrugging off something. "Let's get back to the skinning."

Denvers stood there a long moment, watching Prieto walk stiffly toward his horse, seeing Judah turn toward a carcass with a tight frustration in the twist of his lips. Finally Denvers moved over to a dead steer, surprised to find himself trembling. Reaction? He shrugged. He didn't know. He did know it hadn't been finished here tonight. At least he'd be expecting it next time. He had started to bend over the beef, but he stopped. "Pothook," he said.

Cæsar was stripping off a hide. "Eh?"

"I said this steer carries a Pothook brand," said Denvers. "Esther told me what few steers you run on the island are marked with a Double S."

Cæsar Sheridan's scarred, bullet head turned up. "So?"

"You got a bill of sale?"

Cæsar straightened slowly, his long, thick arms hanging slightly forward from his squat, potbellied torso like a gorilla's. "And if I don't?"

"I might have known as much," said Denvers. "No wonder you made sure Sheriff Giddings was in Refugio tonight. I guess the bottom has really dropped out of the cattle business down here when a man rustles cows for their hides."

A slow grin spread Cæsar's thick lips over his broken teeth. "You got your piggin' string on the right steer, Denvers. Now, get to work."

"I never took a cow that wasn't mine," said Denvers. "Even for the skin."

"You'd kill a man for a wallet that wasn't yours," said Cæsar. "I think you'd better reconsider the cows."

"No," said Denvers. "I don't think I will."

Cæsar Sheridan moved up to Denvers in that quick, catty way and stood there with his huge belly lopping over his tight belt. "You aren't in any position to be choosy, Denvers. The only reason you're safe, coming this far onto the mainland, is because we're with you and because we made sure Giddings and his posses weren't around this section of the coast. Try it alone and you'd run into those posses before your horse had time to dry the sea water off it. Or maybe you'd prefer a lynch rope."

"I'll take my chances," said Denvers, and turned toward the paint.

He was yanked back around by Sheridan's bloody hand on his collar and pulled violently up against Sheridan's gross body, with the stink of blood and sweat and leather almost overpowering him. "Nobody's taking chances, Denvers, least of all me. If Giddings's posses caught you, you'd talk about tonight. I'm not having that. The only

34

reason Giddings can't come on Matagorda with warrants for us is that he doesn't have anything to issue warrants for. The minute he gets positive proof of anything, that channel won't be any more protection to us than a mud fence after a big rain. And I'm not sending him that proof in the person of any witness tonight."

"Sheridan," said Denvers, "I'm leaving. Either you take your hand off me, or I'll take it off for you."

Denvers saw the slow flush creep into the man's sensual face, and for a moment the hand holding his collar trembled. Then Cæsar Sheridan's lips drew back in that ugly grin. He threw back his close-cropped head and laughed. "You're not going anywhere!" he roared. "And if you want to try it. . . ." His voice choked off in a gasp as Denvers's fist sank into his belly up to the wrist. Sheridan bent over spasmodically, and Denvers brought the same fist on up, smashing it into the hand holding his collar. With Sheridan's hand knocked away, Denvers swung his whole body into another blow at the man's gross belly. He felt his knuckles sink into the soft flesh until he thought they had gone through Sheridan. Cæsar staggered backward, his face dead white and twisted in a strange surprise, as if he hadn't believed a man Denvers's size could hit like that.

"I keel 'im!" screamed Carnicero, and they were all in on him, shouting and yelling, Judah bringing his knee up against him and knocking him back into the salt grass. For a moment Denvers went to his knees beneath the weight of their bodies, fighting blindly, head rocking to someone's boot smashing his mouth. Then Cæsar Sheridan came in from somewhere, roaring like a bull, tearing Judah off with an open hand and sending him backward in a spin that crashed him into a cypress, rolling Prieto aside with a backward swipe across the face. "This is mine!" roared

Sheridan, grabbing Denvers by the collar again and yanking him onto his feet. "This is mine!"

Denvers ducked the man's first blow without having seen it coming, felt Sheridan's arm go past his head, and slugged for that belly. He heard Sheridan gasp and tried to tear free of the man, but this time Sheridan had him. He threw his ponderous weight to one side, blocking Denvers's next fist, and Denvers was taken off balance. They both rolled into the salt grass, boots spewing viscid, black mud. Sheridan got on top of Denvers's back and jammed his face in the mud, riding him like a bronco, slugging the back of his neck. Face driven deeper into the muck with each blow, Denvers tried to take a gasping breath and choked on the mud. He writhed over on his back, mud blinding him, reaching up to catch Sheridan's fist as it came down.

Gripping the fist in both hands, he rolled again, carrying Sheridan off him, and then he was on top. Sheridan grabbed him in a bear hug, and for the first time Denvers felt the incredible, driving strength of the man. He was pulled against Sheridan's gross body, unable to hit him, ribs cracking and popping under the inexorable pressure of Sheridan's massive arms. Somehow Denvers got his forearm in between Sheridan and himself, forcing it up until his hand was across Sheridan's face with the heel against the man's nose. Gasping weakly, he shoved upward, forcing Sheridan's head back. Sheridan made a desperate, strangled sound, rocking his scarred head from side to side in an effort to free himself, but Denvers kept his hand jammed against the man's nose, and, finally, shouting in agony, Sheridan had to release his hug in order to tear himself away.

Denvers leaped up, the cypresses spinning around him, Prieto and Judah dim, unreal figures that seemed to sway toward him, bent forward with waiting leers on their warped faces. Then Sheridan was in front of him again, a massive wall moving in to crush him. Denvers spread his legs and once more sought the man's belly with his hard fists, trying to keep free of Sheridan's arms. He heard the man's gasps of pain every time he sank his knuckles into that roll of fat lopping over the broad black belt. Sheridan jumped back, sobbing for breath that wouldn't come, his crazy, roaring laugh echoing through the trees.

"By God, I haven't had a fight like this"—he broke off to grunt sickly as Denvers struck again and jumped on backward, bent almost double, shaking his bullet head—"damn you, Denvers, I'll kill you!"

He took a blow in the face to come in close with Denvers and caught Denvers's next blow with both hands, grasping his arm and swinging him around to slam against a tree. Denvers tried to get his shoulder in between himself and Sheridan, but Sheridan caught Denvers's lank, black hair and began beating his head against the furrowed bole of the tree. Denvers heard someone's desperate shout, realized it was his own, and felt himself writhing helplessly against the weight of Sheridan's gross torso holding him against the cypress, still beating his head against the trunk, and then he couldn't hear anything any more but the roaring in his head, or see anything, or feel anything, and finally even the roaring was gone.

IV

Denvers's first conscious sensation, perhaps, was that of being suffocated. He reached out his hand with a sob, trying to shove away the heavy crimson damask all around him. A cool hand caught his, forcing it gently down again. Then, beyond his muddy boots, he saw the white and gold footboards of the bed, stuffed with the same color damask, and above his head the pulleys which drew the drapery of the four poster bed up, and finally the girl's face. She started to draw away, and he closed his hand on hers to keep her there. Then he felt the first real pain in his head, and it must have shown in his face, because her black eyes suddenly grew large with compassion.

"Nobody's ever whipped Uncle Cæsar," she said. "You were a fool to try."

Denvers sat up, almost fell back, grabbed the fretted bedpost to keep himself erect. "Where's my gun?"

"I guess Uncle Cæsar took it. He isn't mad at you, though. He's funny that way. He likes you all the better for standing up to him. He says you're the toughest"—she broke off to catch him as he tried to get up and almost fell on his face, stumbling against the marble-topped table by the window—"here, you can't do this!"

"I'm getting out!"

She released him suddenly, allowing him to sink back onto the bed against the headboard, and her face was flushed. "The cattle?"

"I never ran wet cattle in my life, and I'm not starting now," he said. "Not even wet hides."

"I know, Denvers. I guess Uncle Cæsar's been doing it ever since Dad died ten years ago. I've tried to make him quit, but what could I do? First it was cattle, rustling them from spreads on the mainland and running them across the channel at neap tide. They'd put them aboard a two-master Captain Garcia had waiting off Mocha Point and, by the time Sheriff Giddings got across with his posse, the only cattle on the island would be our own. Now, since the bottom dropped out of the beef market and this Skinning War started, it's been the same with hides." She stopped suddenly, anger pouting her full underlip. "I don't see what cause you have to be so finicky anyway."

It caused him pain to raise his head. "Hardwycke?"

"What's rustling compared to killing a man?" she said. "You're lucky Uncle Cæsar let you stay. If you'd tried to get through the posses Giddings will have thrown along the coast, you'd be hanging from a cypress tree right now."

"You think I killed Hardwycke?" he said.

"You must have wanted that twelve hundred dollars pretty bad," she said bitterly, "to murder a man for it."

He shook his head dully. "Listen, I've kept my mouth shut because I didn't know where I stood here. The whole business is getting crazier all the time. I don't even know why I should tell you. How do I know you're not in this with your uncle, just as deep as the others?"

Her breath came heavily. "I'm not, I tell you. If I had any way to stop it, I would. But I can't turn in my own uncle to Giddings. I've tried. More than once, I've tried. But at the last moment I couldn't. It just isn't in me, that's all."

He waved a hand jerkily. "I'll take your word. Will you take mine?"

"For what?"

"That I didn't kill Jale Hardwycke," he said. "Bud Richie and me were driving a bunch of steers down from New Mexico to ship at Indianola. We were bedding down that night when we heard the shot. We came across somebody bending over Hardwycke's body there on the Karankawa Trail. The man jumped up and ran away into the brush. The wallet was still sticking out of Hardwycke's hip pocket. I guess we scared the other man away before he'd gotten it. Richie took the wallet out to see if we could identify the dead one. Giddings and his deputies showed up at that moment. I guess they'd been prowling the bayous for your uncle and heard the shot, same as us."

The girl was looking at him intently, and her voice sounded husky. "I want to believe you, Denvers . . . somehow."

He felt sick again and put his head into his hands. The back of his neck was wet, and he saw the china bowl of dirty warm water on the table. The rag beside it showed some blood. Sheridan had really done a job, beating his head against that cypress, then. Denvers became aware that the girl had moved closer, and he looked up. There was a strange, taut look in her face that drew him to his feet.

"I've got to believe you," she said. "You're the only one left."

"What do you mean?"

"Uncle Sheridan, Judah, Carnicero. I can't turn to them, can I? Uncle Sheridan's the one who's kept me on the island. When Sinton Navarra came, I thought, maybe, because he was an outsider"—she turned to one side, shrugging—"but he wasn't any help. He's mixed up in it, somehow. Denvers, please stay. . . ."

"Mixed up in what?" said Denvers.

Lamplight caught in her dark hair, with the vague, frustrated shake of her head, and she crossed her arms to rub her shoulders, as if she were cold. "I don't know, really. I can't name it. Something that's been going on here. Not the rustling. . . ."

"Lafitte's ghost?"

She turned on him contemptuously.

"Carnicero said he saw the ghost last night," said Denvers. "It's sort of a legend here? Your father. . . ."

40

"Arno Sheridan wasn't killed by a ghost," she said angrily. "Whatever killed him was human. My father was found stabbed to death farther up on the island when I was nine years old. I'm not talking about that anyway. The Lafitte legend was here long before I came. This is something different. Something recent. Maybe you saw it. Between Sinton and Uncle Cæsar. Between all the men. They've changed. Watching for something. Waiting."

"You sure it doesn't have to do with this Lafitte business?" he asked. "What's the story?"

"About Lafitte?" She shrugged, turning to look out the window. "He was supposed to have built this house. Called it his Maison Rouge. French, for Red House. The real Maison Rouge was at Galveston Island. Lafitte settled on Galveston after the United States chased him out of Barataria. Then the Americans made him give up Galveston about Eighteen Twenty-One. Nobody really knows what happened to him after that. In fact, nobody really knows anything about the man. He's one of the greatest mysteries of the Gulf, I guess. Most of the stories about him are just legends. This house is certainly old enough to have been built by him. We found some old-fashioned clothes in a chest out in the cypress grove. There's even a story about treasure he buried here on the island. But if you believed the legends, you'd be hunting buried treasure on every island off the Gulf Coast from Padre Island to Gran Terre."

"How about this one?"

She pulled aside the heavy crimson portière, and the open shutter rattled in the wind, and she stared absently outside. "Oh, on his last raid off Matagorda, Lafitte was supposed to have taken a Spanish ship, the *Consolada*, I think, down Cuba way. Half a million in doubloons and gold plate and all the other fixings you hear in one of those

pirate stories. He brought it back here and buried it somewhere. You know his old custom of killing the two men he
took out to help him dig the hole, so he'd be the only one
left who knew its whereabouts? Then his mulatto mistress
murdered him in a fit of jealousy, and Lafitte's men left
Matagorda without having found the treasure. However, so
the story goes, a letter had been written by Jean to his
brother, Pierre, telling where this treasure was hidden on
Matagorda. Such a letter, of course, would have to be carried by a man Lafitte could trust implicitly, so the tale
chooses Dominique, his one-eyed gunner who had fought
with Napoléon."

"You sound skeptical," said Denvers.

She shrugged. "I live here, Denvers. It's no fairy-tale pirate island spilling over with gold doubloons. It's just a
bleak, lonely, empty sandspit, seventy miles long and five
miles wide, full of squawking birds and crazy jack rabbits
and crazy men."

She whirled away, dropping the portière, pacing restlessly toward the door, and he smiled. "You sound fed up."

She was facing him again, and the sudden intense bitterness in her voice was startling. "Fed up? I'm going crazy,
Denvers. Don't you think I want to get off? I'd give my
soul. The farthest inland I've ever been was Refugio and
that was when I ran away. Uncle Sheridan found me there
and brought me back. Even when I do manage to sneak
away, about all I can do is wade across from Dagger Point
and get my feet muddy in the swamps. What would I do if I
went any farther? Ask someone to let me poke their cattle?
I'm not a man. What chance has a girl got? Uncle knows
that. He doesn't even bother keeping a very close watch on
me. A girl can't run away from home like a boy. Nobody
outside would give me a job. I've been in prison all my life.

I've never seen the outside world. You don't know how I envy you." She had come toward him again, and he realized how near she was standing and how uncomfortable it made him. "And it isn't just that I'm fed up with the island, Denvers. I'm afraid. This last year, you don't know how I've been afraid. Something's happening here, Denvers. Something evil. . . ."

He stretched out an arm to express his concern. "Wait a minute, Esther. . . ."

"No." She stood rigidly now, looking down at him with a pale, strained face. "I'm not crazy, Denvers. You know it. You felt it when you first entered the house. I saw your face. I saw the way you looked around. It's something you feel and can't see. Tell me you didn't feel it?"

He frowned, mouth tightening. "Maybe I did. I thought it was because I was a stranger, maybe, coming in on this place, or because the house was so old."

She shook her head. "More than that. Something between Sinton and Uncle Sheridan. Something between all the men."

"Just who is Sinton Navarra?" he asked.

"The son of Esther's mother," said Sinton Navarra, "by her first husband." He closed the door as he came into the room. His black boots made no sound across the faded nap of the Empire Aubusson, and he moved with that light, swinging ease so unfitting for such a large man, and his pouched eyes held that veiled inquisition, and a secretive smile played about his lips. "Yes," said Navarra. "Esther's mother had married before she came to Matagorda. Arno Sheridan was her second husband. Her first was Olivier Navarra, my father, who died of malaria at New Orleans in Eighteen Forty-Nine. I was sent to France to be reared and, while there, my mother married again. Thus, while I am

43

really Esther's half-brother, I had not seen her until I came to Matagorda a few months ago. I take it my sister has been telling you of the horrible evil which hangs over this house. Ah. . . ." He held up a pale, long-fingered hand as the girl started to protest. "I understand, my dear, I understand. Matagorda has just gotten on your nerves, that's all. The incessant screaming of those beastly gulls. The never-ceasing pound of the surf." He cocked his dark head, moving to pull the portières aside. "You can hear it now, eh? You can always hear it. Beating, beating, beating, like some diabolical drum, calculated to drive a person insane. No, Esther, I don't blame you. I suppose she gave you the history of the house, too, Denvers." Navarra moved to the scarred Pembroke table at one side of the window, caressing a heavy, tarnished candelabra there. "She doesn't believe Lafitte built this house."

"I never said that," pouted Esther. "I just say you can hear legends about him almost anywhere along the Gulf and very few of them own a shred of truth."

"Perhaps I am more of a romanticist." Navarra smiled softly. "The clothes you found in that old trunk in the garden, for instance, Esther. Or even the furnishings here. If a Colonial had furnished the house, everything would have been matched, don't you think? I mean Chippendale, or Georgian, or Late Empire. But look around you. The bed? French State, I'd say. And this candelabra? Undoubtedly of Spanish origin. And this Pembroke table. Hardly fitting together in one room. My room's the same. A hodgepodge of Louis the Fourteenth and Spanish Colonial and Chippendale."

"You seem to know," said Denvers.

Navarra's shrug was deprecating. "I dealt in furniture in New Orleans for some years."

"I thought it was France?"

Navarra's heavy eyelids flickered with annoyance. "I have been many places, Mister Denvers. Many places."

"From New Orleans you should be an authority on Lafitte."

Navarra seemed to draw himself up. "An authority? I know every move Jean Lafitte made from the time he was born to the time he died, Denvers. I have been separating fact from fancy about Lafitte all my life. I know more about him than. . . ." He stopped abruptly, looking down strangely at Denvers, his brows raising as if in surprise. Then that soft, secretive smile caught at his lips, and he waved a hand. "But that is neither here nor there, is it? After all, Lafitte is long dead, and. . . ."

The scream came through the open shutter, above the sound of the surf, and Navarra was the one to jump for the door after the first stunned surprise had held them all there. "That wasn't any gull!" he said, and took the stairs three at a time, stumbling across the dancing steps of the elliptical landing. Early dusk cast a dim luminescence through the circular fanlight above the door, limning a weird, shadowy form darting through the hallway. Denvers rose dizzily from the bed, and Esther rushed to help him keep his balance, while below Navarra tore open the front door and clattered across the pedimented porch. A few stunted cypresses surrounded the house, and Navarra thought he saw a form darting through them. He ran into the trees, taking a flagstoned walk, and stumbled across something, going to his knees. It was a man stretched out on the stones. He caught at Navarra's leg feebly. "I found where he stays," he gasped. "Just like Arno Sheridan I was up past Dagger Point and I found . . . where . . . he stays."

The man had stopped talking by the time Denvers and Esther reached him. Navarra shook him without response.

Esther looked at Navarra. "Who is he?"

Navarra toed the dead body with an immaculate boot. "One of Sheridan's hands."

Carnicero came running through the trees, sobbing. "I saw it. *Madre de Dios.* I saw it. Lafitte!"

"Oh, now, Carnicero," said Navarra, raising his hand.

"You don't believe me?" blubbered Carnicero. He bent toward the dead man, pointing a shaking finger at the bloody wound in his side. "Look. Stabbed. The same as Esther's father was stabbed. Not by a knife, *señores y señorita.* Don't you think I've seen enough knife wounds to know? This man was stabbed by a sword!"

V

The stench of rotten meat was so strong it had begun to nauseate Ernie Denvers. The only sound for a long time had been the squealing birds and the dull pound of the surf. *No wonder the girl is fed up,* he thought. *Fed up? A man could go mad in a place like this.* He sat heavily on the paint mare they had given him, slitting his eyes against the biting sand blown up by the morning Gulf wind. Ahead was Mocha Point, a long, rickety pier jutting out from the high spit of grass-topped land, and all along the shore were huge piles of decaying beef, covered black with scavenging birds.

"All legal," Cæsar Sheridan was saying. "Nothing wrong with having our own packery on Matagorda, see? Shank Pierce has one across the bay. That's where most of the cows in Texas are going now. Private packing. Hides and tallow. And who can stop us from packing our own tallow and skinning our own beef here? Nobody. We run our herds on the island, don't we?"

"And if you wade across to the mainland every night after a few dozen of somebody else's hides, who's to know the difference?" said Denvers sarcastically.

Sheridan threw back his head to let out that roaring laugh. "That's right, boy, that's right. A fallen hide belongs to anyone who wants to skin it, no matter what the brand. Just like in the old days a maverick belonged to anybody who put his dally on it. That's the law. And that's the Skinning War. Texas is full of hide rustlers that help a hide to fall by filling it full of holes. That's why Giddings can't prove anything on us. All he's ever seen is the carcasses we leave. Could be any one of half a dozen gangs operating along the coast. By the time Sheriff Giddings gets over here, our shipment of hides will have left aboard Captain Garcia's two-master, brands blotted out and everything."

Navarra had a silk handkerchief held across his nose. "That Mexican who was killed yesterday smelled almost as foul as this, Cæsar. Was he one of the hands you have down here?"

Sheridan nodded. "This Lafitte thing is getting on my nerves. Any more trouble like that and my Mexicans are going to leave the island."

"Have you ever seen this ghost yourself?" asked Denvers.

Navarra waved his handkerchief disgustedly. "Of course, he hasn't. These Mexicans are just a bunch of superstitious animals."

"Why would it necessarily have to be Lafitte's *ghost?*" asked Denvers. "You can laugh off Carnicero's stories, but not that dead Mexican a week ago. Killed with a sword? Who carries a sword nowadays?"

Sheridan frowned at him. "Don't be loco. Those Lafitte stories are so much tripe."

"Navarra doesn't really think so," said Denvers. "When was Lafitte supposed to have died, Navarra?"

"Supposed?" Navarra's voice was sharp. "He did die. You know the story."

"And a hundred others," said Sheridan. "I've hit just about every town along the Gulf, from Port Isabel to New Orleans, and every one has Lafitte dying in their own town hall. I met an old sea captain at San Antone who claimed he saw Lafitte on his deathbed there in Eighteen Thirty-One. I saw another one who swore he found Lafitte's grave near Indianola."

"He died in Eighteen Twenty-Six," said Navarra angrily. "He was in his middle thirties."

"And this is Eighteen Seventy-Five," mused Denvers. "Fifty years added to a man's middle thirties. Have you ever seen all of Matagorda Island, Sheridan?"

The older man shrugged. "No need to. Nothing up at the other end. We don't run cattle down there. Island's too big to use all of it."

"This is fantastic," said Navarra. "Lafitte was a brilliant man, a vivid cosmopolitan, a gentleman of the world. Even supposing he didn't die, a man like that wouldn't isolate himself on a lonely. . . ."

"You said yourself this place could drive a man mad, Navarra." Denvers grinned.

"But fifty years . . . ?"

"I've seen a lot of spry old men past eighty."

Navarra turned away, swabbing angrily at his nose with the handkerchief. "I refuse to discuss it any longer."

Sheridan leaned back in his saddle, slapping his thigh with a raucous laugh. "He's gotcha, Sinton. That dead Mexican didn't meet up with no ghost and neither did my brother. How do you know Denvers ain't right? Maybe that story about Lafitte building this house is true. Maybe the old boy's been running around here with his sword like Carnicero claims."

"Don't be a stupid ass," said Navarra thinly.

Sheridan's laugh broke off abruptly, and he spurred his horse, jumping it around in front of Denvers's paint to bring the animal broadside across the head of Navarra's black. He grabbed the black's bridle, yanking it around till he held its head down by the rump of his horse and was facing Navarra. "Don't call me names, Sinton," he said.

All the indignant hauteur had slipped from Navarra, and his smooth, soft voice formed a sharp contrast against Sheridan's guttural roar. "Take your hands off my bridle. I don't like it."

"Maybe we better make it clear who bosses this island before I do that, Sinton," said Sheridan.

"Cæsar," said Navarra deliberately, "don't threaten me. I'm not one of your Mexican hands. I'm not afraid of you."

Sheridan looked at Navarra a long moment. "No," he said finally. "No, I don't think you are, Sinton. But get this"—he yanked viciously upward on the bridle, causing the black to jump—"I'm running Matagorda and, nephew or no nephew, you'll do as I say when you're here. You've been bucking me ever since you came, Sinton. I don't know what it is. I can't put my hands on it, but it's been there. Don't go any further." He jerked the bridle again. "Don't let me get my hands on it. If you do, I'll tear it apart and you, too."

He threw the horse's head away from him and necked his own fat bay around, flapping both feet out wide to bring them in with a solid, popping sound, and the bay jumped forward. Navarra sat his black there without moving, watching Sheridan go. There was an ineffable evil in the

49

way his thick lids had closed almost shut over his eyes, the network of minute veins giving their pouched, dissolute flesh a sickly blue shadow. He seemed to become aware that Denvers was watching him and turned, glancing at him momentarily. Then, with an angry thrust of his head, he urged his horse forward.

There was a row of tallow vats along the shore near the pier and back of them was the slaughter shanty. Prieto and another Mexican were skinning carcasses by the shanty, and Carnicero was mounting a bloody-hoofed horse preparatory to hauling a skinned cow to the nearest pile of rotting meat.

When Denvers came up, Sheridan told him: "We tried salting the beef, but all we could get for a two-hundred-pound barrel was nine dollars. Even that tallow don't bring much more than what it costs to ship. The hides are the only things that really pay. You help Prieto with the skinning today."

Carnicero disappeared behind the piles of meat, hauling his carcass, and came back to dismount and climb up a ladder on the nearest tallow vat. Denvers was off his paint by then, rolling up his sleeves, when a Mexican *vaquero* came fogging through the piles of carcasses, his sombrero flapping against his back. "Another cut of steers disappeared from our north herd this morning!" he called to Sheridan, hauling his lathered horse to a stop.

"Did you see anything?"

The man crossed himself. *"Madre de Dios,* does one see an *espiritu?"*

Sheridan turned to Navarra, face turning dark. "There's your ghost again. How do you explain that?"

"I don't purport to," said Navarra. "I just say Lafitte died in Eighteen Twenty-Six."

"Hell!" snarled Sheridan, turning to Prieto. "I'm going

out to see what kind of tracks they found this time. You put Denvers to work."

The odor of rotting meat was oppressive, and Denvers reached for his bandanna to slip it over his nose. It was then he noticed how Prieto was watching him. The man's thin, bitter face was turned after Sheridan, riding away, but his glittering black eyes were looking sideways toward Denvers, and they held a sly, waiting light that stopped Denvers's hand with the bandanna just beneath his jaw. Then he heard the squeak of saddle leather behind him. Navarra?

"Did someone really cut out a bunch of steers this morning?" said Navarra.

"Strangely enough, yes," said Prieto, turning fully around toward Denvers, smiling mirthlessly. "I heard about it before sunup and sent word to have someone ride in with the news when Cæsar came. If it hadn't happened that way, I would have found something else to pull him away."

Denvers caught his first sight of Judah coming down between the piles of beef, slapping at the swarm of flies buzzing around his great, black, sweating torso. He had a big meat cleaver in one hand.

"Good," said Navarra from behind Denvers. "Good."

Carnicero was now climbing down the ladder from the top of the tallow vat and moving with heavy feet toward Denvers from the opposite side of Judah. Denvers couldn't keep his eye on all of them at the same time.

"We've been wanting to get you alone like this," said Navarra.

"You mean you don't want Sheridan to know?" said Denvers, and his voice sounded like mesquite scratching saddle leather.

"You might put it that way," said Navarra, taking a

small step around in front of Denvers. "I think you know what we want, Denvers."

Denvers had never wanted a gun so desperately. Four of them. Three on the mainland had been bad enough, and even there with his gun he had gone into it knowing how it would end. But now four. "This is why you didn't let Sheriff Giddings take me?" he said tensely. "What's in Hardwycke's wallet you all want so bad?"

"Surely you know," said Navarra.

"Not the twelve hundred dollars."

"Not the twelve hundred dollars," said Navarra.

"Maybe I don't have the wallet."

Navarra's blue-shadowed lids closed slowly across his black eyes. "I think you have. You can give it to us now. Or we can take it. Whichever way you prefer."

Whichever way you prefer. It almost made Denvers laugh. Whichever way you prefer. Sheridan wouldn't be coming back this time. All right. He still felt weak from the last fight but what the hell. He spread his feet a little in the sand.

"Am I to assume that you wish us to take it?" said Navarra.

"I can't give you what I don't have."

Carnicero had his *saca de tripas* out. That wasn't so much. Neither was Judah's cleaver. It was the gun. He wouldn't stand a chance after one of them pulled a gun. He couldn't let it get that far. All right. That would start it then. The first man to go for his gun would start it. He was still watching Navarra and remembering that French Le Page in the man's shoulder harness.

"If you don't have it on your person," said Navarra, "we'll find out where you put it."

"You won't lay a hand on me."

"We'll find out where you put it. If you don't have it on you. Either way. It doesn't matter. Once more, Denvers.

Will you give us the wallet?"

The surf boomed dismally behind Denvers, and the gulls swarming over the rotten piles of meat made a horrible, raucous din, and the sweat had soaked through his shirt beneath the armpits. *The first man to go for his iron.* Judah's bare feet made a shuffling sound in the sand. Denvers ran his tongue across dry lips. The first man.

"Why waste time?" snarled Prieto.

"All right," said Navarra, and it was he.

There was no thought behind Denvers's move. He had been so keyed up to it that he felt nothing, actually, until he struck Navarra. He must have leaped, because he heard his own grunt, and then he was up against the big, dark man, grabbing for the hand Navarra had snaked behind his coat, and all of them were shouting around him. Denvers's weight carried Navarra backward, and the two of them reeled across the sand, knocking Prieto aside as he sought to draw his gun. For that moment surprise robbed Navarra of any reaction. By the time he had recovered, Denvers had the man's hand twisted around, jerking the big French pinfire from it. Still staggering backward to keep from falling, Navarra floundered into the surf and, with the first wet slap of brine against his legs, Denvers responded to the drive of a heavy body crashing onto his back.

"No, Judah, don't!" screamed Navarra, tearing free of Denvers. "You'll kill him!"

The blow that struck Denvers's head sent him to his knees with the Le Page still gripped desperately in his fist. Through the roaring pain in him he sensed that the giant mulatto was shifting to strike again and rolled sideways through the shallow water, trying to keep the gun held above it. Navarra tried to catch him and got one hand on his shoulder. In that moment Denvers felt the violence of the man's strength. Then he had torn free, with Judah's meat axe slapping the water where he had been a moment before. Still floundering away, he realized the mulatto must have been set to cleave him in two and had shifted the axe in the last moment to strike with the flat of the blade instead of the edge, when Navarra had first shouted.

Prieto's shot sounded sharply above the dull wash of the surf, and Denvers whirled toward him, struggling to his feet. Still stunned by the mulatto's blow, he was surprised to feel the French gun jump in his hand, and the explosion jarred him partly out of his dazed pain. He heard Prieto's shout, and Prieto's gun go off again, and the lead splashed water up at him, and then he had the Le Page going. It sounded like a whole crew of triggermen fanning their irons in front of his face, and he had never dreamed a gun could sling so much lead.

"Navarra," he heard Prieto yell, "stop him!" Then Prieto stopped yelling, and, knowing that was over, Denvers whirled to meet Judah as the mulatto floundered through the water toward him with the meat cleaver. Denvers's shot went into the foaming breaker at his feet, and he followed it, driven down by the man who had leaped on his back. He twisted around, firing blindly against the man's body, but the gun had been in the water now, and it made a soggy, clicking sound. Desperately he pistol-whipped the contorted face above him. Carnicero? It was gone, and he heard the man's pained cries, and he was trying to get to his feet again, gasping and choking, spitting out salt water, when he caught the flash of Judah's cleaver.

His plunge aside ducked his head beneath the sea again, and he threw himself at Judah, blinded by the stinging brine, feeling Judah's arm strike his shoulder with the blow that had missed. Inside the reach of that cleaver now, he struck at Judah's face with the gun. He heard the mulatto's hoarse scream and followed the falling body on back, straddling it to strike again, driving the man's bloody face beneath the water. The next breaker washed Denvers off Judah's limp frame, and he floundered backward, off balance, into Navarra who had been stumbling toward him from the shallow water.

Waist deep they met, and Navarra's hands caught Denvers's wrist as Denvers tried to strike with the Le Page. They reeled back and forth with the breakers carrying them inshore and the backwash carrying them out again, Navarra trying to twist Denvers's arm around so he couldn't use the gun. Finally the heavy man twisted Denvers into position to apply pressure, and the pain brought a strangled shout from Denvers, and he felt the gun slip from his fingers, falling into the water. He tore his wrist free of Navarra's grasp, seeking the man's legs beneath the water. He found them and snaked one foot behind Navarra's knee, suddenly throwing his whole weight against the man.

Navarra stumbled backward, and at that moment a breaker struck them, carrying the larger man down with Denvers on top. It washed their struggling bodies inshore until Denvers was straddling Navarra in shallow water, his knees on the sandy bottom, his head above the sea. He found Navarra's neck with both hands and held the man's head down that way, feeling the thick muscles swell and writhe beneath his fingers as Navarra tried to rise above the water. Another roller foamed over, and Denvers's own head was submerged. When it had passed, he came out, gasping and coughing, still holding the other man under with a desperate grip. Navarra jerked back and forth beneath Denvers in a spasmodic frenzy, hands clawing, legs kicking, but his struggles were growing weaker. A man was on Denvers's back then, tearing him off Navarra. He twisted from one side to the other under the blows, clinging with the last of his strength to the man beneath him.

"*¡Por Dios!*" shouted the one on his back, hooking an arm around his neck. "He's dead now. Get off him, will you? I keel you!"

Navarra's struggles ceased, and Denvers released his hold, turning to thrust feebly at Carnicero. The Mexican had one arm around Denvers's neck, the other drawn back with his knife. Denvers tugged weakly to one side, and they rolled off Navarra. A breaker swept them up on the wet sand at the water's edge. Carnicero rose above Denvers, straddling him. Denvers tried to catch the knife arm, but the whole desperate struggle had left no strength in him, and his grab missed, and his breath left him in a weary gust. Carnicero held the knife suspended above Denvers's chest for a long moment, a strange, indefinable expression crossing his face. Then the first lugubrious tear dropped from his eye.

"I can't," he said, and the tears began to stream down his face. "I was born with a *saca de tripas* in my hand. They pinned my swaddling clothes together with stilettos. I ate my *frijoles* with a Bowie knife from the time I was two. All my life they have called me Butcher for what I can do with a knife. And now, when I get the chance"—he began to whimper like a baby—"I can't keel you!"

VI

Somewhere in an upstairs room a shutter slapped dismally in the wind. The chamber they had given Denvers was dark, and a rotten board creaked every time he paced past the

Pembroke table. He halted at the window a moment, drawing aside the tawdry portières of crimson damask to look out at the somber clouds scudding across the slate-colored afternoon sky. He was hungry, and his boots were still soggy from the fight in the surf, and his head throbbed painfully from the blow Judah had given him with the flat of the meat cleaver. He turned back to start pacing restlessly again, and then stopped abruptly, hearing the rattle of the door. Esther Sheridan pushed it open hesitantly and came in with a candle.

"It's getting dark," she said. "I thought you might like a lamp."

He watched her lift the glass reservoir on the Sandwich lamp, adjusting the wick spout until the candle flame caught. The camphene sent out a pungent odor, and the flickering light rose to glow against the curve of her cheek before she settled the glass again. Then she blew out the candle and stuck it in an empty socket of the candelabra on the Pembroke. It brought her close to him, and, when she turned, there was a searching depth to her eyes. "What is it they have against you, Denvers?"

"Who?"

"Prieto's pretty badly wounded," she muttered, still studying his face. "They don't think he'll live. Navarra must have been pretty nearly drowned. He's still in his bed. Judah's face looks like a side of beef somebody's been chopping steaks off of. Or maybe it's not what they have against you. Maybe it's what they want from you."

He turned away from her, going shakily to the window again, wondering if he still feared that he couldn't trust her, or if it were himself he couldn't trust now. It did something inside him to have her stand that close. Esther was only nineteen, and yet she did something inside him. He couldn't smell the camphene any more. He wondered what made her hair so sweet.

The girl began to laugh suddenly. "I guess they didn't know what kind of *cimarrón* they were stringing their dallies on when they jumped you. Four at once and you haven't even got a scratch on you to show for it!"

"My head hurts, my body aches everywhere, and I have trouble standing up," he said, and shifted uncomfortably as he sensed her beside him again.

"What is it?" she asked insistently.

He turned suddenly, driven somehow by her nearness, by the scent of her black hair, wanting to trust someone. "The wallet, the wallet. What else?"

She drew a sharp breath. "Hardwycke's wallet?"

"Navarra started to ask me for it when I first got here," said Denvers. "Changed his mind when your uncle came into the room. I didn't even realize Navarra had asked me for it. Then Prieto began putting on the screws when we went after those hides on the mainland night before last. Your uncle broke that up again. Yesterday afternoon they got Cæsar away for good."

"They're afraid of him," she said.

"Navarra isn't," said Denvers.

"I don't think Sinton Navarra is afraid of anything," she muttered. "But the others are afraid of Uncle Cæsar. You saw what he did to you. You can lick all four of them put together, but you can't lick Uncle Cæsar. Do you blame them for fearing him? I'm afraid of him myself."

"Maybe they do fear him," he said, "but is that the reason they wanted him gone?"

"If Sinton's up to something, Uncle Cæsar would kill him if he found out. What's in the wallet they want so badly?"

He shrugged. "How should I know? I don't have it."

Her voice was surprised. "Who does?"

"Sheriff Giddings," said Denvers. "He took it from Bud Richie."

"But you took his horse, he said."

Denvers jerked his dark head impatiently. "Giddings followed me here, didn't he?"

She caught at his arm. "But that doesn't mean he found where his horse had dropped beneath you, Denvers. I found you in that canebrake opening onto the sea. How far back had you left the dead horse?"

"At the head of the bayou," he said. "Beyond those canes."

Her voice was rising now. "That's Indian Bog. You must have come through the bog itself. Nobody takes that route. It's too dangerous. We've lost more cattle in there than any other bayou on this coast."

"I found a solid strip in the muck," he said. "They were right on my heels, and I had to take a chance."

"But Giddings wouldn't have followed you that way. It's the only reason you gave him the slip. He'd take the edge of the bog around to the coast before crossing at Dagger Point. And if he came that way, he'd never find his dead horse."

"If the wallet's still there. . . ."

"It might tell us what this is all about!" she cried. "Listen. We can't leave the house together. Uncle Cæsar thinks we're trapped here because the tide's in, and there aren't any boats on this side. He won't be watching so closely. When they all go back into the kitchen to eat, slip out the side door and meet me in the cypress grove."

VII

Cæsar Sheridan was sitting at the big oak table in the living room, playing solitaire, and he grunted as Denvers entered. "You seen Sinton?"

"Navarra? Not since yesterday."

"He ain't in his room," said Sheridan, slapping a queen down disgustedly. Then he turned in his chair, putting a beefy hand on his knee. "What happened yesterday, anyway? What's between you and Navarra?"

"Maybe he doesn't like the way I part my hair," said Denvers.

Sheridan snorted like a ringy bull. "Don't try to put that in my Stetson. Ever since Sinton hit this island, there's been something funny going on. You in it?" Denvers started to answer, but Sheridan went on, turning back to the cards, talking more to himself than to Denvers. "When Sinton first showed up, I let him stay because he was kinfolk. Now I'm afraid to let him go for fear the sheriff will tie onto him, and Sinton will talk. Same reason I'm afraid to let you go. You ain't planning a run-out, are you? I'll bet. Well, it won't do no good. Tide's in now, and you'll get pulled down by the rip if you try to swim. I've got a Mexican down at the barn with orders to shoot if you try to sneak a horse. I swear, Denvers, I don't know what to do with you. Messing up my men. Bringing the sheriff down on my head. Up to something, I swear. . . ."

"Beans on," said Judah from the kitchen door. He stood there, looking at Denvers with murder in his eyes as black as the hide on his bruised, lacerated face. Sheridan shoved his chair back and rose with a grunt. "Coming?"

"I'm not hungry," said Denvers

Sheridan threw back his head to laugh "You mean you don't hanker to go in Judah's kitchen and let him hang over you with a butcher knife. Well, I can't say as I blame you. One time's enough for a while."

He stomped through the kitchen door, growling something at the mulatto. After a moment Denvers moved across the parlor to the side door. It was unlocked, and he slipped out. The cypresses acquiesced to the biting wind with a mournful sigh, heavy foliage beating into Denvers's face as he sought the girl. She startled him by stepping from behind a huge tree trunk. Without a word she led him over the short, rank prairie grass that covered the inland portion of the island, reaching the sandy shore finally. The moon had risen by then, and Denvers took off his high-heeled boots to walk the rest of the way. It took them an hour to reach the spot past Dagger Point where the tall sea grass flanked a bayou that cut back into the island. His feet sank ankle deep into the muck as he dropped down its bank toward the water. Finally the girl parted the growth from the prow of a skiff.

"Uncle doesn't know about this," said Esther. "I came across it last year, hidden up here. Somebody else must have been using it. I've found new pitch in the seams several times."

He helped her haul the leaky, battered skiff into the water. "Anybody else on the island?"

"Some Mexicans on the other end, but that's fifty-six miles. Maybe a few crazy hermits in between. Uncle says you always find them in a place like this. We had a couple helping us brand last fall. Maybe one of them."

He had never rowed a boat before, and they made heavy work of it across the choppy channel. About halfway over they had shipped so much water that Esther had to bail with his hat while he worked the splintery oars. They reached the shore of the mainland and hunted along the coast until long after midnight before finding the mouth of the bayou leading toward Indian Bog. Finally the reeds and muck of the bayou became too thick for further rowing, and they hauled the boat ashore, hiding it in some salt grass. The air here was oppressive with the scent of hyacinth growing along the water, and the festoons of Spanish moss caught wetly at Denvers's shoulders as Esther led him inland. Stumbling wearily through the tangled marshes, tormented by the vicious mosquitoes, they at last found the pipe-stem brake Denvers had broken through that night and hesitantly penetrated the rattling canes. The booming of the frogs rose all about them, and somewhere a panther squalled. Esther's hand was suddenly thrust into his, warm and moist, and her voice sounded strained. "You'll have to lead the way from here on in. Think you can remember?"

The bellow of an alligator startled him. He parted the canes with his free hand, peering into the gloom ahead, hunting for that big spread of water lilies he had stumbled through. Then his foot sank into rotten mud up to his knee, and the girl caught at him with a sharp cry. Indian Bog? Indian Bog. On the right he caught the sickly white gleam of lilies. There was something revolting about the whole place. The canes rattled like hollow bones and the salt grass stank and a foul odor of decay rose from the mud and the wild hyacinth waved feebly in the breeze like dying hands. The first sign they had of the horse was the buzz of flies. The moon was sinking with the coming morning, and they barely made out the rotting carcass, covered with flies and gnats, half eaten away by scavengers. Stomach knotting, Denvers forced himself to approach the animal. The Mexican saddlebags Giddings had carried were called *alforjas,* and, when Denvers bent to open them, the flies swarmed up with a loud, angry buzzing, sending a revulsion through him so sharply he almost jumped back. He ripped at the pocket of the *alforjas* and put his hand inside.

"All right," said a soft voice from behind him. "Pull it out and give it to me."

Denvers took his hand slowly from the saddlebags, turning to face Navarra who stood in the canebrake. The man had recovered his Le Page from the surf the day before, and it was in his hand now. Behind him Carnicero's bucolic face showed dimly in the darkness. The girl stood where Denvers had left her, a taut surprise on her face, her hands to her mouth.

"We came across at low tide," Navarra said. "Been hunting up and down the coast for that dead horse all evening. Thought maybe you'd been telling the truth about not having the wallet. Then Carnicero spotted you coming down the shore in that skiff. We followed you in through the bayou, going along the edge. Give the wallet to me, Denvers."

"The *alforjas* are empty," said Denvers.

He saw the little muscles bunch up beneath the thick flesh of Navarra's heavy jaw. With a muttered curse Navarra rushed at him, shoving him aside to stoop over the saddlebags.

"Never mind, Navarra. Denvers is right. The *alforjas* are empty."

Navarra stiffened perceptibly, then straightened from the dead animal. Denvers saw him then, Sheriff Giddings, standing on past Esther, his big Colts gleaming dully in his hands. Navarra made a small, spastic gesture to raise his Le Page.

"Don't," said Giddings. "Ollie's behind you. Drop the gun or you'll be deader'n that hoss." The sheriff began moving forward. "Think we wouldn't figure on this? When I saw Denvers at your house on the island, I couldn't be sure he was my man. Like you say, it was dark that night of Hardwycke's murder, and even up close I didn't get a good enough look at him to identify positive. But I knew that bullet I'd put in my hoss would drop him eventually. Took us a long time to find the animal. Think you'd reach it before we did, Denvers? When I found that wallet still in the saddlebags. . . ."

"You have the wallet?" Navarra asked.

Sheriff Giddings answered sharply. "That's right. You won't get the twelve hundred dollars, either. I been hunting thieves half my life, Navarra, and I know the way their minds work. Like I say, when I found that wallet still in the saddlebags, I knew Denvers would be back. I knew just how his mind would work. It was that twelve hundred dollars he killed Hardwycke for, and it would draw him back like a fly to molasses. Soon's he discovered he'd left it on the hoss, he'd be coming. So I just squatted with my posse. Looks like I got a bigger catch than I planned. That's all right, too. There's a little matter of some Pothook steers I'd like to discuss with you. It's getting near dawn now. Ollie, you get the horses, and we'll take these folks to Refugio."

Ollie Minster made a short, squat shadow back in the canes, moving to get the horses. Denvers saw the shift of other posse men. Two of them were closing in from behind a cypress, holding carbines. Denvers was half turned toward Carnicero when he saw the Mexican staring past the two men who had just appeared from behind the tree. He raised his hand to point, and his voice was hardly audible.

"*Madre de Dios*. There it is. Believe me now? See for yourself. *Madre de Dios*. Jean Lafitte himself!"

Denvers didn't actually see anything beyond the two men except that first shadowy movement in the trees, and then they turned with their guns. One of them shouted hoarsely, and the Spanish moss whipped around them with their scuffle. Then the man who had shouted staggered backward, gasping. The other began pumping his gun.

"Giddings!" he shouted, and his voice was drowned by his racketing Winchester, "I saw him, Giddings! Damn my eyes if I didn't! I saw him!"

"John," shouted Giddings, whirling that way, "stop, you fool! Carterwright! You'll get sucked down in that bog, John. Come back."

The posse man who had staggered backward was crouched down on his knees now, hugging his belly, and Denvers realized he must have been stabbed. The one Giddings had called Carterwright was running into the cypresses, still shouting. Giddings made a small, jerky move after him, shouting again. "John . . . don't!" he called, and for that moment was turned away from Denvers and Navarra. "Carterwright!"

Denvers jumped toward him, and Navarra bent to scoop up his Le Page. Giddings was whirling back as Denvers's body struck him. They went staggering into the canes, one of the sheriff's six-shooters deafening Denvers with its explosion. Denvers caught the gun between them, feeling it leap hotly beneath his hand as Giddings thumbed the hammer again. Giddings tried to beat at Denvers with the other gun. Denvers ducked the blow, tripping the man. They crashed down into the brake, and Denvers let his body fall dead weight onto Giddings. He heard the man grunt sickly, and for that instant the sheriff's body was limp beneath him. Denvers tore a Colt free from Giddings's hand, struggling to his feet. Navarra came in from behind him before he was fully erect, slugging at him with the Le Page. Denvers rolled aside, getting the blow across his neck instead of on the head. Dazed, he caught at the canes to keep from falling. Navarra bent over Giddings, striking him on the head with the barrel of his pin-fire. Giddings sank back, and Navarra pulled something from the sheriff's pocket. "Carnicero!" he shouted. "I've got it! Come on! I've got it!"

The Mexican stumbled through the brake from somewhere, panting. Then the sound of horses came to them, and Ollie Minster was shouting. "Giddings, Giddings? Where are you? Giddings?"

"Over in the brake!" shouted the one named Carterwright, coming in out of the bog. "Navarra and that other ranny jumped Giddings."

The canes crashed as Minster drove his horse into them. Navarra dived to one side, disappearing in the pipe stems, but the horse was on Denvers before he could follow. Then it went through his mind. Just in that instant while the horse was looming up above him big and black. Just the name. The name he had known so long before. All the way down from New Mexico. And the time even before that. Bud Richie. He didn't even try to get out of the way. He lunged for the animal, the shock of striking its chest knocking him aside. Then he had his hand on the stirrup leather, and the horse was dragging him off his feet. He had the Colt he had taken from Giddings, and he had that last moment before he had to let go. "Remember Bud Richie?" he screamed up at Ollie Minster, the canes rattling and slamming all around him as he was dragged through them, his foot giving a last kick at solid ground. "Remember Bud Richie?"

Minster twisted on the horse, face ugly and contorted above Denvers, trying to bring his gun around in time. "Don't, Denvers! I didn't . . . Denvers!"

Denvers's Colt cut him off, crashing just once, and Denvers saw Ollie slide off the opposite side of the horse with the pain stamped into his face. Then Denvers couldn't hang on any longer and let go of the stirrup leather to roll crashing through the pipe stems. He came to a stop and lay there, hearing Carterwright call something from behind. He got to his knees finally, shaking his head, and crawled through the canes till he could no longer hear the man. He figured the girl would have made for the boat and tried to take a direction that would lead him to the bayou.

He had found the slippery, mucky bank of the bayou and was stumbling down it toward the sea when the horses crashed through the canes behind him. He whirled, raising the Colt, hammer eared back under his thumb before he saw it wasn't Carterwright. "Ollie was leading the other posse men's horses!" cried Esther, throwing him the reins of the animal she had been leading. "He let them go to follow you, and I got them."

He caught one pair of reins and threw them back over the head of a big buckskin. The heavy horse wheeled beneath him as he stepped aboard, and he slapped into the saddle with the animal already in its gallop. The other two horses followed Denvers and the girl for a while but soon trailed off and disappeared behind. Dawn was lighting the sky when he and the girl reached Dagger Point, and he saw the two horsemen ahead of them out in the channel.

"Neap tide came while we were on the mainland!" called the girl. "It's about time for high tide to come in again. Looks like Navarra's already having trouble. It's suicide if the rip catches us before we're across. Want to chance it?"

Denvers pointed back of them along the coast. "We'll have to."

The girl took one look at the pair of horsebackers fogging across the shore from the direction of the bayou and turned her own animal into the rollers. Denvers could feel the rip-tide catch at his buckskin as he followed. He remembered the first time they had waded across here and realized how much deeper it was as the horse sank up to its belly in the first shallows. The animal threw up its head, nickering, and tried to turn back. Denvers bunched up his reins and drove it forward, water slopping in over the tops of his boots suddenly, then reaching to his knees. The undertow swept the buckskin helplessly to one side, and Denvers felt the animal's hoofs go out from under for an instant.

Esther's horse was a little pinto, maybe two hands shorter than the buckskin, and its head was already under. Fighting it, she turned in her saddle to shout above the growing wind. "Don't let your horse start swimming! The rip will sweep you away from the shallow part as soon as its hoofs leave bottom, and you'll never be able to touch down again! Hurry up, Denvers, hurry up!"

The solid feel was gone from beneath him, and he realized the horse was trying to swim. His reins made a wet, popping sound against its hide as he lashed it and yanked its head viciously from side to side. Long years of habitual reaction to that made the buckskin put its hoofs down and try to break into a gallop. Ahead the pinto was floundering helplessly, black tail and mane floating on the water. It began slipping to one side, and Denvers heard the girl's frantic cry. He raked his buckskin under water with his spurs, and the frenzied beast heaved forward, whinnying in pain, tossing its head. The pinto was already being swept away by the rip tide as it strove to swim, no longer able to touch bottom. Denvers unlashed his dally rope from the buckskin's horn, shaking out several loops and heaving the length to Esther. "You told me yourself!" he shouted at her. "Don't try to fight that pinto! You're off the bar already! Grab my rope before you're out of reach! This buckskin's taller! Maybe he can make it!"

Esther jumped from her pinto into the water, grasping desperately at the rope. Coughing, gasping, she pulled herself in. He hooked an arm about her wet, lithe waist, pulling

her onto the buckskin behind him. Ahead he saw that
Navarra and Carnicero had reached the surf and were
climbing onto the island. Denvers raked the buckskin with
the rowels again, hearing the horse's nicker above the wind,
feeling it surge forward. The undertow kept sweeping at it
malignantly, and every time the animal sought to lift its legs
and swim, Denvers bunched his reins and yanked its head
from side to side. His hands were raw from tugging on the
leather, and the brine brought stinging pain to the abra-
sions. Soggy, dripping, they finally reached the surf, and the
buckskin broke into a weary trot, urged on by the rollers at
its rump. Navarra had dismounted on the sand dunes, and,
when he approached near enough, Denvers saw that the
man had a wallet in his hands.

"It was on Giddings," said Navarra, throwing up his
head to look at Denvers, voice suddenly ironic. "I suppose I
owe you an apology, Denvers."

Still sitting his horse, Carnicero shouted and pointed toward the channel. Sheriff Giddings and Carterwright had
driven their horses into the water and were coming across.
Denvers didn't realize how strong the wind had grown until
the girl screamed. "Go back!" she called, and Denvers himself could hardly hear her voice above the whining blow.
"Giddings, don't be a fool! High tide's coming in! We
barely made it ourselves! You'll be swept off the bar!"

She stopped shouting as Carterwright was abruptly turned
aside, his horse floundering in the choppy sea a moment, then
shooting down the channel. Giddings tried to turn his horse
back, but the rip caught it, and a high swell hit him. When the
horse showed, topping the swell, Giddings was out of the
saddle. Esther put her face in her hands, and her shoulders
began to shake. Denvers felt sick at his stomach, somehow,
and turned away. He became aware that all this time Sinton

Navarra had been pawing through the wallet. Money lay scattered all over the sand, and Navarra was tearing the last greenbacks heedlessly from the pocket of the leather case. "It isn't here, Carnicero. It isn't here!" He threw up his head suddenly, wind catching at the white streak in his long, black hair, and the wild light in his eyes was turned sly and secretive as his bluish lids drew almost shut over them. "You've got it, Denvers. You had it all along."

"What?"

"You know!" almost screamed Navarra, and his suavity was swept away now. "You know what I've wanted all along! That's what you were after when you killed Hardwycke! Not the money! Are you from New Orleans? Give it to me, Denvers! I'll kill you this time, I swear I will!"

"That's all, Navarra!"

Navarra had reached for his Le Page, but his whole motion stopped with his hand still beneath his coat. Denvers had stuck Giddings's Colt in his belt, and that was where he had drawn it from.

"I told you he could get it out pretty quick," said the girl, laughing shakily. Then she cast another look out to sea, and a sick horror crossed her face. She caught at Denvers's arm. "Whatever we do now had better be back at the house. This is a real blow coming up."

Denvers hardly heard her. "Navarra," he said, "what did you want in that wallet?"

VIII

The ancient house trembled to the blasting malignancy of the wind, and somewhere on the second story a loose

70

shutter clattered insanely against the warped weatherboards. The cypresses bowed their hoary heads and wept streamers of Spanish moss that were caught up by the storm and swept away like writhing snakes to tangle at Ernie Denvers's feet as he stumbled through the grove, one hand pulling Esther along after him. They hitched their horses to the rack in front of the long, columned porch. Denvers waved the Colt impatiently for Navarra to go ahead. He had taken the Le Page from the man, but had been unable to force Navarra to tell what he had wanted from the wallet. The front door creaked dismally, and Carnicero went in and stopped. Navarra went in and stopped. Denvers saw why as soon as he stepped through the portal. Revealed by the light of a single candle on the table, Judah was crouched over Cæsar Sheridan, lying sprawled on the floor. The mulatto was looking at them, and the whites of his eyes gleamed from his black, sweating face.

"It killed Uncle Cæsar," whispered Judah, and his voice got louder as he spoke. "It's here in this house. I saw it. My own eyes. I saw it."

Carnicero worked his lips a moment before he could get the words out. "Who?"

"You know who," said Judah. "All dressed up in his satin knee breeches and cocked hat, like he was going to a party. Rings on his fingers and gold buttons on his coat. You know who."

"¡La fantasma!" choked Carnicero, and crossed himself. "Jean Lafitte. . . ."

The laugh stopped him. It came, crazy and warped, on the howling wind, partly drowned out by the clattering shutter. They all turned to look at the stairs, circling up the dancing steps to the top landing. It was a shadowy form, at first, moving down out of the darkness. The candlelight flickered across the gold buttons on the long, blue tailcoat, then caught the gilt *fleur de lys* embroidered across cuffs and collar. Denvers had seen pictures of the dress worn in the early 1800s. He recognized the black of the high Hessian boots gleaming against the skin-tight Wellington trousers, the short regimental skirts of a white marseilles waistcoat. There was something unearthly about the eyes, sunken deeply in their sockets, gaping blankly from the seamed parchment of the face. The hair was snow white, done in a queue at the back of a stiff, high collar. The apparition threw back its head to laugh again. "Yes!" he screamed. "Jean Lafitte! Did you think you could come and take my house like this? You'll all be spitted on my sword."

The wind outside changed direction, whipping in through the door, and the candle snuffed out, plunging the room into darkness. Denvers staggered back under the impact of a heavy body, felt the hard bite of a ring against his belly as a hand clawed the Le Page from where he had stuck it in his belt. He tried to tear it away but, when his own hand reached his belt, the Le Page was gone. Then the gun bellowed down by his belly, and he felt the bullet burn across his ribs. He fired blindly ahead of him, and then stopped because the girl was calling, and he realized he might hit her.

"Denvers, Denvers, where are you . . . ?"

The mad laughter echoed through the high-ceilinged room, and Denvers stumbled across a heavy body. Sheridan? He brought up against the solid mahogany center table, trying to right himself, and another man charged into him. He slugged viciously with the Colt. Six-gun iron clanged off a steel blade, numbing his hand. He sensed the man's thrust, and the blade tore through his shirt as he leaped aside. The cackling laughter rose from in front of him. Ducking another thrust, he tripped over the stairway and stumbled violently backward, having to climb the stairs to keep from falling.

"Denvers, is that you on the stairs?"

Again he held his finger on the trigger for fear of hitting Esther and, cursing bitterly, backed on up the stairs.

"Strike your colors!" howled the madman, charging at him.

"Denvers?"

"Esther," he called, "don't come up the stairs! I'll hit you if I shoot downwards."

A volley of shots came from down there, and the man in front of Denvers laughed crazily. "You can't kill me. I'm Jean Lafitte."

There was another thunder of shots, and Denvers shouted hoarsely: "Navarra, stop that! Esther's on the stairs."

"The devil with the girl!" shouted Navarra from the lower blackness. "Get that madman, Denvers! Get him, I say!" He stopped yelling, and there was a scuffle from down there, and Denvers heard the slam of the front door shutting. Then it creaked violently as if someone had torn it open again, and Navarra's voice sounded muffled by the wind. "Denvers? I thought you were on the stairs . . . ?"

The insane laughter drowned that out, and the man suddenly loomed up on the stairs in front of Denvers, leaping upward with his sword. Denvers lurched forward to meet him, trying to knock the rusty blade aside with his gun. The clang of iron on steel rang through the house again, and Denvers was thrown back, hand numbed as before, barely able to hang onto the Colt. Hot pain seared his shoulder, and he felt the slide of steel through the thick muscles there. With the blade caught in him, Denvers went to his knees on the dancing steps that led to the top landing above him. He hugged his shoulder in to keep the man from pulling the sword out again and turned as he rose, trying to stumble up those last few steps to the level hallway. Jerking desperately at the sword, the man threw himself against Denvers, and they both tripped on the final stair and stumbled across the hall to crash into the opposite wall. A blurred figure rose from behind the newel post and ran past them with a wild shout. Denvers got to his feet again, striking blindly with the gun, rolling down the wall in an effort to free himself from the screaming, clawing madman. He caught the line of light seeping from beneath a door. Then the door was thrust open and that second man who had crouched by the newel post was silhouetted in the lighted rectangle for that moment. "Carnicero?" called Denvers.

"Jean Lafitte!" screamed the madman, grasping Denvers's gun wrist with the bestial strength of the demented, finally managing to pull the sword free. Denvers threw himself back from the man's thrust, bounced off the door frame, fell into the lighted room. He flopped over on the floor, tripping up Carnicero as the Mexican tried to jump over him and get out the door. He got one look at the Mexican's dead-white visage. *"¡Madre de Dios!"* screamed Carnicero frenziedly. *"¡La fantasma!"*

"Jean Lafitte!" howled the demented creature and lunged at Carnicero.

Carnicero jerked aside, and the sword went through the leg of his flopping white pants, carrying him back against the table, the other man crashing up against him. Denvers shook his head, trying to rise. "See?" he panted. "Carnicero? It's no ghost. Get him, Butcher. He's real, and he's loco, and he'll kill you. Get him!"

Carnicero pulled his long *saca de tripas* out of his belt

with a spasmodic jerk, catching the man's sword arm and whirling him around. Now it was the Mexican on the outside, bellied in on the other, holding him against the table. The man gibbered insanely, clawing with dirty, broken nails at Carnicero's face, trying to tear his sword free. Carnicero had the knife back above his head, holding the man by the throat.

"Get him!" shouted Denvers, stumbling to his feet and falling against the wall, pain blinding him. "He's crazy, Butcher! You've got to stop him!"

"I can't!" bawled the Mexican, still holding his gets-the-guts up in the air. "I never keel a man in my life, Denvers. That's why I couldn't stab you the other day. Not because you save my life on the mainland. I just never keel a man in my life."

"Jean Lafitte!" roared the crazy man, tearing his arm loose finally and twisting from between Carnicero and the table. Leaning feebly against the wall, Denvers tried to line up his Colt on the man, but Carnicero's heavy body blocked him off. The Mexican was crying pathetically: "I can't . . . I can't . . . !"

The man caught Carnicero's shirt front in one hand, slamming him around against the table and shifted his feet to lunge. With a last, desperate effort Denvers threw himself toward them, gun clubbed, left arm flopping uselessly from his bloody shoulder, but he saw the sword flash up and knew he would be too late. He didn't see exactly what happened then. He saw that Carnicero had dropped his knife arm down to try and ward off the thrust. The two bodies were up against each other for a moment, their feet scuffling on the floor. Carnicero was hidden almost entirely by the other man. There was a last spasmodic reflex; someone gasped. Denvers stopped himself from falling into them, and the crazy man slipped down against Carnicero, his face turned up in a strange, twisted pain. His arms were around the Mexican, and he slid all the way down, until he was crumpled on the floor with his arms still clasping Carnicero's legs.

"*Dios.*" Carnicero's voice was barely audible, and he glanced dully at the bloody knife in his hand. "It was so easy. I keel him. I didn't think it was like that. Just slipped in so easy. *Dios.* I keel him."

Denvers dropped beside the other man, pulling him off Carnicero's legs, shaking him. "Listen. Who are you? Really. What is all this?"

The man's eyelids fluttered open, and he cackled feebly. "Jean Lafitte. My island. They think Marsala killed me? They think many men killed me. There are a thousand legends. This is the only truth. My island. My Maison Rouge. . . ."

"You killed that Mexican the other night?"

"Aye, and Arno Sheridan," panted the man. "When Sheridan brought his family to this island, he drove me out of the house. Said I had no right to live there. I was just a crazy hermit. I'm not crazy. I'm Jean Lafitte. My house, understand? I caught Sheridan out on the range one day so long ago. He found where I was hiding. I put my sword through him. Just like I put my sword through that Mexican. He was riding herd on the cattle, and he found where I was hiding, too, and I killed him. I'll kill all of you. I'll drive your cattle into the sea and take my house back. . . ."

"It was you cut those cows out the other day?" said Denvers.

Blood frothed the man's lips. "I've been cutting them out for years and driving them over the bluffs above Dagger Point. I had a skiff hidden up there. Somebody took it last night."

"What were you doing on the mainland last night?"

"I go there often. Often. You'd be surprised what I know. A man can hide in the canebrakes and hear many things. I heard Sheriff Giddings and his posse go by. They were talking about that dead horse everybody was hunting. I heard Sinton Navarra and Carnicero go by. They wanted the dead horse, too. I found it before anybody else." He giggled idiotically, coughed up blood. "I was very clever. I took the letter out of the wallet."

The sudden stiffening of Denvers's body caused pain to shoot through his wounded shoulder. "Letter?"

"Yes." The man laughed weakly. "I took it from the wallet, but I left the money in it, and put the wallet back into the *alforjas,* and nobody knew I had taken it, did they? You don't think I'm Lafitte? In my breast pocket. I wrote it. To my brother, Pierre, in Eighteen Twenty-Six. From this very house. How they got hold of it, I don't know, but I wrote it. My letter. You can't have it."

He tried to catch Denvers's hand, but Denvers already had the parchment halfway out of the coat, bloody at one corner. It was then that Esther stumbled in, dropping to her knees beside Denvers. She made a small sound when she saw his wounded shoulder. Then she was looking at the man. "Denvers, who is he?"

"You said it yourself," Denvers told her. "Lot of crazy hermits on this island. Probably got hold of some of those clothes you found in that chest. Navarra?"

Her head rose at that. "Judah ran out the front door, and in the darkness Navarra thought it was you. He went out after Judah. He must have found out his mistake by now."

Her hands slipped off him as he got to his feet, moving toward the door, and his voice was unhurried and deliberate

now, because that was the way it stood inside him. "Stay
here. I don't want you in the way this time. Stay here till it's
over."

IX

"Denvers . . . ?"

The hall was dark lower down, but here a candle gut-
tered, suspended in a cast-iron holder, and he went down
slowly into increasing shadows with his good shoulder
against the wall to conserve his strength.

"That you?" asked Navarra.

Denvers decided he must be at the very foot of the stairs.
"It's me. You wanted the letter out of Hardwycke's wallet."

Navarra's voice trembled slightly. "You had it all the
time. I'm coming after it."

The creaking started slowly, deliberately, with a small
interval between each groan, as a man would make
mounting the old stairway unhurriedly. Denvers felt the
skin tighten across his sweating face. "You killed
Hardwycke for the letter?" he said.

The noise stopped down there, and for a moment
Denvers thought he could hear Navarra's breathing. "Not
personally, Denvers. Prieto killed Hardwycke. Prieto and I
left New Orleans together, but he stopped off at Refugio
while I came on to Matagorda Island. If Prieto missed
Hardwycke on the mainland, I'd get him when he arrived
here."

"Why should he come here?"

There was a long pause, and Navarra might have been
trying to place Denvers exactly during it. Then he spoke.

"In New Orleans. Hardwycke had acquired some real estate that originally belonged to the Lafittes, and among the titles he found that the Sheridans had no legal claim on this end of Matagorda. Ostensibly Hardwycke was coming here to force the Sheridans off. However, one of the properties Hardwycke had acquired was the site of the old Lafitte blacksmith shop in New Orleans, and a Negro retainer of Hardwycke's let it leak out that in the floor of the black-smith shop they had unearthed some old papers of the Lafittes, among them this letter. When I heard that, I knew why Hardwycke had really headed this way. I told you I was an authority on Lafitte. How do you think I became an authority? I've tracked down more of his legendary trea-sures than any man living and never found a doubloon. But this is the real thing. It's the most gold Lafitte ever had in one spot. I've been hunting that letter half of my life, Denvers."

"You aren't Esther's half-brother?"

"She had a half-brother under the circumstances I told you who died in France," said Navarra. "I was a friend of his, and he left me in charge of his personal effects. The Sheridans knew of him but had never seen him. When this came up, I took advantage of that. Prieto was my man. Judah hated Cæsar Sheridan and feared him, and what man wouldn't have turned against his master for a share in half a million dollars? Carnicero is an old fool afraid of his own shadow. He was Sheridan's man, but he feared me as much as Sheridan and would do whatever I told him. And now I'm coming, Denvers. I'm coming. . . ."

Denvers saw the sudden shift down there, and Navarra made a shadowy figure behind the curving railing, charging up from the bottom tier of stairs and jumping for the pro-tection of the newel post on that first elliptical landing. He covered his rush with a volley that seemed to shake the house. Denvers ducked down with the lead slapping into the wall behind him, snapping a shot at Navarra, and saw the man throw himself down behind the dancing steps.

"Hold it, Navarra!" shouted Denvers. "Let me read you the letter!"

"Don't try to stall me, Denvers!" called Navarra. "I've come this far, and you won't stop me now. How many shots have you got left in that Colt? Is that what you're doing? You can't bluff me, Denvers."

Denvers spun his cylinder and was surprised to find in the flickering light only one fresh shell. Had he fired that many? He wiped a perspiring palm against his Levi's. "It doesn't matter how many shots a man has, Navarra," he said. "Only how he uses them. Listen to the letter. It's dated June Eighteenth, Eighteen Twenty-Six. 'Dear Pierre.' That was Jean's brother?" There was just enough light so that he could make out the ancient script.

" 'Dear Pierre,' " he read, holding the letter in his left hand, trembling slightly from the injury to his shoulder, " 'I am writing you from Matagorda Island, where I have taken abode after I left Galveston. Do not believe any rumors that might reach you of what is happening here. Only what I write in this letter. The men are growing restless, and already one ship's crew has left in the *Pride*. The only one I can trust now is Dominique, and it is with him I shall send this letter. Even Marsala has turned on me. She left the house this morning in a fit of jealous rage and didn't come back until late into the night. Something about a Creole I have been seeing in New Orleans. Which one could that be? There will undoubtedly be talk of a treasure I took when I boarded the *Consolada* last month. It will be false. . . .' "

"Denvers!" Navarra's voice had a hoarse, driven sound.

"You're lying. You're making that up to stall for time. There was a treasure, I tell you, and I'm coming. You can't bluff me, Denvers. You can't stop me. Twenty shots, Denvers."

Denvers eared back the hammer with his right thumb. *I'm coming, Denvers. One left against twenty shots.* He went on reading the letter, deliberately, barely able now to make out the old-fashioned script. " 'It will be false. Already there has come to my ears a rumor that I have buried treasure on Matagorda. There is no treasure on the island. . . .' "

"Stop it, Denvers!"

Denvers caught the shift that must have been Navarra setting himself to rise from his crouching position behind the dancing steps. He grew rigid, the buzzing in his ears louder now, his feet feeling as if they were sinking into a soft, puffy cloud. *Twenty shots.* He remembered that fight on the shore, and what little chance Prieto had stood against that Le Page. *It doesn't matter how many shots a man has, Navarra. Only how he uses them.* Denvers read the last lines of the letter tensely, waiting for Navarra's rush. " 'There is no treasure on the island. The *Consolada* was the only prize I took during my stay here, and she was nothing but a blackbirder off the Gold Coast bound for New Orleans. The few Negroes I took off her didn't bring me enough to buy Marsala a new dress. . . .' "

"Stop it! Damn you!"

Screaming that, Navarra jumped erect on the landing, throwing himself up the last stairs with his gun bucking madly in his hand. Lead whining around him and hitting the back wall in a wild tattoo, Denvers dropped the letter from his left hand and with his right he curled his fingers fully around the Colt's butt. A bullet plucked at his shirt and another clipped his ear. He still couldn't see Navarra very well. The stairway seemed to spin before his eyes. One shot. Navarra shook the whole balcony, coming on up, his gun flaming in his hand. A veritable arsenal. Navarra rounded the turn completely and made a looming target over the Colt's front sight in the flickering light. *It doesn't matter how many shots.* Denvers flexed and winced as a bullet hit him somewhere in his left side. Then his finger pressed the trigger. He heard the boom of the Colt and saw it buck in his hand. Over the sights, Navarra's body stiffened, stumbled up one more step, hovered there, then crashed backward. Denvers swayed forward, dropping the Colt to catch himself before he fell. He was dimly aware of Esther's voice somewhere back of him. Her hands were on him, soft and supporting.

X

The wind made a faint whine now, fluttering the tails of the three horses as Denvers and Esther and Carnicero headed them up the last dune before the beach. Denvers was still weak from loss of blood, and his shoulder throbbed painfully, but, as long as a hand could fork a horse, he was all right. Esther looked across at him, hair blown over the curve of one flushed cheek. "I can't believe I'm leaving this place. What's it like on the outside, Denvers? Do women really wear satin dresses? My mother used to tell me. And that stuff they use on their hair to make it smell sweet."

"Perfume? You don't need perfume, Esther."

"You'll have to help me, Denvers," she said. "I guess I won't even know how to act."

"You'll know how to act," he said. "And as for helping

you, I'll be there as long as you want."

Carnicero giggled. "It's funny, Denvers. All the time I've lived here, and she never looked at me like that."

The girl flushed, and then, to hide her confusion, looked back toward the old house. "I guess it was best, that crazy man dying there. I don't see how an old man like that could be so strong. He must have been past eighty." She shivered suddenly, eyes darkening as she turned to Denvers. "Who do you think he was, Denvers, really?"

"Jean Lafitte," Denvers said, and there was only wonder in his eyes as he added, "or maybe just his ghost."

The Ghost Horse

I

When Eddie Rivers saw the cut-under mountain wagon laboring up the grade and into the little Wyoming valley, he dropped his hayfork and ran as hard as he could to the creek bottoms behind the shack. He threw himself down into the chokecherry thicket. Panting, wide-eyed, he watched the woman draw the team to a halt before the shaggy, dog-run cabin. It was June Weatherby, the schoolmarm from Jackson. She stood up in the seat of the wagon and called:

"Jim . . . Calico Jim! Are you there?"

In a moment Eddie's tall, broad-shouldered father appeared in the doorway. "Yes, ma'am," he said in his drawling voice. "Mostly."

"I've come to get Eddie," she said. "The Hembres are ready to take him into their home."

Eddie felt the bottom drop out of his stomach. This was what he had dreaded. This was what had kept him awake at night for the past weeks. This was what made him so miserable that he couldn't eat his breakfast. What right did they have to take him away from his father? He'd been closer than ever to Calico, since his mother had died five years before. Calico was all he had.

It was an untamed sort of life, running wild horses up here in the Wind Rivers with Calico. But it was a good life that could get into a boy's blood and make him fight like a hog-tied steer if somebody tried to take him away.

June Weatherby was getting out of the wagon now. She was a tall woman, awfully old, almost twenty-three. Her hair was blonde and piled high on top of her head. The wind kept flicking little curls out like it was trying to tear it free and drop it down over her shoulders. Her cheeks were whipped red as apples by the wind. Her eyes were so big and blue Eddie could see them sparkle even from this distance. He thought that she'd be almost as beautiful as his mother had been, if she wasn't a schoolmarm.

"It's no use trying to hide him now, Jim." Her voice came clear as a bell to Eddie on the thin mountain air. "This is the last time I'm coming up to get him. If he doesn't come with me now, I'll have to send the sheriff for him."

Jim came out of the doorway, smiling his shy sidelong smile that he always seemed to have around women. He was never shy with horses or men. He never tucked in his chin and looked up at them from under his sun-bleached eyebrows the way he did with Miss June, almost like he was afraid to meet her eyes. He never kept making little designs in the dust with the toe of his boot, either, watching them more than he did her. It disgusted Eddie to see how polite and squelched he was in front of nothing more than a schoolmarm.

"Ma'am," Calico said in his drawl so close to a chuckle, "I'm not hiding the boy. He just doesn't want to go. Anyhow, I don't see what all the fuss is about. I'm teaching him his three Rs. Ask him, if you don't believe me. He's probably holed up out there in the bushes some place. If you wanted, you could turn him up soon enough."

June said, low-voiced: "It's not so simple as that, Calico.

You know that education's more than learning the three Rs.
I was his mother's friend and I'm not going to stand by and
see Cora Rivers's son raised like a wild boy. Eddie has to
learn to live with people. Most of all, he needs the friend-
ship, the association, of others his own age."

"At the expense of losing his father?" Calico asked. "I
have to stay here, you know. It's where I make my living."

"You could come down and see him," June said.

"Once a week?" Calico asked. "I'd be a stranger, June.
He may need other kids, but he needs a father worse."

June Weatherby was plainly exasperated. "We've gone
over all this before, Calico. Each time you've outtalked me.
But you won't this time. By law, every child has to attend
school. And you're breaking that law by not letting Eddie
go when he has the chance. The Hembres are willing to
take him and you haven't the right to hold out any longer.
Now don't make it bad all the way around. Please go out
and find him for me."

For a minute Calico kept making designs with his boot.
Then, head down, he turned and came out toward the hay-
fields. Eddie's heart sank. He knew he couldn't escape
Calico. The man came plowing through the stubbled hay.
He was tall, immensely tall, and his hair was red and curly.
He rarely ever grinned and yet he always seemed to be grin-
ning. Maybe it was the way his sky-blue eyes kept twinkling
and darting back and forth beneath his bushy red brows.

"Now, Eddie," he said, "you got to come with the lady.
You don't want to cause her any more trouble."

Eddie felt sick as Jim's eyes dropped to the ground by
the hayfork. There wasn't a better tracker in all Wyoming
than Calico. Eddie was sunk for sure now. But the man's
eyes twinkled as he raised them again. And, instead of
following the tracks, he turned off toward the haystacks on

the other side of the field. He picked up one of the hayforks and began jabbing viciously into the stacks.

"I know where you like to hide, you little devil!" he shouted. "Come out of there or I'll jab this clear through you!"

"Jim!" screamed June. "Stop it! You'll kill him."

Jim kept jabbing. "You want to find him, don't you? I know he's in there somewheres."

"Not that way!" she cried. "Don't be foolish!"

He threw the fork down disgustedly, shaking his head, and wandered aimlessly around among the haystacks, peering at them like a bear just out of his cave. Finally he went back to the schoolmarm.

"I can't find him. Boy's like a fox, when he takes to hiding."

Eddie saw June's yellow curls bob with the exasperated shake of her head. "You did this on purpose. I'm sick of playing blindman's bluff with you and that boy. You force me to do this, Calico. The next time I come up, it will be with the sheriff."

Eddie watched her climb back into the wagon and spin it around, its wheels kicking rocks and dirt angrily up against the side of the log house. Not until long after she was out of sight did he creep from his hiding place. He saw Calico in the corral out behind the cabin, saddling up his mule, Billy-goat. He went up to the fence, peering through the bars at his father.

"Something the matter with your eyes?" Eddie said.

Calico smoothed out the saddle blanket without turning around. "Why?" he asked.

"Those tracks I left in the creek bottom was plain as day."

"Guess I better see the doctor," Calico said. "I couldn't see a thing."

Eddie felt a grin come to his freckled face. "Then you knew I wasn't really in those haystacks?"

"I did. But the schoolmarm didn't. Plum scared her to death, didn't it?"

Eddie couldn't help laughing. "I thought you were sick of all this. Thought you were going to send me back with Miss Weatherby the next time she came."

"Looking at her, I got to thinking what four walls do to a man. They say you turn purple and get big yellow spots all over your face if you stay inside too long. You wouldn't look good with yellow spots all over your face."

"Guess I wouldn't," Eddie agreed. "Where you bound to now?"

Calico grunted, lifting his heavy double-rigged saddle onto the mule. "I figured it was about time I looked for that Appaloosa again. I could get five hundred dollars for a horse like that in Jackson, if he was gentled and trained right."

"Need a helper?"

"I could use one."

"That schoolmarm isn't so likely to be wandering around out in the Wind Rivers after a boy like me, is she?"

"I don't even think the sheriff could find you up there."

Eddie grinned again, broadly. "You got your helper."

II

For two days, Eddie and Calico Jim rode into the mountains. Calico was mounted on Billygoat, Eddie rode a black pony named Midnight, and led their pack horse. They flushed mule deer from the open glades, saw a lumbering black bear eating chokecherries beside a mountain stream, passed a band of moose grazing belly deep in swamps made by a beaver dam. Behind them the magnificent Tetons rose in towering, snow-clad peaks. To the northeast loomed the rugged Continental Divide, its summits veiled in a delicate blue haze, the upper crags all bent in one direction like the banners of an army. And always, behind them, down at the bottom of the long, timbered avenues through which they rose, the waters of Jackson Lake shimmered like sheet lightning under a bright sun.

Soon they were in the Appaloosa's country. Calico had been trying to trap this wild horse ever since he had sighted it two years before. But the animal was clever and wily, and always escaped them. Finally, six months ago, Calico had built a trap at the head of a valley that overlooked one of the Appaloosa's favorite watering spots.

They had not tried to drive the horse into the trap then. The hated man smell would have kept him from entering it. But now the smell had worn off. Eddie and Calico had not been near the valley since that time. The Appaloosa and his band would feel safe to return.

This was Calico's hope, as he scouted for fresh signs along the way. Near evening of the third day, he found tracks of a wild band heading northward. He could not be sure it was the one they wanted, but they were heading into the country where the trap stood, and Calico and Eddie followed.

They rose to the high ridges and started using the binoculars. Finally, near noon of the fourth day, Calico spotted something. He stepped off Billygoat, pulling him behind a ledge of rock and signaled Eddie to do the same. They stood there with the wind whipping through the manes of their horses and skittering gravel across the exposed ridge.

Eddie saw interest tense Calico's big shoulders, deepen the laugh wrinkles about his blue eyes.

"We're in luck for sure, Jigger," he chuckled. "Take a gander."

Eddie held the glasses to his eyes. He was looking down into some of the wildest country in Wyoming—virgin timber that covered the shoulders of a mountain as black and matted as a beard, open parks that looked like jade pools, mountain meadows rippling with waist-high grass— all tumbling down beneath Eddie into the valley below. Finally he found the band of wild horses grazing peacefully in one of the lower meadows. There were duns, browns, flea-bit grays, blacks with the winter hair still making them shaggy. Then Eddie caught his breath. Up on a rock, muzzle raised, long mane whipping in the breeze, the look-out stallion stood outlined against the sky. His unusual coloring was enough to make him stand out in a whole herd of animals. His chest and neck were a solid steel-blue, but that faded toward the rear into a pure white, like a creamy blanket draped over his back and rump, and on this blanket were daubed great red spots, as if some painter had carelessly splashed them there.

Calico had told Eddie that the Nez Percé Indians had originally bred these animals for war horses up in the Palouse country of Idaho. Eddie could well imagine this stallion riding into war, as he watched him standing there on the rock. With his broad chest, his powerful legs, his gracefully arched neck, he looked all grace and muscle and wind-blown power. He was the kind of animal that came once in a horse runner's life. The vivid, untamed spirit of him seemed to reach out and grab at the boy's heart. With the glasses still clamped to his eyes, Eddie tried to pronounce the name.

"Appalarchoo . . . Allarchooler. . . ."

Calico tossed his head back and laughed. "Took me ten years to learn how to say it, Jigger. When I was a kid, I used to call 'em Apples."

"That's a good name," Eddie said. "If we catch him, can I call him Apples?"

"Apples it is," Calico said. "But let's not start counting our chickens. We're lucky enough to spot him so soon, let alone catch him. You remember how many times he's escaped us before. Let's start drifting 'em toward that trap."

As Calico talked, his mule had been nuzzling his shoulder, as he always did. But it was only to get near the tobacco sack in Calico's shirt pocket. With a sly look, Billygoat wrinkled back his lips and caught the strings of the sack between his teeth. Calico felt the tug and slapped Billygoat's nose, jerking the sack from his mouth.

"I don't know where you got your taste for my makings," he said. "Sometime I'm going to let you eat it all and you'll get so sick you'll think you swallered some locoweed."

Chuckling, Eddie mounted Midnight again. Calico tightened the girth on the mule, and then swung aboard. They started moving unhurriedly downslope toward the horse herd.

Calico knew that a band of mustangs could be driven by a man in almost any direction he chose, if he did not press them too closely. The mere appearance of a rider on their left flank would turn them right, or upon their right would turn them left. But they would only drift, unless he tried to get too close.

As Eddie and Calico drew near, the stallion's head lifted, pink nostrils fluttering with their scent. Then he wheeled, catching sight of their movement in the trees. He bugled shrilly at his band.

Grazing heads popped up. Mares whinnied at their colts. The Appaloosa galloped down to herd them together and they started drifting up the cañon. Calico and Eddie followed on their rear until they reached a fork in the cañon. The right fork would lead toward the trap. But the stallion started leading his band into the left.

Calico waved his arm at Eddie and the boy urged his mount up on the band's left flank. The startled horses wheeled wildly, kicking up rocks and dust, and headed for the other fork. They ran down the narrow gorge for a quarter mile, but gradually slowed down, as Eddie and Calico did not press them any more. Finally they were drifting at a walk again. They stopped to graze here and there until the nervous leader circled back to nip at their heels and urge them on.

The tangy sweetness of balsam and pine was swept down the cañon by an afternoon breeze and the breathless excitement of the chase filled Eddie. This was what the schoolmarm wanted to take him away from. It made him sick to think about it. How could June Weatherby know what it was to camp beside a boiling mountain stream with Calico? To see the morning sun explode on top of a mountain peak? To run a wild bunch through cañons that maybe white men had never seen before? Only someone who had tasted the raw wildness of the land could know. Eddie would be happy to spend the rest of his life up here with Calico. He even wished they never had to return to the cabin.

As the afternoon waned, the horses grew tired and nervous with the constant presence of the men. They became harder to drive. Calico and Eddie had to press them closer and watch their flanks more carefully.

The cañon was growing narrower. The timbered humps of the mountain cast black shadows across the trail. In the distance, the towering Garnet Peak was almost lost behind a blue haze. Glaciers sparkled on the north shoulder of the peak. Giant slides spilling down the rocks gleamed like rivers of silver in the sun. Finally the band came to another fork in the cañon, the left one leading into the valley that held the trap.

Calico moved onto the right flank of the herd, aiming to turn them into that fork. But the Appaloosa grew suspicious and wheeled to nip at the heels of his mares, trying to turn them the other way. Calico called to Eddie. The boy left his spot to join the man. Still the big stallion tried to break through them, shouldering against his band, circling back and forth, bugling angrily. The cañon echoed to the frightened whinnies and the clatter of hoofs on shale. Then, through all the other sounds, came a thunderous gunshot.

The cañon seemed to rock with it. The echoes struck the walls and came back and multiplied until the place was ringing with a series of gigantic thunderclaps. The Appaloosa reared, eyes rolling wild and white in its head. Then he bugled again, shrilly, frantically, and wheeled to charge straight at Eddie. With a frantic whinnying, the whole herd followed, racing by the boy in a stream of flying hoofs and whipping manes.

Vainly Eddie tried to turn them, but they stampeded by heedlessly. Calico joined his son, both their animals running. He was staring up at the peaks above them. There was another shot, filling the cañon with its deafening echoes.

"Are they shooting at us?" Eddie shouted. His voice was almost lost in all the noise.

Calico turned to him. "I don't know. We'd better forget those horses and find cover."

He wheeled Billygoat and clambered up the steep slopes into timber. Eddie followed, breathlessly booting Midnight

94

over rock slides and up steep creekbanks. For some reason, Calico did not stop. He forced Billygoat higher and higher, until they reached the ridge. Here, with the animals lathered and laboring for breath, his father halted. Eddie could see that he was looking down into the timber ahead of them. There was movement through the trees. A man came into view. Eddie saw that he was still intent on the running horses at the bottom of the cañon and had not seen Calico or the boy.

"It's Haskins," Calico snapped. "We can't let him get that Appaloosa, Jigger."

He started Billygoat off again, scrambling him down out of the talus. He reached timberline and plunged into the trees. Eddie tried to follow, praying that Midnight would not lose footing and fall. He saw Haskins again, still stalking through the trees, trying to get in another shot. He was a horse rancher from across Jackson Hole, a big, surly man, black-haired and black-browed, dressed in age-whitened Levi's and basket-stamped boots. He must have heard the crash of Billygoat coming through the trees, for he wheeled about. When he saw Calico charging down on him, he jerked his rifle up to shoot. But Calico ran his mule into the man, knocking him aside, and then jumped off on him before he could use his gun.

The two men rolled down the slope, locked together, smashing through the buck brush and red monkey grass, scraping against rocks. Eddie pulled Midnight to a stop and jumped off, running after them. In the thick timothy of the meadow, the two men came to a stop.

Calico tried to tear free but Haskins brought a knee up into his stomach. Calico rolled off with all the wind knocked out of him. Haskins lunged to his feet and scrambled back to where he had dropped the rifle. Eddie tried to reach the gun before the man, but Haskins got there first. He scooped it up and wheeled around on one knee to shoot Calico just as the red-headed man started to rise.

But Eddie threw himself at Haskins, knocking the gun skyward as it went off. Then he caught the rifle barrel in both hands and tried to tear it free. But Haskins gave it a jerk, pulling Eddie off his feet.

The boy still clung grimly to the gun, hugging the barrel in across his stomach with both hands. Haskins cursed and kicked him in the ribs. The pain blinded Eddie, but he refused to let go.

"You little devil!" Haskins muttered savagely, and started to kick Eddie in the face.

But Calico lunged in on the man, catching him by the shirt, swinging him around and hitting him across the jaw. Haskins straightened up, his face blank with shock, then he toppled over like a fallen tree. Calico towered above him, rubbing his knuckles and grinning wickedly.

"Easy as eating striped candy," he said. "Why don't you get up and let me do it again?"

Haskins rolled over dazedly, then sat up, holding his jaw. He looked at Calico's fist and made no attempt to rise.

Calico glared down at the man. "What are you shooting at that Appaloosa for? You won't see another horse like him in fifty years."

"I've been stalking that horse for three days now," Haskins said harshly. He got to his feet, dusting himself off with vicious slaps. "Some of those horses in that band are my stock. The stallion has enticed them away from my ranch and turned them wild." Blood rushed into Haskins's face as he thought about it. "The Appaloosa's a devil. He even gets 'em out of a pen somehow. I've lost three of my best mares to him this last month. If he keeps it up, I'll be ruined."

"Wait a minute," Calico said. "How long did you say you've been stalking him?"

"Three days ago he hit my ranch, run off a couple of my stallions and a good mare. I followed the tracks clear across Jackson Hole into these mountains. I lost 'em this morning but kept on going. Then I caught sight of him down in this cañon. Didn't even see you behind the band."

Calico frowned, then said: "But we've been following that horse a whole day, and the tracks didn't start down by Jackson Lake, the way they would if the band had come across Jackson Hole from your place. They started 'way south of the lake. They just wouldn't've had time to come across Jackson Hole, do all that traveling, and be up here by now."

Eddie saw Haskins frown a little, as if trying to figure it out. Then he shook his head. "I can't help it. I saw that Appaloosa taking my horses. He was just hitting timber when I shot at him. By the time I'd saddled up and got on his trail, I had to follow the tracks instead of him. It was the Appaloosa, Calico. I swear it."

Eddie didn't like Haskins, but he sounded like he was telling the truth. He could see his father thought so, too. He waited, shifting uncomfortably, until Calico spoke.

"I can't figure it out," he said. "No horse in the world could have made it over here that fast, especially driving a whole band with him."

"I told you he's a devil," Haskins said. "The quicker he'd dead the better."

Calico shook his head. "Tell you what. The horse can't steal your animals, if somebody traps him and tames him. Give us another chance to capture him before you try to kill him."

The man studied Calico with sullen black eyes. Then he

scratched at his stubble beard, grimacing. "All right," he said. "But if you don't get him this time, I'm coming out here again. I'll get him next time, Calico. I'll get him for good."

III

The gunshots had driven Apples to utter desperation. Even after he and his band were out of sight of the riders, even after the man smell was no longer borne on the breeze, it seemed he could still hear the deafening crack of that gun. And hearing it, he tore along faster and faster, eyes protruding wildly from their sockets, muzzle foamy with lather, for the Appaloosa had once known man well.

Born wild, he had been captured when still young and broken to the saddle. They had put something heavy and stiff on his back and burned his hip. They had jammed a cold piece of iron in his jaws that cut his mouth whenever they jerked on it, making him turn left or right at their will. He had escaped before they could make him a gelding, and had fought a roan stallion for the right to lead this band. Now, five years old, he had been running the wilds for three years. But the painful memories associated with men only added to his instinct of escape whenever he caught their hated scent.

On and on the band drifted, ever deeper into the box cañon country. Apples ran with his mate, a pretty bay mare. Gradually the first terror receded. The pine-scented air began to smell good again, free from that man taint. The wind ruffled his mane like a soothing hand. He crossed a springy carpet of pine needles, nipping playfully at the bay's heels. She turned to frolic with him, nuzzling his shoulder, nickering affectionately. They stopped to graze in the deep grass of a meadow, and all was peace again.

Sometimes this companionship with the bay brought back memories, too. But they were not painful memories like those associated with man. They went further, so dim they were like a dream. The stallion could recall running with another horse like this, frolicking across the high parks, drinking at the chill streams, grazing on the sweet grasses. That other horse had been the same color—blue across the chest, with the red-daubed white blanket over the hips. As Apples saw the mares in his band with their colts, he thought that perhaps it had been his own mother. But he couldn't be sure.

He herded his band on into pine-fringed foothills that twisted and turned until they tumbled off into the Wind Rivers. The river led them into a cañon where deep green pines clung to ledges high on the crimson walls and the sky was a turquoise strip above them.

They were deep within the cañon when a new scent joined the damp odors of granite and pine needles. Apples raised his head, pink nostrils twitching. Was it the man odor again? He felt panic running through him, and wheeled about, searching the shadows. Suddenly they appeared, far to the rear, riding the shallows of the river. He saw that it was the same two who had followed him before. They must have picked up his trail again.

One was a tall, red-headed man riding a grunting mule. The other was a boy on a black horse. There was something wild about the boy, with his Indian-black hair, his sunburned face. It seemed to touch the wildness in Apples, and hold him a moment, as if in some kinship. He had never felt this with a man before, and could not understand it. Then the man smell was swept to him again. With a shrill whinny he turned and nipped at the bay's heels, startling his band into flight.

The river cañon twisted before them like a snake. Centuries of erosion had carved out spur cañons every few hundred yards. But Apples knew they offered no escape. They were box cañons, merely traps that led back a half mile or so and then came to an abrupt end, their walls so high and steep that no four-footed animal could scale them.

As they reached the first one, he saw that the man and boy had gained on him and were right on his flank. They came in close, shouting and slapping their hats against their legs. It frightened the mares and young stallions, and they tried to veer into the box cañon. Sensing that was what the men wanted, Apples circled swiftly to the inner flank of the band, turning them away from the mouth of the trap. They ran on, snorting and coughing in the dust raised by their flying heels. For a time they were ahead of their pursuers.

Then Apples saw the mouth of another box cañon ahead. The pair spurred their mounts closer to the wild band once more. The black-haired boy was at the rear of the herd, preventing them from turning back. The red-headed man was on their right flank, and they could not wheel that way. Dead ahead, growing out from the mouth of the spur cañon, was a thick line of tamarack and scrub pine. Horses hated dense timber where branches would whip at their eyes and the alligator bark would scrape hide off and the trunks would bump tender noses. The only opening it left was the mouth of the spur cañon, on their left flank. As the band approached the timber, they realized this, and started veering into that spur.

Again Apples sensed the trap. He tried to work onto the inside of his herd and turn them. But the mares and young colts were tiring now. They were driven to panic by the shouting figures pressing in on their tails and flank. They only knew that they had a choice between the hated timber dead ahead and the open mouth of the cañon. It was natural for them to choose the cañon.

If Apples had run wild all his life, he might have made the same choice. But a horse that had been caught and had escaped was twice as smart as a wild horse that had never known man. As he saw how hard the men were trying to turn them into the spur cañon, he knew it was a trap.

With a sharp whinny, he threw himself against a mare, knocking her off balance, forcing her to turn aside. Then he nipped at the heels of the next horse, a young stallion, and he veered away with a squeal of pain. A pair of colts came afterward, and Apples reared up above them, frightening them into a turn.

This wheeled the band toward the timber. They tried to break before Apples' generalship. But he kept them going, nipping at heels, biting shoulders, running boldly into panicky mares that sought to turn back. Apples saw the red-headed man try to run across their front. But it was too late. The whole band ran, squealing, into the timber.

Matted undergrowth clawed at Apples. A branch whipped across his eyes, blinding him. Another one scraped at his hide and he bugled shrilly in pain. The crash of brush was all about him. When he finally broke into the open, he saw that his whole band had scattered through the timber. The only one close to him was the bay mare. He tried to round up the mares and colts as they came one by one from the timber. But the riders burst into the open and forced him to run again, with only the bay at his side.

On and on they galloped, past more spur cañons, through another stretch of dense timber, with the roar of the river always filling the cañon. Time and time again the riders tried to force the two wild horses into one of those spurs, only to be outmaneuvered by Apples. But he could see the bay was tiring. As twilight filled the gorge with a pearly haze, she began to stumble, whinnying pitifully in exhaustion.

Apples sensed that they would capture her if she could not soon escape, and it roused an instinct within him as old as time. One of the stallion's main functions was the protection of his mares and colts. Apples had fought wolves to protect his band, had killed bobcats to keep them safe, had spent many a bloody afternoon in combat with other stallions that wished his mares. Now he was facing a new enemy.

Perhaps it did not form in his mind the way it would have in a human's—the deliberate resolve that his mate should not know the pain of the branding iron, the agony of spurs, the cruel tug of the bit. But those memories were brought to him again, and filled him with the savage instinct to protect the bay.

They were approaching another spur cañon. The pursuers appeared out of the twilight again, their mounts also stumbling and lagging with exhaustion. They got on the bay's flank, driving her against Apples, trying to turn the pair onto the spur. Apples attempted to shoulder the bay out again, but the mare stumbled and almost fell.

The riders were crowding close, swinging their ropes. Apples knew what that meant. The red-headed man made a toss and the rope barely missed Apples' neck, sliding off his shoulder. The boy spurred in behind the bay, swinging his rope. The mare squealed in panic and turned directly into the spur cañon. Apples veered to follow, nipping at her heels, trying to turn her back. But she was too weary, too panicked.

Desperately he lunged against her, biting her shoulder. With a hurt look in her eyes, she spun away. It took her beyond the men and past the cañon mouth. But Apples saw how close the riders were. If he turned back, too, it would lead them up on her again. That protective instinct flared in him anew. He had lured more than one wolf away from the band by deliberately making himself the target. With a last look at the mare, now beyond the cañon mouth, he wheeled into the cañon.

He saw both riders turn to follow him, and knew he had saved the bay. It kept him from turning back, even though he realized he might have stepped into a trap. He led his pursuers at a heavy gallop up the twisting rock-walled gorge. Finally he reached the box end, where the walls towered on three sides, too steep to climb. He wheeled to face the enemy. His labored breathing made a husky roar in the narrow notch. His heaving flanks were shiny with sweat and his eyes were wild and savage. The riders appeared in the haze of dust and twilight, charging toward him, swinging their loops. He heard one of them shout: "We've got him, Jigger! We've got him!"

IV

It took Calico and Eddie three full days to get Apples back to the shack, roped and hobbled. Even so, he never stopped fighting. They turned him into a pen, and took a much-needed sleep themselves. Calico was out doing chores when Eddie finally rolled out of his blankets. It was mid-morning, with the powdery smell of dust and the sweet tang of curing meadow grass hanging thickly in the air. The boy grinned a good morning to his father and the two of them went over to the Appaloosa's pen.

The animal trotted around the inside of the fence, snorting defiantly at them. The power in the broad frame awed Eddie. The animal did not stand much over fifteen hands, but he had a broad chest and powerful rump, the muscles rippling beneath the silken skin like fat snakes.

"Look at the size of that throttle," Calico said. "He must have some Arab in him. There's enough wind in there to run a week. We never would have caught him if he hadn't turned in the box cañon to save the mare."

"We going to work him today?" Eddie asked hopefully.

"Might as well." Calico nodded. "See that brand on his hip? He's been caught once, just like I thought. It won't be like busting a wild bronc'. But he'll probably buck a while anyway. He's got too much spirit to knuckle under without a fight."

They got their ropes and went into the pen after the horse. It took them some time to corner him and put a rope on his neck. Then Calico had to put him in a Scotch hobble, too, a hitch that doubled his left hind leg up and left him only three hoofs to stand on. He had to fall over a couple of times before he realized how helpless he was, and quit fighting. Then they cleared the big holding corral of horses and worked Apples into it. He started to buck and fight when they tried to put a saddle on, and he fell once more onto his side. They helped him up, and he stood, quivering and snorting, while they put the rig on. Then Calico looked into his mouth.

"Somebody put a bit on this horse too soon," he said. "I can still see the scars on the roof of his mouth. We'll start him with a hackamore."

The hackamore was a rope bridle with a big knot that

tied beneath the jaw. It was what most horse-breakers used in the beginning stages of training a horse. A wild bronco did not understand the signals used to make it turn and stop. In the beginning, there was naturally a lot of jerking and pulling on the reins to teach the horse. If a bit was used, this hard reining would cut a horse's mouth cruelly. With the hackamore, the mouth was saved. By pulling on the bridle ropes of the hackamore, the rider could press the knot into the tender flesh just beneath the jaw. The horse soon learned that it could avoid this pain by turning or stopping as the rider wished. When the horse finally knew the signals, and a bit was put in, it only took the slightest touch of the bit on the tender roof of its mouth to make the animal respond.

Eddie got a pepper-and-salt hackamore out of their tack shed, and helped his father adjust the knot under the snorting, trembling stallion's jaw. Then Calico took off his bandanna and tied it across the Appaloosa's eyes. As he stepped back, an outraged bray broke the stillness. Calico chuckled.

"Billygoat is jealous," he said. He turned to look at the mule, whose ugly dish-face was shoved over the fence. "Don't you act like a baby just 'cause I like to top another bronc' once in a while!" he shouted.

The mule brayed again and all the other horses in the bigger corral began whinnying and snorting. Still chuckling, Calico put a toe in the stirrup and made a motion as if he were going to swing aboard. The Appaloosa braced itself but did not start bucking. Satisfied that he would be able to reach the saddle before the show started, Calico put his weight on the stirrup and swung into leather. The horse crow-hopped, almost fell over again, then settled down, trembling. Calico gathered up the hackamore ropes.

"Take off the Scotch hobble, Jigger."

Breathless with excitement, Eddie undid the hobble, lowering the hind leg. Muscles bunched like fists across Apples' chest, but still the blindfold kept him from exploding.

"Now that bandanna." Calico grinned. "And jump back like a rabbit."

Eddie reached up to yank the blind off, jumped quickly back, and ran for the fence. Even as he did, Apples gave a wild, bugling whinny and erupted. He started out in a high-roller, bucking straightaway across the corral. Eddie watched him from behind the fence. He gripped the bars in a frenzy of excitement, wincing every time the horse hit and Calico's body snapped with the shock.

The Appaloosa started to sunfish, twisting from side to side so far its belly flashed in the sun. Then it started weaving, never coming down in the same spot twice. The sharp hoofs cut the earth to ribbons and raised banners of yellow dust that swirled around the grunting, pitching Appaloosa and the yelling rider.

The horse hit for the clouds and Calico lost a stirrup and Eddie thought he was through. But he got his foot in the stirrup again before the stallion hit the ground, and took the shock with a slack body. Then Apples began pioneering all over the corral, bucking in circles and figure eights until Eddie was dizzy. He didn't see how Calico kept the saddle.

At last, the Appaloosa realized it couldn't unseat Calico with the fancy bucking and started bucking straightaway once more. Calico took each shock of landing with a body as slack as a dishrag. But it was beginning to tell on him. His face was loose with exhaustion and a painful grunt left him every time they hit.

Yellow ropes of lather furled the horse and his sweat-shiny flanks were heaving like bellows when he finally quit pitching and went into little crow hops around the corral. Even that ceased after one trip around, and he stood, trembling and wheezing and beaten beneath Calico. Eddie ran in as his father dismounted. Calico leaned against the horse, his eyes closed, his face pinched with the beating he had taken. Then he opened his eyes and grinned feebly at Eddie.

"Wasn't I right, Jigger? You wouldn't beat a bronc' this quick. Apples has a lot of fire, but he's got sense, too. He remembers it wasn't any use to fight. We'd bust him sooner or later. How about topping him while he's still whittled down?"

Eddie gulped. "Me?"

"Why not? Broncs' are part of the business. You've got to top one sooner or later. He may pitch a little and it'll give you the feel of things."

Eddie's stomach felt tight; cold sweat broke out on his hands. But it wasn't fear. It was merely excitement. He had dreamed of sitting this horse from the first time he had seen him. It was a dream come true.

He put his weight into one stirrup, testing the horse as Calico had. When the animal showed no signs of pitching, he swung aboard. But as soon as he touched the saddle, Apples dipped his head between his legs and hunted clouds. Eddie found himself sailing through the air.

The next moment he struck the ground. It seemed to rock the whole world. He turned over, squinting his eyes against the tears. It didn't seem to hurt so badly when he opened them and saw his father running toward him, grinning broadly.

"Take another dive like that and you'll break every bone in your body," Calico said. "You were stiff as a stick.

107

You've got to make like you're a sack of oats. You drop that sack and watch what happens. It just spreads all over the ground and comes up laughing. How many times have I got to tell you?"

The boy rose, shaking his head groggily. "I know. I just keep forgetting."

His father came over and laid a big, calloused hand on his shoulder. It felt warm through his shirt. "You've got a lot to learn about horses, Jigger. But if you come up grinning like that every time it knocks you, you've got the thing licked."

"Gosh, I hope so." Eddie stared ruefully at Apples, who had run to the other side of the corral. "How about me using spurs this time, Calico? I'm not the rider you are, remember."

Calico shook his head. "No, Eddie. One of the things that's made this horse spooky of us is somebody handling him rough. I think he's decent down under, and you don't need spurs for a decent bronc'. Now, how about forking that leather again?"

Calico went after the stallion with his rope. Apples was too tired to fight much. The man cornered him and got the loop on his neck and held him while Eddie blindfolded him again. Then he mounted and settled himself firmly in the saddle. Calico walked down the rope, threw it off, and put his hand on the blindfold. The horse was quivering beneath Eddie.

"Set tight?" Calico asked.

The boy nodded, crawling inside. Calico tore the blindfold off and Apples dipped his head again. But this time Eddie was ready. One moment he was heading toward the clouds, the next moment the world seemed to come up and hit him on the bottom. He was surprised to see he was still in the saddle. He didn't know how the horse was bucking, straightaway or pioneering or what. He only knew the corral spun around him. First he was looking at the ground, then at the sky. Something came up and hit him like a wet board, pounding his backsides. Then the wind was whistling past his ears.

Then it was over. He was still in the saddle, and Apples was cat-backing around the corral. He stopped that and broke into a trot. Flushed with victory, Eddie sat up straight in the saddle. His insides felt like jelly and his head was still spinning, but he tried not to show that as he trotted the Appaloosa around the corral. He had obviously been trained to rein before, for he responded to the slightest pressure of the hackamore knot under his jaw. Eddie needed only to touch the right side of his neck with a rein and give the smallest tug, and Apples turned left for him. Then he pulled back and the horse came to a stop before Calico. The laugh wrinkles deepened around the man's twinkling eyes.

"There you are, Jigger. Easy as eating striped candy. I'll bet you thought you were up there an hour."

"More like a year."

"It was only three seconds, and three bucks. But that's the way it is. You don't know where you are and you lose all sense of time. How about off-saddling now? I think he's had enough work for one day."

Eddie got down and began to uncinch the heavy, double-rigged bronco saddle. He set it down and turned back to the horse. Apples was blowing heavily and dripping lather, but showed no more fear of Eddie. The boy reached up to pat his neck. The horse started to pull away. Then, feeling the gentleness of the hand, he stopped and turned to touch Eddie's arm with an inquisitive nose. It was like velvet, soft and warm. And the light in the eyes was warm and liquid—like that of a dog adoring its master.

"Look at that," marveled Calico. "You've made a friend already, Jigger."

It struck Eddie suddenly that there was something special about this horse. He had never felt such a deep and certain kinship with Midnight or the other animals he had ridden. As he reached up to twine his hand in the silken mane, a wagon rattled into view on the road. A man and a woman sat in the seat. Eddie stiffened as he saw the sunlight gleam on the woman's yellow hair and wink on the tin star pinned to the man's cowhide vest.

"It's the schoolmarm, bringing Sheriff Kinsale," Eddie said sharply.

He raised desperate eyes to Calico. But the man stared at the wagon with a confused frown on his face. The impulse to run gripped Eddie like a spasm. He stood rigidly by Apples, poised for flight, as the wagon pulled to a halt by the pen. June Weatherby sat, straight and prim, on the seat, spots of color glowing in her cheeks.

"We've come to take the boy back to town, Calico," she said. "If you try to stop us, the sheriff will serve a warrant on you for obstructing the law."

Calico did not answer. He shoved his hat back on his curly red hair. He stared confusedly at the ground, drawing little designs in the dirt with his boot toe. It riled Eddie once more to see how much the schoolmarm always embarrassed Calico. He turned toward the woman, saying hotly: "I won't go along."

The sheriff wheezed as he climbed out of the wagon. He was a graying, paunchy man with a luxuriant beard and glowing mustaches in which he took great pride. He made a snoring sound when he spoke, and his breath fluttered the mustaches.

"Come now, Eddie. Don't make us any trouble. You need a home like the Hembres can give you."

The boy felt his hand tighten on Apples' mane. "I won't go."

"We've tried to be reasonable with you and Calico long enough, Eddie." Impatient anger made the sheriff's voice rough. "Don't make me come in there after you."

Calico held out his hand. "Now hold on, Kinsale. . . ."

"You keep out of this, Calico. You've been breaking the law, keeping this boy out of school. Your teaching him just isn't enough. I can put you in jail, if I have to. You coming, Eddie?"

The boy did not move, staring hot-eyed at Kinsale. The sheriff's face grew red. He let out a snoring breath again, fluttering his mustaches, and pulled open the gate. Eddie wheeled and ran across the corral. The sheriff followed, wheezing heavily. The horse saw him coming and reared up in a startled way, whinnying shrilly. Then the animal wheeled around Kinsale and ran for the open gate. Calico shouted and ran at him but it only startled Apples more. He shied away from Calico and dashed though the gate.

Horrified, Eddie stood on the other side of the corral, watching the Appaloosa gallop down the road. A hundred yards from the pen, the horse halted and looked back for a moment, as if seeking Eddie. Then, almost reluctantly, he turned and galloped on into timber.

"You let him go," Eddie told Kinsale accusingly. "Calico said a horse like that comes once in a man's lifetime, and you let him go."

Still running toward Eddie, Kinsale wheezed: "I didn't mean to, son. You can have another horse. Dog-gone it, you and this here hawse-runner make me more trouble than a whole passel of stage robbers. Come along, now. . . ."

"No!" Eddie cried, and wheeled to duck through the bars. He ran like a deer across the hayfields, hearing Kinsale shout behind him, and then crashed through the chokecherry thickets into the creek bottom. Soundless tears of rage and loss were squeezed from his squinted eyes as he thought of Apples' being gone. He'd never go back with Kinsale now. Never!

He ran upstream until his heart was pounding and his lungs seemed ready to burst. Then he had to slow down. But he turned off through the thickets and dense scrub timber to a box cañon that only he and Calico knew about.

It was really no more than a deep gulch, the buck brush across its mouth so thick a man would go right past without even knowing it was there. He scratched his face and ripped his shirt clawing through the brush. Then he scrambled to the dead end and sank to the earth there, exhausted, bleeding, defeated. The loss of Apples was like an ache in his chest and he hadn't wanted to cry so much since he was a baby. But he bit his lip to keep back the tears, trying to figure what was next.

He knew he couldn't go back to the cabin. Maybe the sheriff would wait there for him to show up. But where else could he go? If he had a horse and some grub, he could have gone deeper into the mountains and hole up, like Calico said the train robbers always did when the posse was after them. But he didn't have a horse or grub. He didn't have anything.

Night came down and the chill mountain air began to eat into his bones. He crouched against the dank earth, shivering, hungry. He had never felt so lonesome in his life.

As the moon began to rise, spilling yellow light down through the foliage, he heard a crackling along his back trail. Somebody was coming. Had the sheriff tracked him down? He flattened on the ground, eyes glued to the spot where the light filtered across the trail.

A mounted figure appeared, leading two other animals. Eddie's breath ran out in a great gasp of relief. He recognized his father's unmistakable silhouette. He called out, jumping to his feet. Calico pulled up and dismounted, chuckling deeply in his chest, and everything was all right again.

"Figured you'd be up here in our hide-out, Jigger. The sheriff's left, but I've a notion he'll be back tomorrow, or sometime soon." He paused, looking dubiously at Eddie. "Are you sure you don't want to go with him?"

Eddie said: "Why do you think I ran away?"

Calico shook his head helplessly. "You don't think I'm doing wrong, do you?"

"I don't know," Eddie said. "All I know is I couldn't stand being away from you."

A strange brightness came into Calico's eyes. He grinned and reached out to touch Eddie's mop of hair. "I guess I feel the same way about you, Jigger. How can it be wrong for a man to want to keep his own son?" He looked off at the mountains. "Why don't we hit the trail? I've had enough of those busybodies for a while."

V

Calico and Eddie went deeper into the mountains that night and made their camp. The next morning they backtracked to pick up the Appaloosa's sign. Calico found the hoof prints on the wagon road near the shack and followed them into the mountains. The trail was cold but he did not have much trouble uncovering it that day. Both Eddie and Calico were surprised that it led them out of the Wind Rivers, across Jackson Hole, and into the Snake Mountains. It was not a wandering trail. The horse seemed to be traveling with some definite goal in mind. Calico could not figure it out.

They crossed South Park where the waterfowl rose from swamps with a muffled whirring and birds chattered in the cattails. They left the park and crossed the Snake River, climbing the trail to the Narrows. The gorge below them was filled with the hollow boom of the rapids, and the water was whipped to a sudsy foam by the sharp rocks. The two riders rose higher, through towering peaks and ridges, and finally reached a wind-swept ridge that looked down into a round green valley. White barns and a log house lay like toy blocks 1,000 feet below. Corrals looked like a pattern of jackstraws dropped haphazardly on the tawny earth.

"Haskins's ranch," Calico said, taking his binoculars out for a look. "That bunch of broke horses in his corrals does look smaller than the last time I was here. He had a big red bay he was really proud of. I don't see it down there."

He handed the four-power binoculars to Eddie, and the boy searched the corrals in vain for the red horse. Finally he shook his head, and Calico said: "Haskins was telling the truth about some wild one stealing his best horses, then." He frowned, scratching his stubble beard. "I still don't see how it could have been Apples. No horse could've reached the Wind Rivers from here in that short a time, not even traveling alone."

"Maybe it was another wild stallion."

Calico shook his head. "Haskins swore it was an Appaloosa. If there was another Appaloosa in this section, we'd know it, Jigger. So would Haskins. No two Appaloosas are colored exactly the same. The spots are dabbed on different, or the shape of the rump white's different, or the chest color is bay instead of blue. If you saw another one, you'd know it wasn't Apples in a second."

"Then either it was Apples that Haskins saw, or Haskins was lying."

"He'd have no reason to lie. He may be a rough one, but he's too good a horseman to kill Apples for nothing." Calico shook his head again helplessly. "We're up against a mystery, Jigger. Maybe we'll find the answer over here in the Snakes."

They reached another loop of the Snake and lost Apples' tracks in the marshy bottoms. Calico hunted until nightfall but failed to find where they led out. Finally, with the light gone, they had to give up and make camp. Eddie tried not to show his disappointment. He was so tired every muscle in his body ached. But he would have ridden the rest of the night, if it meant they would find Apples. He unsaddled the animals, hobbled them, and turned them out to graze. Calico had already lit the fire, started the coffee, and was making biscuits in the top of the sack. After dinner the night seemed to press in against them. The only sound was the chirping of crickets in the deep meadow grass or the far-off snort of Midnight.

It was lonely and a little spooky and Eddie was glad for the fire and his father. After a while, Billygoat wandered in and nuzzled Calico's shirt front, trying to pull out his tobacco sack. Calico brushed him absently away, not even speaking to him.

"Thinking about Apples?" Eddie asked.

"No," Calico said. "About you." He was silent for a while, sitting cross-legged before the dying fire, staring off into the black shadows beneath the towering pines. Finally he said: "Sometimes I think maybe June's right about a kid needing a home like the Hembres' and an education. Look at me. I was an orphan. I had to start cleaning out stables for a living when I was ten. I got something of an education, but not enough to go very far. Horses are all I know. Got nothing but a few head of scroungy bronc's, an old shack, and one dirty shirt to my name. Never make more than tobacco money, sometimes not that. I've got no right to hold you down to that."

Eddie sat up straight with surprise. "But I like it, Calico. I don't ever want anything else."

"You're too young to want it now, Jigger. But when you're my age, you might begin to realize what you've missed. Then it's too late."

"Now you're talking like June Weatherby."

"Maybe I am. But it's only one side of me talking. The other side wants to keep you." He glanced at Eddie, then looked quickly away, as if embarrassed. His voice sounded husky. "Nobody wants to give up his own son."

"Gee, Calico. I never knew it was like that. I thought you was plumb set on making me a horse-runner."

Calico shook his head. "I don't know which way to turn. Sometimes I feel I'm doing you wrong by keeping you away from school like this. But I can't seem to give you up, when it comes right down to it. Be mighty lonesome up here without you, Jigger." He glanced at Eddie again, then rose with a gruff chuckle, slapping at his buckskin breeches. "Well, that's something we can't settle tonight, anyway. How about rolling in?"

Before Eddie could answer, Billygoat tossed his ugly head and snorted. Calico wheeled around, staring at a spot between two lodgepole pines. A man appeared in the circle of firelight. He was a tall Indian with a porcupine roach in

116

his hair that made him look even taller. He was wrapped in a matted buffalo robe worked in yellow and red quills. At his waist, dangling from a belt, was a beaver-pelt medicine bag in which he carried his tobacco and powder and lead and such. The only part of his body showing was his bare ankles, shining like old pennies in the fire glow. His face was as empty of expression as a mahogany mask. His black eyes glittered at Calico.

"Howdy," Calico said. "Throw in and have some chuck."

The Indian looked at the coffee pot for a long time. Eddie felt the skin crawl down the back of his neck. Did the man understand English? He didn't move. Eddie began peering around the black shadows. Maybe there were more Indians out there, just waiting to shoot or something. He felt the perspiration break out on his palms. Then the Indian sat down, so abruptly it made Eddie jump. Calico poured some more water in the pot and dumped a handful of coffee after it, kicking a new chunk of wood into the dying fire. Then he got out some more bacon to fry. The Indian licked his lips and threw back his robe, exposing a brawny, copper chest.

"What tribe?" Calico asked.

"Hunkpapa Sioux," the Indian said.

Right after he spoke, he gave a jump and slapped at his medicine bag, looking around. Eddie couldn't see anything behind the man except the mule, standing with his rump toward the Indian. He was complacently gnawing on the bark of a juniper.

"It's just old Billygoat having his supper." Calico grinned. "Leave him there long enough and he'll have that tree stripped, head to toe."

The Indian settled down again. Calico went on frying the bacon and asked him if he'd seen an Appaloosa around anywhere. The Indian nodded solemnly.

"Spotted horse. Over in Paiute Cañon. Bad medicine. Indian stay away. Big Devil."

"Big Devil?" Calico asked. "You can't mean the Appaloosa."

The Indian nodded again. "Same horse. Bad Medicine. You chase?"

"That's the one we're after, all right."

"That's why he go to Paiute Cañon. Him born there. Always go there when men chase. . . ."

The Indian broke off, slapping at his medicine bag and jumping a second time, looking around behind him. Again, all Eddie could see was the mule, still chewing on the bark. Muttering, the Indian settled back. The coffee was boiling, and Calico poured him a cup.

"Let me get this straight," Calico said. "You say this Appaloosa is bad medicine. . . ."

"Heap bad medicine. Like ghost. Steal Indian horse. Kill Indian horse. Kill Indian man."

Calico let his breath out in a long whistle. "Killed a man?"

The Indian nodded solemnly. "Man-killer. Ghost horse. All Indian stay away. You stay away."

"He's crazy," Eddie said, unable to contain himself any longer. "He can't be talking about Apples. That horse wouldn't kill anybody."

Calico shook his head. "Seems to know what he's talking about, Jigger. And he sure means an Appaloosa. I hate to believe it, but it ties in with what Haskins said."

As he finished, there was a ripping sound. The Indian jumped to his feet, grabbing once more at his medicine bag. But this time it was gone. Eddie spotted part of the swarthy beaver pelt extending from either side of Billygoat's mouth. When the Indian saw the mule chewing on his bag, he gave a shout and yanked a wicked-looking knife from his belt, lunging for Billygoat. Calico snaked a long leg out and tripped the Indian, and he fell flat on his face. He rolled over and came to his feet again, wheeling toward Calico.

"Watch out!" Eddie shouted. "He's going for you, Calico."

To Eddie's surprise, Calico held his hands up in front of him and backed away, laughing. "Look out now," he told the Indian. "Billygoat didn't mean any harm. He just hankered after that tobacco in your medicine bag. Tell you what. How about this turnip in repayment?" He took his big gold watch from his pocket, holding it out to the Indian. "My grandpa give it to me. Tell the time of day even after the sun's down."

The Indian stopped, gaping at the watch glittering in the firelight. "No sun?"

"All night long, tells time. And ticks. Listen to that noise. Better'n crickets."

Intrigued, the Indian leaned forward to listen. The anger left his face. He accepted the watch, frowning at it. He held it to his ear. Then he shook it. Then he looked at it and grinned. He put his knife away and gathered his robe about him and sat down to drink his coffee. Then he ate the bacon, listening to the watch and grinning and nodding at Calico. When he was finished, he stood up again and the grin faded. He looked toward the east.

"Paiute Cañon. Devil horse. You stay away."

Ceremoniously he wrapped the robe about him and rode into the night. Eddie stared after him. There was a gulp in his throat. He didn't want to believe that about Apples. He looked pleadingly at his father. Calico stirred the fire, shaking his head.

"Please. . . ."

"All right," Calico said gruffly. "We'll see for ourselves."

★ ★ ★ ★ ★

All next morning the man and boy rode toward Paiute Cañon. It was wild country. They sought the high slopes, and the timber beneath them looked black as a beard on the trail. Woodchucks heckled them from rocks and Billygoat heckled right back. The booming of the wind through the pines sounded like distant cannon sometimes. Finally they reached a ridge overlooking a narrow gap that Calico said was the cañon. The ridge became the edge of a cliff and they followed it until they came to a shelving trail slanting sharply into the notch.

Grazing on a slope far below them was a band of horses. And sure enough, high up on a rock stood the sentinel stallion, an Appaloosa. His chest shone like blue steel in the bright sun and the red spots on his white rump were as bright as wet paint. Calico turned to look questioningly at Eddie.

"You still want to do it?"

The boy's heart was pounding with excitement. "We can't go back now. We've got to get him."

"All right," Calico said soberly. "I know this cañon. It runs back a mile. The sides get so steep a horse couldn't climb them. I'll go to the other side. You stay here. We'll drive the horses in from both ends and have them trapped between us. Give me about half an hour and then start down that trail yonder. But remember this, Jigger, don't you try and get that Appaloosa. Just work him into the notch easy and he won't try to get past you. Wait for me to come. Savvy?"

Eddie grinned happily. "I savvy."

The man nodded and turned on down the cliff, disappearing back in the trees. Eddie waited impatiently until he thought the half hour was up, then started down the steep, shelving trail. It made him dizzy to look down from such a height at first, but he got over it. He left the cliff and rode out onto the slopes, getting closer to the herd. It seemed to him that Apples looked different, somehow. He seemed jumpier, more suspicious, moving restlessly on the rock and sniffing the air. Then Eddie grinned wryly. After that long chase, anybody would be jumpy.

As he drew closer, Eddie saw a big red bay among the mares and colts. Haskins's horse. He didn't want to believe it, but there it was, right before his eyes. But that didn't mean Apples was a killer. And maybe the red bay had just joined him of his own free will.

Eddie wound down over the sage-covered slopes, slipping up on the flank of the herd before they caught his scent. When they saw him, they fled down the hill toward the gorge. The stallion nervously circled their rear, head up, taking in everything he could. Eddie waited a little before he slipped up on the other flank. He didn't want to rush them but just keep them going. A few of them got away, but the bulk of the band, including the Appaloosa, was finally herded into the gorge. They began running ahead of him now, in a great flurry of dust and squeals and flashing hoofs. Then they disappeared around a bend. For a moment Eddie thought he'd lost them. But he had ridden on only five or ten minutes when the Appaloosa appeared, coming back. His heavy ears lay flat, his magnificent body seemed fired with smoldering fury as he raced along.

Eddie knew what had happened. The band had met Calico and he'd let the others through but had blocked the Appaloosa. Excitement mounted in Eddie. The Appaloosa stopped when he saw the boy. Eddie saw Calico's rope trailing from the animal's neck. His father had apparently roped him and then lost his rope. Eddie knew, if he could only get his hands on it, he would have the horse. Suddenly, as if reading his mind, the stallion gave a shrill whinny and wheeled away, running back into the gorge. The next moment he disappeared around a bend. But Eddie knew that the horse would meet Calico and turn back again.

Pushing back his hat, Eddie scratched his head the way Calico did when he was trying to figure out something. And, sure enough, it worked. He thought of a plan to catch Apples. He took off his jacket, his hat, his bandanna, the blankets from his saddle, even his boots, and strewed them across the bottom of the gorge. He knew that the man smell on them would spook the wild horse and keep him from going through. All Eddie had to do now was get hold of the free end of the rope when Apples stopped and snub it around a tree. That was all.

Eddie quickly hitched his horse in the timber, then ran in his stocking feet to an outcropping of buck brush that grew out into the trail. He heard the thud of hoofs and knew the stallion was coming back. The animal flashed past him. Then he stopped abruptly, rearing up, in front of the clothes, nostrils flaring at the hated man smell. The rope was dragging from his neck, the free end only a few feet from Eddie. The boy jumped out into the trail, grabbing up the rope before the horse could wheel. Then he ran back around the tree with it, winding it twice about the trunk. The stallion twisted and lunged, trying to get free. But the stout rope held him, the slipknot digging into his neck every time he pulled back. He fought with much more savagery than Eddie remembered in Apples, squealing and bugling, pawing and kicking, biting at the rope. At last he seemed to realize he was beaten. He stood with his head down, dripping lather and blood-flecked foam, quivering all over.

Eddie drew a long breath. He wished Apples hadn't

fought him so hard, but now the stallion was broken for keeps. And wouldn't it be swell if he could be aboard the horse when his father came up? Calico'd be mighty proud of him then. Eyes shining, he ran and got his boots and put them on. Then he went back and unsaddled his own horse, lugging the gear back to the Appaloosa. But the stallion wouldn't let him come near. Baring his teeth, he lashed the air with thrashing forehoofs.

"Listen, Apples," Eddie pleaded, taking a step forward, "I'm not going to hurt you. We're friends . . . remember?"

The stallion screamed and reared up. Then he came down and wheeled on the boy. His whole body trembled with fury. There was a strange glare in his little deep-set eyes. That look sent a chill down Eddie's spine. He'd never seen that cold, crafty expression in Apples' eyes before. And Apples hadn't kept his ears flat against his head all the time, either.

The puzzle grew in Eddie's mind as he spoke in soft, cajoling words and tried to get the saddle on the animal's back. When nothing he said or did soothed the Appaloosa, Eddie began to get mad. He ran to get his own rope. It took him three throws to catch the Appaloosa's hind leg. Then he walked toward the horse, keeping the rope tight all the time so the animal was stretched between the two lines. When he got near enough, he snaked the rope around the horse's other hind leg with a quick throw, drawing the two hind legs together so he couldn't kick. He hobbled them that way, tying the knot as Calico had taught him so it could be released by a quick tug on the rope. The horse was hobbled so tightly that, if he tried to move, he would fall over. He stood, quivering and snorting, the muscles twitching all over his body, as Eddie lifted the heavy saddle on. He cinched it up, and then made a war bridle from his lead rope. Then he untied the rope on the stallion's neck. Still the hobble kept him from moving.

"Now, Apples, when I get to you, you'll remember me well enough. You won't be scared at all. I'll bet you won't even buck."

The horse grew rigid as stone when Eddie put his toe to the stirrup. There was a wild, savage look to his eyes that scared the boy, but he swung up anyway. The stallion remained dead still, all his muscles standing out tautly. Eddie frowned, wondering how Apples could forget him so soon. Had Sheriff Kinsale frightened the horse that much? He reached down to give the rope a tug that would release the hobble.

As soon as the hind hoofs were released, the Appaloosa gave a savage scream and exploded. Eddie was taken by surprise. He barely managed to keep from flying off. The horse hit the ground with all four legs like ramrods. Eddie tried to take the grinding shock with a slack body, as Calico had taught him, but it seemed to shatter the world right inside his head. He felt the horse switch ends and blindly clawed for the saddle horn. The animal started pioneering. He jerked Eddie's body back and forth in the saddle, slamming him against the seat one minute and tearing him out of leather the next. Then the boy felt the stallion rear up on his hind legs. He thought the animal would stop and come down. But he didn't. Higher and higher he rose. This was the trick of the killer horse, to fall back on his rider and crush him. Eddie knew, if he didn't tumble off now, he would be caught beneath 1,000 pounds of bone and muscle.

With a wild shout, he kicked free of the stirrups and rolled off. He tried to hit slackly as a sack of oats, the way Calico had told him to do. It did seem to take some of the shock out. He rolled over, expecting to see the horse running away.

But the Appaloosa was coming back at him. Lying on one elbow, he saw the stallion wheeling and charging down on him, eyes blazing with murder. Eddie tried to get up, shouting: "No, Apples! You aren't that kind of a horse. . . ."

The animal didn't halt. Eddie was still on one knee when the stallion reared above him in all his savagery, eyes glistening red with hate, deadly hoofs flashing. There was a blinding explosion of pain, a shattering blow against the boy's left arm. Eddie heard himself cry out in agony.

"No, Apples!" he shouted at the stallion again. "You aren't that kind of a horse. You can't be. . . ."

Dimly he realized he was on the ground and rolled over, sobbing with the pain in his arm. The animal had wheeled and was starting back. The ears lay flat. The eyes held a cold stony glare, far more terrifying than the blazing hatred of a moment before. Eddie's heart stopped beating as the Appaloosa reared above him again. This time he couldn't defend himself, he knew.

At that instant a rider flashed into his vision, charging out of the gorge and knocking the stallion aside. Vaguely Eddie saw that it was Calico on his mule. The Appaloosa staggered back, then wheeled, and lunged in at the mule. Billygoat dodged the deadly charge, whirling as the horse wheeled again, rearing up, bugling wildly. Calico was tugging his Winchester free as he reined the mule around.

"No!" Eddie gasped. "Don't shoot him. . . ."

"It's the only thing that'll stop him, Jigger!" Calico shouted. "He's crazy . . . !"

The horse charged again before Calico could cock his gun. Billygoat waited until the last minute, then dodged aside, braying raucously. The stallion ran by. Calico cocked the Winchester and fired wildly. It was a snap shot, and missed the horse.

But Eddie saw the sudden change in the Appaloosa. The horse wheeled around. The rage and hatred in his little eyes were turned to utter fear. With a shrill whinny, he whirled and ran up the cañon. Eddie turned back, weak and dizzy with pain.

Calico stopped Billygoat and jumped off, running to his son. "It was all my fault, Jigger," he said. "I should've come up sooner. I kept holding back, thinking we could get him quiet-like by moving in slow. It looks like your left arm's broke. You hurt anywhere else?"

Eddie gritted his teeth. "All over. But I guess my arm's the only place that's broken."

Calico pulled out his bandanna, wadded it up, and shoved it into his son's mouth. "Bite down on that. I'm going to splint that arm. Then we'll take you back to Jackson." He squatted back on his hunkers a moment and looked up the cañon, taking a deep, shaken breath. "I guess this ends it, doesn't it, Jigger?"

Eddie felt a sharp fear stab at him. "What do you mean?"

"I hate to say it, Eddie, but we can't have that horse. Haskins and the Indian were right. No animal would act that way unless he was a man-killer."

VI

It took Calico and Eddie three days to get back to Jackson. It was a nightmare for the boy, with his arm hurting him so much. A couple of times he passed out and his father had to hold him on the horse as they rode. On the afternoon of the third day, when they reached town, Eddie was so sick he could hardly see the row of false-fronted buildings that lined the main street. He dimly heard the voices of men, the stamp of cow ponies at hitch racks, the creak of a big hay wagon passing them. Then they came to Doc Purcell's office, in the second story of the bank. Calico stepped down and tied their mounts. When he lifted up his arms to help his son down, everything went black again for the boy, and he fell against his father.

When Eddie came to again, he was lying on a table. His arm was throbbing like fury. He saw that there was a new splint on it, instead of Calico's old bandanna tied around a couple of willow sticks. The doc must have reset it and put all those white bandages on. The boy looked up to see a round red face bending over him, full of concern. It was Doc Purcell, a little on the sawed-off side, so dignified in his frock-tail coat that he reminded Eddie of a bantam rooster all puffed up with his own importance. But Calico had said that this was just to hide a heart as big as a wagon wheel.

"He has come to," Doc Purcell announced.

Calico came toward the table and bent over his son. His face looked sort of drawn and pale. "Better, Jigger?" he asked.

"He'll be all right," Dr. Purcell said. "Most of his pain came from the jolting on that long ride. I suggest you put him to bed immediately, Calico."

At that moment the door opened and somebody came in—somebody with yellow hair and a pretty, flushed face. The schoolmarm, feeding off her range again! Eddie felt sick all over. Why couldn't she leave them alone, anyhow?

"I saw you come into town through the schoolhouse

window," she said in a breathless voice. "What's the matter with Eddie?"

Calico gulped. He took off his hat and whistled on it with his breath. Then he explained haltingly what had happened, all the time working his hat around between his hands. When he had finished, June Weatherby burst out indignantly, her blue eyes snapping.

"I told you that was no life for the boy. See what it has brought him now?"

"It wasn't his fault," Eddie blurted, gritting his teeth against the pain. "I ran away from the sheriff myself."

"I don't care," June declared, her pretty pink face puckered with anxiety. "Calico had no right to take a boy your age out into the wilderness after those savage beasts."

Calico asked wryly: "Ma'am, what do you know about boys? He's ten times more of a man than any town boy his age."

June flushed. "Are you a man when you smell like a goat and can't write your own name?" she demanded scornfully.

Calico lowered his head and started to draw designs on the floor with the toe of his boot. "Meaning me?" he asked in an abashed way.

Dr. Purcell chuckled. "I guess she put you in your place, Calico."

"It doesn't matter," June said. "The main thing is we've got Eddie here now, and he can't run away in that shape. If he must stay in bed, we might as well move him to the Hembre house. They were ready to take him when he ran off into the hills the last time."

"I'm not going," Eddie stated flatly.

Calico turned and leaned over his son. "Maybe she's right, Jigger," he said. "Maybe the time's come for you to have a little better life than I can give you. Clean clothes, good home-cooked meals . . . all that kind of thing." He tried to grin, and patted Eddie's leg. "You aren't filling out very good on that bacon and beans we eat out at the shack."

Calico straightened and looked at June. Eddie noticed that the two didn't mean to be as mad at each other as they ought. There was a funny flushed look to her face and her eyes were shining. For a minute, Calico was meeting her eyes more squarely than he ever had before. Then suddenly he dropped his gaze and began working his hat between his hands again.

"I got to ramble now, Eddie," he said. His voice sounded strange and husky. "You understand how it is. I couldn't take you back to the shack in that shape. A man like me isn't any good at nursing. Needs a woman's touch. I'll come down to see you as often as I can. You understand, don't you?"

He grasped his son's shoulder, but Eddie pulled away, turning his head aside. He couldn't help but feel that his father was deserting him. He didn't want to stay here. They were all strangers to him. It would be like a prison after the wild, free life he had lived. He heard Calico leave and dropped his head sickly.

Too weak to resist, Eddie let June and the doctor help him out to the buggy, standing in front of the office. In heart-broken silence he rode along, propped up between them, until they came to the Hembres' big, white, two-story frame house on the outskirts of town.

June got out and ran up the walk. She knocked on the front door, and after a minute a man opened it. It was Ezra Hembre, owner of the livery stable in town. He was a middle-aged man, heavy-boned and big, with a ruff of grizzled hair above a ruddy face. The two talked in undertones, glancing back at the buggy, then they both came back down the walk.

"Hello, there, Eddie," Mr. Hembre said heartily. "Glad you decided to come. We sure need a boy around the place. Ma's got Polly Jane to help her, but I ain't got nobody."

Eddie didn't know what to say, so he just ducked his head the way his father did and kept quiet.

Doc Purcell climbed out and went around the buggy. Eddie glanced up and saw them all looking at him. "Can you make it alone, Eddie?" June asked anxiously.

Eddie nodded and managed to step down. His legs felt as if they weren't attached to him and everything was swinging in a big circle. But somehow he made it up the walk, leaning on Ezra Hembre's brawny arm.

A woman opened the front door of the big white house. She was plump and motherly. Her bare arms were powdered with flour up to her elbows and the scent of cinnamon and cloves and cooking apples floated out to meet them. Ezra Hembre helped Eddie forward.

"Here's Eddie, Ma, come to live with us," he said. "He got stomped by a wild stallion and needs to rest up a bit. When he gets well, he's going to help us around the place and show Polly Jane more about horses."

Eddie took off his old, beat-up sombrero as Ma Hembre smiled at him. Then she gathered him into her arms. "We've wanted you a long time, Eddie," she said with a warm smile. "You'll have your own room and tomorrow we'll buy you some other clothes."

For a moment it was so much like it had been with his own mother that Eddie forgot how much he wanted to escape. Then Pa Hembre helped him climb up the stairs, while Ma went ahead to turn down the bed. They took him to the big room at the end of the hall and sat him on the bed. While Pa Hembre got one of his nightshirts for Eddie, June and the doctor told him good bye.

"You're going to be all right here," the schoolmarm said. "And if there's anything I can to do help, just let me know."

He tried to scowl at her, but they had all been so nice to him he couldn't do that. He just thanked her with a gulp and a nod of his head. When they were gone, Hembre came back in and helped Eddie get out of his clothes and into the nightshirt. After Eddie was under the covers, the man grinned down at him.

"Ma's gone down to fix you some soup now. We'll send Polly Jane up with it. You must have seen her once in a while when you was in town with Calico. She's only a year younger than you, Eddie. She can ride as good as a cowpuncher already, but she'd sure love to talk with a kid that's topped wild bronc's."

As Hembre went out, Eddie groaned to himself. A girl was coming—and him like this! A moment later he heard quick steps on the stairs and the door opened. Eddie slid down under the covers, a hot blush covering his thin face.

"Hello, Eddie. I guess you don't remember me. I'm Polly Jane."

He looked around to see a girl standing beside the bed, holding a tray with a bowl of steaming soup on it. She was willow-slim, her face had a deep tan, and her curly brown hair was streaked yellow by the sun. She was wearing a plaid shirt and Levi's tucked into small, scuffed boots.

Eddie turned his head away. The smell of the soup made his mouth water, but he wasn't having any while that darned girl was here. He waited silently while she set the bowl on the small table beside the bed.

"Roll out, Eddie, roll out while it's hot," Polly Jane said, rattling the spoon against the tin tray like a dinner gong.

"No, thanks," Eddie muttered glumly. "Don't want any."

When she just sat there, he darted a furtive look at her from the corner of his eye. She was shoving her hair back with an uncertain gesture and there was a worried expression on her face. It made him feel kind of rude. Blushing, he sat up in bed. "Well, I might have a little," he said gruffly to hide his embarrassment. "Sure smells good."

Smiling, she put the tray down on the bed in front of him. "I really wanted to hear about how you broke your arm," she said in a breathless voice. "Pa says you were breaking a wild stallion. Aren't you sort of young for that, Eddie?"

"Naw," he said. "I've been busting horses ever since I can remember."

"But not this kind," she insisted. "Pa says you must have the makings of a real top hand to stay on him as long as you did."

"He wasn't so bad," Eddie said. "It took me a little time to get my wood on him, but once I hit the kak and got my toes in the oxbows, I stuck tight as a cocklebur. If he hadn't started windmilling, I never would have sunned my moccasins."

"Wait a minute . . . wait a minute!" Polly Jane laughed. "I thought I knew cow talk but that comes from too far out on the range for me. What's wood and what's a kak?"

He grinned self-consciously. "Wood and kak's the same thing . . . a saddle."

"And oxbows are stirrups," she said. "But what's windmilling?"

"That's when a horse swaps ends completely, right up in the air. And you sure know what sunning your moccasins is."

Her chuckle was like the gurgle of a little creek. "I guess that must be falling off."

When he nodded, Polly Jane asked him more about Apples and before he knew it he was telling her all he knew about the horse. How for several years Calico had been seeing the Appaloosa in the Wind Rivers. How at last they'd been able to trap him. How strangely he'd acted, so gentle and willing the first time they'd caught him, so wild and savage the second.

Round-eyed, she dropped to the floor beside the bed and listened with her arms clasped around her knees. Eagerly she begged for other stories about the wild horses he and Calico had caught. Hardly knowing how it happened, Eddie found himself explaining how Calico trapped them and sometimes sold them to the Army, sometimes trained them for cow horses, selling them to outlying ranches for thirty or forty dollars each. She sat so quietly and drank it all in so admiringly that Eddie found suddenly he didn't dislike girls as much as he'd thought. When Ma Hembre came up and said he had to go to sleep, he was almost sorry.

But Eddie couldn't go to sleep right away, sick and tired as he was. He kept thinking about Polly Jane, wanting to like her, but determined that no filly was going to make a town sissy out of him. He told this to himself again and again, scowling ferociously. No, sir, as soon as he was able, he was going to run away. This took his thoughts back to Apples and he began going over and over what had happened back there in the valley.

"There's gotta be some mistake . . . there's gotta be some mistake," he kept muttering, unable to believe that the beautiful horse was really a killer. "I must've done something wrong. I can't understand it."

An early morning sun slanted through the window when Eddie woke up. For a moment he lay there, relishing the comfortable bed. He'd never known one could be so soft. It was like sleeping on a cloud. Then he shook his head angrily. He couldn't let them break his resolve. Maybe the bunks up at Calico's were a little harder, but at least you didn't have to be afraid to touch them for fear you'd get them dirty. Then the door opened and Polly Jane came in with a bowl of hot mush and a jug of milk on a tray. She had a blue polka-dot dress on this morning and she'd tied red ribbons on her pigtails. He remembered to scowl. Maybe she'd tricked him into talking to her last night but it wouldn't happen again. She didn't seem to notice, though. She just put the tray down on the table and sat on the foot of the bed.

"We get all kinds of stories about your father down here in town," she said. "Does he really get drunk every night and go around chasing the bears?" Eddie frowned at her, biting his lip to keep from answering. How could they get such crazy ideas about Calico? But she went right on. "Did he really break a bottle of corn whiskey on that man's head when the man wouldn't let him play the piano in his bare feet?"

That was too much. Eddie couldn't keep quiet any longer. "It isn't true!" he explained indignantly. "I never saw my father drunk. Those are just crazy stories they cook up about anybody that's different. Just 'cause he lives out there alone and maybe gets tired of wearing his boots once in a while. . . ."

She gave that little gurgling chuckle again. "He does have a mule called Billygoat, doesn't he?"

"Well," he said, "I guess so."

"Why is the mule named that? Does he have horns and a beard?"

"No," Eddie answered defensively. "He just eats everything he can get his teeth into. He likes tobacco most of all.

134

Once he almost made an Indian massacre us by stealing the fellow's tobacco. My father had to give the Indian his granddaddy's watch to quiet him down."

This made her laugh outright and he couldn't help laughing, too. Looking back, it really was funny, although at the time Calico'd been just about ready to shoot Billygoat for his greediness. Quickly Polly Jane asked Eddie to tell her more stories about Billygoat. Before he remembered that he wasn't going to talk to her, he found himself telling her more about the mule. They were both still laughing when she told him to eat his mush before it got cold. He'd finished the whole bowl before he realized how she'd tricked him into it. But then he couldn't be mad at her because things looked different to a man on a full stomach. He was really sorry when she got up and said: "I'd like to stay and hear some more about Billygoat, but I've got to start to school."

He watched her through the window as she went out the front door and joined a big, curly-haired, loud-mouthed boy who stuck out his chest like a pouter pigeon and showed off for her by walking along the fence. Eddie downed a twinge of jealousy. He tried to tell himself he didn't care. But he couldn't help wondering who the boy was.

Eddie was surprised how fast the next few days passed. Polly Jane brought up his meals and read to him in the afternoon—about places like India and China and a country named Arabia where the Arabian horses came from. He'd never heard of that and got her to read to him about it again and again. Sometimes for hours on end he'd forget about his father, about running away. Then he'd remember again and feel guilty, vowing that, when he was strong enough, he'd escape.

In a few days Eddie was able to get up. He stayed around the house with his arm in a sling, or went down to the livery stable with Ezra Hembre in the morning. The Hembres had given him some new jeans and a plaid shirt to wear. They had tried to make him wear shoes, too, instead of the moccasins Calico had made for him. But he would not go that far, and stubbornly refused to put on the heavy brogans. June Weatherby dropped in everyday. They were all so nice that Eddie couldn't stay resentful. He talked with them and he could see that they thought he was resigned to his fate. But down underneath he was just waiting for the time when he'd be strong enough to leave.

It was several weeks before the doctor took the splint and bandages off, and said that in a couple more days Eddie would be well enough to go to school.

School! It made Eddie sick inside. He'd heard his father talk about it. They made you sit on a wooden seat that flattened you out behind so much you couldn't fork a horse any more. They cramped your fingers around a slate pencil till they got so bent you couldn't hold a rope. Time you got out, you could spell Mississippi and do sums and write a lot of big words, but what good would that do you when you went to get a riding job at some ranch?

Eddie just couldn't stay around for that. He knew that, if he was going, it had to be tonight. That evening, when the Hembres were all asleep, he got up and dressed in his old clothes. He sneaked downstairs, took half a loaf of bread and a couple of apples, put them in a sack, and went out the door. The chill spring night made him shiver. For a moment all the warmth and kindness of the household rushed over him and he almost wanted to go back. Then he shook his head stubbornly and pulled his hat tightly over his eyes like Calico always did when there was a tough job of work to do. Nothing was going to keep him from his father any longer. Nothing!

VII

All that night Eddie trudged along across meadow and foot-hill land. At dawn he got a hitch in a farmer's wagon that took him to the foot of the Wind Rivers trail. It was ten miles up the trail to his shack. He reached it early in the afternoon, stumbling from exhaustion, his arms aching, his head throbbing like a drum. But Calico wasn't there. Eddie realized that his father must be out running some more wild horses. Weary and discouraged, he threw himself on the bunk and fell asleep. He woke up with the owls hooting and didn't even know what time of night it was. He tried to cook himself some supper but the biscuits wouldn't rise and he burned the bacon. He ate it anyway and went back to sleep.

His aching arm woke him at daybreak and he got up and went outside. Midnight and a couple of other horses were in the pen. It was hard to saddle up with only one arm but Eddie finally got the rigging aboard. Putting some biscuits and jerked beef into the saddlebags and lashing the blanket roll behind the cantle, he started off in search of Calico. He knew his father would be watching one of the horse traps in the Wind Rivers.

Eddie reached the first trap in the afternoon. It was one he had helped Calico build a year ago. But there was no fresh sign around it, and Eddie rode on. Night found him high in the mountains. He hobbled his horse and made camp, eating cold meat and biscuits and drinking icy water from a stream. It was chilly and the fire didn't seem to warm him. A wolf began howling on some distant ridge, and the small rustlings of the night filled the forest. It seemed powerful dark and cold and a fearful loneliness began to fill the boy. For the first time, he realized what a big job he had tackled.

He had been through a lot of this country, but never alone. He began to think of Indians and bears and mountain lions. Then he set his jaw grimly, kicking more wood into the fire. He couldn't return now. He'd rather be scalped by an Indian than have them put him in that school.

Despite his grim resolve, Eddie did not get to sleep for a long time. When he did, he was troubled by bad dreams. He started off at dawn the next morning, forcing himself on.

He found another trap near noon, but it had not been used, either. Leaving it, he rode into a country of sharp rock faces that gleamed like ice in the blazing sun. They seemed to glitter at him everywhere he looked and pretty soon his vision began to play tricks on him. He was drenched in perspiration and he got so dizzy he almost fell off. Finally he dismounted, leaning against his horse. His arm throbbed unmercifully and he felt sick all over. He sought shade and tried to eat, but had little appetite.

After a while he forced himself on, swaying in the saddle. He found a shadowed cañon and the coolness made him feel better. But he realized he had lost his way. He knew a moment of panic. Then he clenched his teeth, forcing himself to be calm. He sought a ridge and surveyed the surrounding country until he found a familiar landmark. It guided him to a broad valley in which another of their traps was built. It was almost dark now, and he hoped and prayed his father would be at this one. But he wasn't.

Eddie spent another miserable night, shivering in the mountain chill, awakened a dozen times by strange sounds that made him lie still in the blankets, waiting for a bear to jump him or an Indian to start hollering. But nothing happened. He ate the last of his food for breakfast, and knew he was done for if he didn't find Calico soon.

In the afternoon Eddie topped a ridge that overlooked another section they often used to trap the horses. It was a deep cañon with many favorite watering places for the wild animals. Eddie rode the ridge, stopping to peer down at each shadowed pool as it appeared below him. He was about to give up when he finally saw the thin smoke of a campfire. Turning down the steep slope, he came into sight of a tall, red-headed figure squatting over the fire. With a whoop, he booted Midnight down through the trees.

Calico turned as Eddie rode out of the timber. For a minute he just sat there, jaw hanging. Then he jumped up and came running. "Jigger!" he yelled.

Eddie kicked Midnight's flanks and rode up to his father. "Howdy," he muttered sheepishly. "Thought you might be hankering for a little company."

"I sure am." Calico helped the boy down and over into the shade. He sounded jubilant and his face wore a broad grin. "Leaving you swiped the silver lining off my cloud, Jigger. But how in tarnation did you make it through all this rough country, the fix you're in?"

Eddie leaned back against the rock, wiping his hand over his wet forehead. "I dunno," he said shakily, "unless I just wanted to be with you so bad nothing would stop me."

Calico sobered. "I don't know if I can let you stay or not," he said dubiously, dropping down beside the boy. "We've gotten into enough trouble already. The sheriff might really put me in jail this time."

"But, Calico," Eddie pleaded, "you don't know how terrible it was down in town. I got big purple spots all over my face from being inside four walls so long. And there was a terrible little girl at the Hembre house that made me eat mush and soup and all that dude stuff."

It looked like a grin that was tugging at Calico's mouth before he turned away. He got up and walked over to where Billygoat was hobbled, fumbling absently at the mule's mane. Billygoat turned his head, wrinkling his lips back off his teeth, and tried to get the familiar tobacco sack. Calico cuffed him affectionately, shaking his head.

"Sulphur and molasses, Jigger. I should send you back. But I can't. Not when you went through all this just to get to me again."

Eddie settled back against the rock, completely happy at last. They stayed there the rest of that day and the night, to rest the boy, and then started looking for horses the next morning. Before dawn they rode to the ridge and moved farther down, waiting for horses to appear at the water holes Calico had not tainted with his man smell. His father told Eddie he was after horses the Army would buy. Their demands were rigid. They wanted animals of one solid color, under sixteen hands, close-coupled and flat-backed.

Just after sunrise, a band appeared at the water hole. Calico and Eddie flushed them and drove them down the cañon. They spotted a gray and a couple of bays that would fit the Army's requirements. Gradually they cut the other horses away, allowing them to escape over ridges and down side cañons, until only the three they wanted remained ahead. Then they dropped back, allowing the trio to slow down, not pressing them. They drove them easily, guiding them in the direction they wanted by merely appearing on

their flanks or at their rear. Soon they reached a broad
cañon and turned northward in its bottom timber. Eddie
recognized familiar surroundings. There was a trap at the
head of the cañon, he knew. They had built it for the
Appaloosa over six months ago. It was the one they had
been heading Apples for when Haskins had shot at him.
Eddie felt a stirring of excitement. Had it been long enough
since that time? This was favorite country for the
Appaloosa. Was there any chance that he would have forgotten the frightening experience by now, would have
drifted back to his watering places?

As Eddie was wondering, Calico pulled up and stepped
off his mule, hunkering down. Eddie saw fresh prints in the
dirt, too many to be made by the three horses they were
driving. Calico looked up suddenly, as if thinking the same
thing that was in his son's mind. He saw the strained,
hopeful expression on the boy's face, and shook his head.

"Don't get your hopes up, Jigger. I doubt if the
Appaloosa would come back so soon. Even if he did, it
wouldn't do us any good. I told you that. We can't use a
killer."

Eddie's face grew somber as Calico mounted again. It
seemed to rob him of all the pleasure of being back with his
father. He followed him gloomily on up the cañon. They
saw the three horses top a low spur ridge ahead and hurried
after them. Calico topped the ridge ahead of Eddie. The
boy saw him pull Billygoat in sharply, reaching for his binoculars. He was staring through them at something in the
valley beyond when Eddie reached him. Eddie saw that the
three horses they were following had stopped. Beyond
them, milling suspiciously about the trap that surrounded
the water hole, was a new band of horses. Eddie didn't need
the binoculars to recognize the leader, even at this distance.

It was a big horse, with a blue chest and a white rump, dabbed with vivid red spots. It was Apples!

Calico sent one dark look at Eddie, then kicked Billygoat into a gallop down the slope. He quartered between the three horses they had been following, cutting them off from the other band. Eddie dropped the rope of the pack horses he had been leading and raced after Calico. He saw that his father was driving the three horses away from the trap.

"Get up at their head!" Calico called. "I'm not letting them get mixed in with that other bunch. We're liable to lose them if that devil gets hold of them."

"Look," Eddie called, "we could drive them all in the trap! They're right up in the wings . . . !"

"Don't be crazy!" Calico shouted. "You know how smart that Appaloosa is. He'd get away and take these horses with him."

"Please, let's give Apples one more chance. Maybe something was wrong before. Maybe there was a burr under his saddle or something. . . ."

Calico reined in close, shouting angrily. "He's a killer, Eddie! I've seen 'em before. That blank, crazy look in their eyes, the way they move like a tiger. There isn't any use trying to trap him. Now you do as I say. I'm not losing these horses, too."

The three animals had been driven up the slope into timber. They were scrambling for a ridge, squealing and snorting, and Calico pushed Billygoat after them. Eddie lagged behind, looking down into the valley at Apples and his band. They were milling nervously around the pen. Apples had trotted free, staring up at the slope. Eddie stopped completely, gripped by the wild beauty of the animal.

The sound of Calico, chasing the other horses, faded up

the slope and died completely. Eddie was in the timber, and invisible to the Appaloosa now. The wind blew against his face, and he realized it would not have carried his scent to the horses. Perhaps he had been too far away for the Appaloosa to see him, also. The horse would think it was merely some other animal, then.

That must have been the case, for Eddie saw the band quieting down, saw the Appaloosa at last turn back, sniffing cautiously at the trap again. The fence extended out into wings from the gate, their ends widely apart, gradually narrowing down until they reached the gate. This formed a funnel that would lead the horses right through the gate, once they were between the wings. Eddie felt a tense excitement fill him as he saw the horses drifting nearer and nearer to the gate. He looked up in the direction in which Calico had gone. He had passed over the ridge now. Eddie knew that for once in his life he was going to disobey his father.

VIII

Apples was still bothered and suspicious. He had not been able to identify the noise on the slope down the cañon. His eyes were not as keen as his scent, and he had been able to make out only the blurred motion of some animals among the trees. He kept sniffing the wind, but could smell nothing dangerous.

The rest of his band was pressing forward. They had run most of the day without coming across a stream and were frantic with thirst. But Apples kept nipping at their heels, shouldering them back. Something was bothering him and he was unwilling to let them go to water yet.

They had often seen fallen trees in the forest, and it was what the wings of the trap looked like to them. But Apples had known the corrals and fences of men, and the fences of the trap bore a suspicious resemblance to these. Yet he could not be sure. There was no man smell on the poles, only the scent of dead wood and decay.

The bay mare rubbed against him affectionately, telling him with her snorts and whinnies how wonderful it was to have him back again with the band. After his escape from Calico's cabin, he had searched all their favorite watering places in the Wind Rivers. Finally he had found his band, running under the leadership of a younger stallion. It had not been much of a battle for Apples to regain his leadership, as the other horse was young and inexperienced.

The horses of his band were now snorting and fiddling all about him, striving to get by and reach the water. As there was no more noise from the cañon, he allowed them to pass. They bunched up in the narrow opening, and then spread out beyond, running knee deep into the water. He waited until they had all drunk, acting as look-out. He circled the strangely fallen logs that looked so much like the man-made corrals, sniffing the air, watching the dark wall of timber. The band began drifting back out, water dripping from their muzzles, and sought the sweet graze nearby. When they were all finished, Apples went in for his drink, the bay mare following. He lowered his head to the cool water and sucked it in greedily. Then he heard a snorting and whinnying run through the band, and raised his head.

They had begun to run before the sudden appearance of a horseman who had ridden out from the trees. Apples rushed for the narrow opening in the fence. But the trees stood near the trap and the rider reached the opening first.

Apples saw that it was a human now, and wheeled

144

around, galloping down the fence, seeking another way out. But there was no other way. He wheeled back, snorting defiance. The human had dismounted and dropped a log across the opening, cutting the stallion off from all escape.

He stood with his rump against the fence, quivering and snorting. The bay mare shouldered against him, whinnying in fright. Then Apples saw that it was the black-haired boy, coming toward him. He was surprised that he felt none of the fright, the hatred, the impulse to escape that usually came with the presence of men. He could remember no pain with this youth—only kindness, a soft, friendly voice and hands filled with gentleness. He heard the boy speak.

"Now, Apples, you know me. It's Eddie. You aren't going to act the way you did last time. Something was wrong then. You were sick or something. You aren't a killer. My father must be mistaken. Your eyes aren't cold and crazy. They look as soft and drippy as his eyes do when he looks at that schoolmarm. You don't even seem jumpy as you did that time."

The habit of escape surged up once more and made Apples run down the fence. But he stopped again, looking back at the boy. Eddie had turned and was coming toward him, that soothing voice going on and on. Somehow it quieted the stallion. This time he let the boy approach him, touch him. A shiver ran through his body. But all Eddie did was pat him softly, grinning at him. Even the mare quieted down, when she saw no harm came to them.

Eddie left them, stooping out between the bars, and unsaddled his black horse. He brought the saddle and a rope back in. Again Apples was torn between his desire for escape and his attraction to this wild and strangely gentle boy. He ran around the corral a couple of times, the mare trailing. But finally he came to a stop again, snorting,

pawing the earth. He allowed the boy to approach again. He
sidled away from the saddle. But he could not even remember any pain from that, when Eddie and Calico had
put it on before. And the boy was still talking gently, softly.
He swung the saddle up. Apples snorted, sidled away. But
the fence trapped him, and the saddle didn't seem so heavy
anyway.

He allowed Eddie to cinch it up, and put the hackamore
on his snout. When the boy mounted, Apples started to cat-
back around the corral. But he didn't start really bucking.
There seemed no cause for that. Nothing hurt him. The
boy's weight felt familiar now. At last he stopped and stood
still, snorting disdainfully to show that he was merely
putting up with it, that he could get rid of all this if he really
wanted to. Eddie drew a sharp breath, patting his neck.

"Good boy, good boy."

Apples liked the warmth of the boy's hand on his neck,
liked to hear the voice speaking to him. He saw the mare
cowering in a corner of the corral, staring in a puzzled way
at him. He snorted and whinnied, trying to tell her it really
wasn't so bad at all. Then he saw the red-headed man
riding down out of the timber and shouting at the boy.

"Get off that horse, Jigger! Have we got to ride that trail
all over again?"

"Apples isn't a killer," the boy answered. "He remembers me. Just watch."

Apples felt the hackamore laid against his neck, and
turned aside obediently to the familiar signal. Then its pressure changed, and he turned the other way. The boy's heels
touched his flanks and he broke into a trot. Then the boy
pulled in the rope and there was pressure against the tender
spot beneath Apples' jaw. The horse knew it would hurt if
the boy pulled any harder, and stopped. The man had

reached the fence, and sat his ugly old mule in an amazed way, shoving his hat back on his head.

"Sulphur and molasses! I never saw anything like that. I was all ready to clip your horns, thinking they'd got too much spread. But it looks like I was wrong."

"I told you," Eddie said, grinning broadly. "Apples isn't a killer. He was just sick that day or something. We can take him home with us, can't we?"

Calico cinched at his pants. "We'll try it. But I'll be worried as a frog waiting for rain in Arizona till we're sure you're right."

IX

Calico roped the bay mare and put her on a lead line with Midnight and the pack horses. He led all these horses, leaving Eddie free to ride Apples back. The boy's injured arm ached from the roping and saddling he'd done with his other arm. But he was so happy and proud he hardly felt it. He knew he'd give a lot more than that to be on the Appaloosa.

They started back to Calico's shack, crossing the meadow and seeking a trail that led them through balsam and spruce that shone like silver against the dense green background of lodgepole pines. Ahead of them the mountains were a gigantic panorama of tumbled slopes and shadowy gorges. They climbed a rock-littered incline. Calico hauled Billygoat out of a patch of lupine he wanted to stop and graze in. Eddie had been so excited at getting Apples back that he'd forgotten the three Army horses until now. He asked his father about them. Calico said he'd let them escape so he could come back and see what had happened to Eddie. The boy was genuinely sorry. But Calico said that, if it was true about Apples, he was worth a dozen Army horses.

Apples was as bridle-wise as Billygoat, and Eddie took the lead, guiding the horse proudly across a wind-swept ridge and down into a thick stand of tamarack. But the bay mare was balky, jerking on the rope and spooking at the rustle of a woodchuck in the brush. Billygoat turned disgustedly back toward her, peeling his lips comically off his long, yellow teeth and emitting a raucous hee-haw.

Then, suddenly, Calico pulled the mule to a halt. He was looking up through a stand of cinnamon-barked trees where a jay scolded somewhere high in the branches. The sun slanted down through the timber and painted the needle-matted ground with broad yellow stripes. Into one of these stripes rode Haskins, on a huge dappled mare. He wore a plaid wool shirt and blue jeans, filmed with the dust of a long ride. There was a black beard stubble three or four days old matting his jowls. His red-rimmed eyes looked as if he had lost a lot of sleep. They danced with anger when they settled on Apples. He had a rifle across the horn of his saddle. He kept it pointed at the Appaloosa as he kicked the gray into a heavy trot down the slope.

"Git off that devil, Kid. I'm going to blow his brisket out right now."

With a touch of his reins, Calico spun Billygoat in between Apples and the oncoming man. "You want to remember the last time you tried to use that rifle, Haskins."

The man hauled his horse down five feet from Calico. His bushy brows collided over his hard, black eyes. His heavy jowls turned red as turkey wattles beneath their bristly beard stubble.

"Look here, Calico," he said, "two days ago that Appaloosa stole two of my best mares right out of my corral. He gnawed the rawhide lashings off the corral poles and pushed them down so the mares could get out. . . ."

"No horse is that smart," Calico said.

"This horse is. It scares me sometimes, how smart he is. And he wasn't satisfied with that. He enticed one of my prime stallions into an upper meadow and killed him. It's the last time that devil gets away with it. I've been tracking him for two days and two nights and I'm going to kill him."

Calico looked at the ground. "You aren't following tracks now."

"I lost them in a creek about an hour ago. But he was heading due east with them two mares and I kept going till I topped a ridge and saw you."

"He had a whole band when we caught him."

"Then he must have picked them up over here," Haskins said. "I know it was him. Three nights ago I saw him in my upper pastures and shot at him. Only thing in the world he's afraid of is a gun. I missed him, but I thought I'd chased him away. Next morning I found my best stud dead up on that same hill." Haskins tried to wheel around Calico, jerking the gun toward Eddie. "If you don't get off him, kid, I'll shoot him out from under you."

Calico reined Billygoat aside until the mule bumped into Haskins's horse, blocking the man off. "Your story doesn't hang together any more than it did last time," Calico said. "If he had wings, that Appaloosa couldn't have got over here from your ranch that fast."

Haskins jerked angrily away as Billygoat took a nip at his hip. "It had to be the same horse, Calico. There ain't another Appaloosa in these mountains. Even if there was, you know there wouldn't be two of 'em marked just alike. The spots was exactly the same. That chest color slanted back over his barrel the same. His tail touched his hocks that way. It's this horse and I'm goin' to. . . ." He broke off, slapping at Billygoat's snout as the mule sought to nuzzle his hip again. "What ails this animal?" he demanded angrily.

"Nothing tobacco won't fix." Calico grinned.

"What's tobacco got to do with it? You're too good a horseman to protect a killer, Calico. I heard what he did to the boy the last time. You're a fool to let the kid get on that horse."

"It's the way Eddie wants it," Calico said. "You promised us you'd give us a chance to catch the Appaloosa. We've got him now and you can't go back on your word."

Haskins was purple with rage. "I didn't say I'd sit around and let him kill my best studs while you was chasing him. Get out of my way."

He tried to swing around Calico once more, jerking up the rifle. For an instant he got its muzzle past Calico, pointed at Apples. Eddie's whole body went rigid in anticipation of the deafening shot. But Haskins had made the mistake of putting his hip within range of Billygoat again. Before the man could pull the trigger, Eddie saw the mule reach forward with his long snout, teeth bared. There was a great ripping sound. Haskins was jerked backward and his horse jumped. It spilled him from the saddle.

He rolled over on the ground, clapping a hand to his hip. A great hole had been torn off the seat of his pants and the white flesh showed through. Then Eddie saw the ends of the cloth and a tobacco tag on a string hanging from either side of Billygoat's mouth. There was a complacent triumph on his ugly face as he chewed it up. Calico leaned back in the saddle and roared with laughter.

150

"After this, you better keep your tobacco in your shirt pocket, Haskins." The man snarled in rage and scrambled to his feet, lunging for the rifle he had dropped. But Calico thumped his heels against Billygoat's flanks, jumping the mule to the gun ahead of the other man. Haskins stopped, still holding his hip, staring at Billygoat dubiously. Chuckling, Calico said: "You better give up now, Haskins. I seen a lot of tough gents in my time, but I never did hear of one coming to a shoot-out with no seat to his pants."

Haskins began to tremble with rage. But Billygoat was standing over the rifle, long yellow teeth bared in his comical gesture, as if he'd just love to take another bite at the man. Finally Haskins wheeled and hiked over to where his spooked horse had run. He mounted with an angry grunt and turned to face Calico.

"You win this time. But mark my word, one day I'll kill that mule as well as that Appaloosa."

After their meeting with Haskins, it was a two-day ride before Calico and Eddie reached their cabin. They turned Apples and the bay into the pen with the other horses and went in to have supper. They were both dog-tired. Calico fixed them something to eat, and over the meal began puzzling again about Apples. He just couldn't believe the horse could make it from Haskins's ranch in such a short time. Haskins had started two nights before he had seen Eddie and Calico, yet they had seen signs of the horse all that one day before they met the man. That left the stallion only one day to travel the whole distance. Such a trip would have been impossible. Even if, by some stretch of the imagination, the horse had made it, he would have shown signs of such a grueling run. His hoofs would have been sore, his body rimed with dried lather, his eyes feverish. Apples had showed none of that. He had been fat and prime and rested when they first came upon him.

Finally Calico shook his head, unable to solve the mystery, and started talking about what they would do with the animal. If he displayed no more signs of viciousness, they could gentle him and polish him and turn him into a regular show horse that would bring maybe $500 from the right buyer.

Eddie felt his heart sink. He realized he had been mistaken in thinking of the horse in terms of his own animal. Yet he couldn't help it. He had kept his faith in Apples when Calico had given up, had captured him, had ridden him all the way back. The spirit and beauty of the Appaloosa had gotten under his skin. But it was more than that. Somehow he felt they belonged together. The very way the stallion acted toward him showed that. He had never felt such a deep kinship toward Midnight, or any other horse. He knew he wanted the Appaloosa more than anything else in life.

But he knew, too, how badly Calico needed the money. Eddie had given his father a bad year, causing him so much trouble with running from the sheriff and the broken arm and everything else, that Calico hadn't much time to run his mustangs. Now he'd even given up those three Army horses to go back and see what had happened to Eddie. The money from Apples was the only thing that would tide him over during the winter.

It was a bitter sacrifice for Eddie to make. But he kept his mouth shut as Calico went on with his glowing plans for training the horse. They washed the tin plates and cups and rolled into their blankets. As tired as he was, Eddie could not go right to sleep. His mind was filled with the defeat of losing Apples again, after going through so much to get him.

The Ghost Horse

★ ★ ★ ★ ★

It was some time in the middle of the night that Eddie came awake. He lay there a moment, wondering if he had dreamed of the sound. Then he saw Calico climb out, slip into his pants and boots, and shuffle to the door. Puzzled, he put on his own pants, his worn moccasins, and followed his father.

A cold wind blew down off the snow-capped mountains as they stepped softly out the door of the shack. Eddie shivered and hugged himself. Then he forgot the cold and stood there, staring. Apples had gotten out! He was running up and down the outside of the fence, snorting and prancing, eyes rolling wild and crazy in the white moonlight. The mare was running excitedly up and down the fence on the inside. Behind her the other horses were snorting and running and bunching up in the shadows beneath the shed roof.

"We'll have to get Apples back in before he runs off," Calico muttered. "You sneak around and open the gate, Eddie. I'll try and drive Apples through it."

Eddie nodded. Making the most of the cover offered by the shack and the sheds, he crept toward the corral. He knew the slightest of noises might startle Apples away. The other horses were stirring nervously in the deep shadows beneath the shed and trotting up and down the far fence. But the only ones he could see clearly were the bay mare, on the inside of the fence nearest him, and the Appaloosa, running up and down on the outside.

He reached the corner of the corral and waited until they had run up to the far side. Then he darted around to the gate. It was still fastened. How had the Appaloosa gotten out? He couldn't understand it.

But the bay and the stallion were turning and would see

him in the next instant. He had to get the gate open so his father could drive the Appaloosa back in. He unfastened it, started to pull it aside. Calico had circled through the trees and appeared from their shadowy cover, running toward the upper end of the corral. This startled the Appaloosa. He wheeled and ran blindly toward Eddie. The boy jerked the gate wide and then ran out to the side. It blocked the stallion from veering away from the corral. His only escape from the two humans was now through the gate.

He halted, wheeling around. But Calico was on his tail, waving his arms and calling. It made the stallion turn back. At the same moment there was a loud whinny from within the corral. One of the horses milling around on the far side charged for the opening. Before Eddie could reach the gate and get it closed, the animal plunged through. He stared blankly at the horse. It was an Appaloosa, too!

Eddie stopped in his tracks. For a moment the two Appaloosas were very close together, on the outside of the pen. He couldn't tell them apart. The bright moonlight showed their markings to be exactly alike. The shape of the chest color, the placing of spots on the white rump, the length and thickness of the mane and tail—all these were identical.

"Pop!" Eddie cried blankly. "Which one is Apples?"

Calico had stopped, too, in complete surprise. He shook his head, then shouted: "It's crazy, Jigger, but the one from inside the pen must be Apples! They must be twin brothers. It don't happen but once in a million times, but they must be twin Appaloosas."

Even as he spoke, the Appaloosa from within the pen had veered away from the other horse and was heading for the timber. But the bay mare had come out the gate and was following him. The second Appaloosa ran toward her, trying to cut her off. Apples saw that and wheeled around, biting savagely at the other stallion, which veered away, snorting in surprise. Apples shouldered against the red mare, driving her toward the trees.

But once more the other Appaloosa got around on her flank, nipped at her heels, and turned her away. The mare ran back to the pasture fence and halted, unable to go farther. Apples wheeled around and raced for her, reaching the mare before the other Appaloosa could. He stood with his legs braced, snorting in angry defiance. The other horse circled back and forth as if looking for an opening. Suddenly he stopped. For one brief moment all three animals remained sharply etched against the sky, long manes ruffling in the wind, eyes white and wild, nostrils red as blood in the moonlight. They made a strange and savagely beautiful sight. Eddie started running toward them.

"We can get them now!" he shouted. "They're played out."

"Stay away, Eddie!" Calico called sharply. "They always stop like that before a battle. I think they're going to fight over that mare."

Eddie pulled up, staring at the stallions in cold panic. Calico was right. The two Appaloosas reared up and were moving toward each other on their hind hoofs. Their mouths were open and their eyes glittered like balls of fire. Then they came together and the shock of it seemed to jolt the earth. Viciously they lashed out at each other with their razor-keen hoofs and snatched at whatever part they could reach with their powerful jaws. They fought with maniacal abandon. They cast their whole immense weight upon one another, their glittering teeth slipping loose from the hide to click together with the loud report of a gun.

Apples was the first to go down. But as the other stallion

reared to trample him, Eddie ran in. With Calico screaming at him to stop, the boy threw himself wildly against the strange stallion. He knocked the animal off balance long enough for Apples to gain his feet again. Then the other stallion turned on Eddie and a flashing hoof knocked the boy back against the fence.

Too dazed to move for a minute, Eddie watched the frenzied animal rush Apples. There was a wild snorting and squealing. Dust boiled yellow as buckskin against the moon. For a while Eddie couldn't tell which was which as the pair wheeled and kicked and bit at each other. Then he saw the strange stallion rise above Apples in all his savagery, hoofs flailing wildly, eyes shining red with hate.

Apples dodged the hoofs and rushed in to rip at his antagonist's belly. Bleeding from the gashing teeth, the strange stallion twisted around, biting savagely at Apples' rump. The latter tried to kick out with his hind hoofs. The other evaded that and reared up over Apples again, flailing at him with those deadly front hoofs. He knocked Apples off balance, driving him down. Apples rolled in the dust, broad belly exposed to those deadly hoofs, sharp as knives. Eddie staggered to his feet, trying to rush in again.

"He's going to kill Apples!" he screamed.

"And you'll get killed with him, if you don't stay out of there!" Calico yelled, running across in front of his son and catching him by the arm. Panting, sobbing, he watched while Apples fought to move from those deadly hoofs. At last, Apples managed to fend them off by using his own flailing legs, and rolled away. Bleeding and snorting, he scrambled to his feet. Yellow froth dripped from his muzzle. His eyes were bloodshot and protruding from his head. His sides were heaving so hard Eddie was afraid they would burst.

"His legs are wobbling like rubber," Calico said. "He can't stand this much longer."

"Get a gun!" Eddie panted. "That stallion's the killer Haskins has been after. He's the one that broke my arm . . . not Apples. We can't let him kill Apples."

Calico nodded. "You promise you won't run in there, if I go to the cabin?"

"I promise." Then the boy tore free from his father, running toward the house. "I'll get it myself. I can't let him kill Apples."

He heard the horses squealing and snorting behind him, heard the ground shake with the awful impact of their bodies as he ran through the door. He grabbed Calico's .45-70 Winchester from the corner, praying it was loaded. But as he ran back out, he heard his father shouting.

"Hold it, Jigger! Apples has got him now. All he's got to do is go in there and tromp the stallion's head to sawdust."

Eddie stopped just outside the doorway, the rifle gripped in his hands. He saw that it was the strange stallion that was rolling on the ground now, hoofs flailing, and Apples who was lunging in. But something was the matter. Apples' feint above the stallion's head was only a half-hearted one. As the prostrate animal kicked at his conqueror with his forehoofs, Apples veered away.

"Run in there, you fool!" Calico shouted. "All you've got to do is step on his head."

The strange stallion rolled back the other way and tried to scramble to his feet. Apples wheeled around, biting at his haunches, preventing him from rising. The other horse kicked wildly, squealing like a stuck pig, and tied to roll in the other direction.

"Now you got him!" Calico shouted. "Stomp on him!"

Eddie felt his heart leap into his throat as he saw Apples

157

lunge in and rear up above the rolling horse. But in the last instant the strange stallion rolled back toward Apples. Screaming in savage rage, he hit Apples' forelegs. He missed and his teeth snapped together with a gunshot report. But Apples dropped back anyway, a strange, wild look in his eyes.

"You fool!" Calico groaned. "You let him scare you off."

The downed stallion used the chance to regain his feet and lunged wildly at his adversary. Apples veered away, looking over his shoulder like a dog that has been kicked.

"Don't turn yellow on us!" Calico shouted.

As if responding to Calico's voice, Apples wheeled to meet his opponent. But it was too late. The stallion crashed into him broadside, knocking Apples off his feet. Then he reared above him and came down with a wild whinny. There was a scream of pain, a crunching sound as the sound of the stallion's front hoofs struck Apples' flailing hind leg. Eddie began running toward them, cocking the gun. Apples tried to roll over but the stallion came down on him again, cutting through hide and flesh with his deadly hoofs.

Eddie knew that the stallion was going to kill Apples this time. The animal had that same crazy look in his eyes he'd had when he'd trampled Eddie. He was screaming with the same insane fury. The gun was too heavy for Eddie to lift to his shoulder. He fired from the hip, on the run. In the darkness and confusion he knew that he had missed. But the shocking sound made the strange stallion wheel toward him. He fired again. The horse reared up with a wild scream, and then wheeled. For a moment Eddie thought he was going to charge down on him. Before he could fire a third time, however, the animal turned and ran into the timber.

Eddie dropped the rifle and ran to Apples. The horse was lying on his side and could not rise. The bay mare kept circling around, veering toward the timber, then darting back, as if unable to leave without Apples. Calico came up and knelt beside the horse.

"That devil," he muttered with a harshness in his voice Eddie had seldom heard before. Then he looked up at his son. "Maybe you'd better go back and pick up that gun, Jigger. His leg's cut up terrible. It might as well be broken."

"Please," Eddie said with tears in his eyes, "you can't kill him . . . not Apples."

"You know they can't do anything with a horse when his leg's ruined."

"He can be healed," Eddie pleaded.

Calico shook his head. "I don't think it can be done. And what if he could? You wouldn't want this horse."

"What do you mean?" Eddie asked.

"You wouldn't want a horse without any heart in him. You saw what happened out there. This horse hasn't got any courage. He's yellow!"

X

Both Haskins and Calico Jim had called that other Appaloosa a devil. And that was what he looked like, running in the wind, his teeth shining bone-white in the moonlight, his eyes cold and deadly. He was still quivering with rage and the fear of those shocking gunshots. It was the one thing in the world he feared. There was still a scar on his hip from the bullet that had hit him long ago. Haskins had shot him three years before when he'd been stealing one of the man's mares. It had only wounded him and he'd escaped. But he could still feel the burning pain of the bullet whenever a gun went off, and it sent him wild with panic.

He finally stopped on a ridge, looking back down into the valley. In the bright moonlight, he could see the cabin and the corrals, the tiny figures of Calico Jim and Eddie crouched over the fallen horse. He had been following them for two days now, ever since he had caught sight of them in the Wind River Mountains. It was just after they had captured Apples. Eddie had been riding the Appaloosa, and Calico Jim had been leading the bay mare.

Devil had been herding the two mares he had stolen from Haskins, but had left them immediately. They did not compare with the bay. She was a mare whose beauty and spirit made her a thing sought after by any stallion that saw her. Devil had twice given chase before, but she had eluded him each time. Now he was determined to capture her.

He had followed Eddie and Calico home, waiting until nightfall, then approaching the cabin. He had an almost human cunning. It had enabled him to free Haskins's mares by gnawing loose the rawhide lashings that held the corral poles to the upright post. But he had been given no time to do that on Calico's corral before the man and the boy appeared.

He wondered now if he had killed the other Appaloosa. He was a veteran of many battles, but this was a special triumph for him. He had fought with Apples before, over mares, and had stolen several from his band. His memory of Apples, however, seemed to go back even further than that. Devil seemed to recall days long ago, when they had played together as colts. They had run with a mother and father who bore the same coloring as they—the white blanket over the rump, daubed with vivid red spots.

Once, during the battle, this sense of kinship had come to Devil so strongly that he had almost stopped fighting. But the killer instincts that all his contacts with man had developed were too strong. They had blotted out his dim feeling of belonging in some way to the other Appaloosa. He had come for the mare. That was all he knew. He would kill the other Appaloosa to get her, as he had killed other stallions that had stood in his way.

He knew the mare was free now. She was somewhere down in the timber between this ridge and the cabin. Fear of the gun had kept him from going back. He worked up and down the ridge with a fierce impatience until he finally saw her, picking her way daintily up the hillside. She kept stopping to look over her shoulder as if reluctant to leave the other Appaloosa. It angered him. He began to move toward her, struck again by her beauty. The ripple of muscle under the silken hide of her shoulder, the graceful arch of her neck, the aristocratic flare of her pink nostrils, all excited him as no other mare had ever excited him before. It drove him down after her.

When she saw him coming, she gave a shrill whinny of fear and dived back down the hill, a bright bronze flash among the trees. Devil ran after her, leaping from ledge to ledge, racing along steep ridges. Then he pulled up short, a crafty light gleaming in his eyes. He'd let her think she was getting away. She'd slow up then and make it easier for him to circle around and come out below her. He swung to the left and started weaving down through the trees. He could hear the mare crashing blindly through them, trying to escape him. He kept track of her by the noise. He raced faster and faster down the side of the running horse.

Finally, as he was worrying about getting so close to Calico's shack, the thunder of her hoofs died down and stopped. Devil's ears flattened, his eyes began to glitter. Snorting at every jump, he leaped out at her from behind a sheltering tree, nipping at her heels, crowding her back up the steep hillside.

Whinnying wildly, the mare plunged upward. Reaching a flat covered by a wedge of aspens, she ran across it, heading for the trees. Devil knew she might escape him if they got mixed up in the timber. His powerful haunches took him in great leaps over the sage-covered ground. And then he was in front of her, blocking her off.

Eyes rolling white with panic, flanks lathered with sweat, she wheeled and struck out in the other direction. But Devil was an old hand at this. At full speed he circled after her relentlessly back up the hill. Gradually her frenzy of fear gave way to weariness. Only her utter desperation kept her going. The mare moved slower and slower, stumbling now and then, dripping with sweat. Devil knew she was near the point of exhaustion.

Dusk had fallen before the mare gave up. Sides heaving, she stopped in a growth of scrubby tamarack. As Devil came up to her, she made no move to fight. Her head was bowed and she was trembling all over.

He halted beside her, snorting in triumph. He was tired, too, his flanks covered with dirty yellow lather. But he herded her on again, allowing her to walk now, moving slowly through the night. They stopped to browse, and near dawn found water. He was heading back toward the country in which he had left the two mares he had stolen from Haskins. When the first rays of the sun reddened the sky, he caught their scent and began to follow it. He rose to a high ridge, pushing the bay before him, and stopped to survey the country below.

Finally he saw something that brought a hot snort of

162

anger from him. A black-bearded, heavy-set man on a gray horse was driving the two mares westward toward Jackson Hole. Devil recognized him as Haskins, his old enemy.

Despite the fact that he had gotten the bay, he still wanted those other two. He pushed the bay ahead, down the ridge, until he was directly above Haskins. He saw that the man was approaching a shelving cliff that overhung a river far below. He followed farther until the cliff became a steep slope, falling off into the rock-studded shallows of the river. He knew a man on horseback would be lost on such a steep and rocky drop-off. He nipped at the weary mare's heels, forcing her down through the pines toward the man. Haskins was herding the other two mares along in the open, chuckling huskily.

"Git on there, you two broomtails. This is one time that devil don't outsmart me."

Eyes smoldering, Devil drove the bay right to the edge of timber, then gave her a nip that made her bolt into the open. He followed at a dead run. Haskins wheeled in the saddle, mouth gaping in surprise. Devil drove against the man's gray horse with his shoulder, knocking the animal off balance.

Fighting to keep erect, the gray stumbled over the edge of the drop-off. Devil saw his feet go out from beneath him, saw Haskins pitched from the saddle. Then the Appaloosa wheeled and ran after the mares, driving the bay and the other two into a bunch and herding them on down the edge of the steep slope. It finally tapered off into the river and he drove them across the rocky shallows. He emerged on the other side, splashing and snorting, and ran them into timber, up a slope to a ridge.

He would drive them across Jackson Hole and into the Snake Mountains, into Paiute Cañon. It was where he and

Apples had been born, where they had run as twin colts. Sooner or later they had always returned there, when hounded by man. It was a hidden, twisting gorge with so many spur cañons running off into the steep mountains that it would be impossible for a man to trap them.

With the mares running across the ridge and down the opposite slope, the Appaloosa stopped for a backward look. He saw that Haskins's gray horse had tumbled all the way down the slope and into the river. He had apparently been unhurt and was just regaining his feet, shaking off the water in a fine spray. The man had crawled back to the top of the drop-off and was standing with his face toward the Appaloosa, shaking his fist in rage.

The horse raised his head and bugled in triumph. There was something evil about his silhouette stamped blackly against the sky. Calico and Haskins had named him well: Devil!

XI

That night was a bad one for Eddie. He didn't know how long he pleaded with his father to let Apples live. He pulled out every argument he could think of but Calico kept hesitating, looking toward the pen, and shaking his head. The raw, chilling fear of losing his horse drove Eddie nearly frantic. It was all he could do to keep from bawling like a baby. But at last his father looked at him, a smile softening his lean face.

"Sulphur and molasses!" he said. "If you're that set on it, let's get going. Go get a tarp and we'll rig up a sling."

They laid the canvas tarp on the ground beside the dazed

horse, pulled him onto it, then moved the animal into the shed by dragging the tarp across the ground with him on it. Once they had him lifted in the sling, Eddie offered to ride to town for Doc Purcell, who acted as veterinary for the community when the need arose. But Calico told him he'd better go instead.

"You just stay here and look after the horse," Calico said. "It won't hurt if you get a little sleep, either. There's nothing much you can do till Doc Purcell gets here."

But sleep was furthest from Eddie's thoughts. Eyes wide, shoulders hunched, he watched beside the still half-conscious Apples as the night dragged on. The only sounds were the wind in the timber and sometimes a faint moan from the stallion. Whenever he heard this, Eddie got up from where he sat against the wall and put his arm around the horse's neck. Apples never moved. Except for the warmth coming from his body, he might have been dead. It made Eddie shiver with fright. Was there nothing he could do? What if Doc Purcell wouldn't come? What if the doc thought it was foolish, too?

Eddie lost track of time. Once he fell asleep with his back against the wall, but awoke at a groan from Apples. A wild fear beating through him, he jumped up and rushed over to the horse. As he began rubbing the bloody neck and murmuring softly under his breath, Apples turned his head and laid it against the boy's arm. Thrilled and happy, Eddie let it stay like that until his arm didn't have any feeling left in it.

As the first light of dawn came creeping through the cracks, Eddie heard hoof beats stop in front of the shack. Then Calico and Doc Purcell came in.

"Th . . . thanks for coming, Doc," Eddie stammered, wondering if the man would make fun of him for holding a horse's head like that.

But Doc Purcell was too busy looking at Apples to notice. His round red face looked tired and his frock-tail coat was powdered with the dust from his long ride. But his eyes held the same kind look they had with Eddie.

The boy waited with his insides all hollow while the doctor examined Apples. Anxiously he watched while the man rolled back the Appaloosa's eyelids, felt of his legs, listened to his heartbeat. A wave of uneasiness swept over him at the slow way the doctor turned

"The horse is done for, Eddie," Doc Purcell said soberly, putting a hand on the boy's shoulder.

"But, Doc. . . ."

"Just as well face it, boy." Doc Purcell's voice sounded husky. "Even if he did get better, I doubt if Calico'd let you go anywhere on him. It wouldn't be safe."

The boy felt as though he couldn't breathe. He stood there, staring at Apples with his powerful legs and deep chest. His beautiful, proud head was turned a little way toward Eddie, as if for help. Let them shoot a horse like that? "Couldn't I try and cure him, Doc?" Eddie asked. The anxiety in him made his voice go high like a girl's. "If I took all the care of him?"

Doc Purcell smiled ruefully. "This horse means a lot to you, doesn't he, Eddie? I'd like to say yes, but it wouldn't be any use. His leg muscles are torn up too badly. If the leg did heal, he'd likely never walk on it. You may as well let Calico put him out of his misery."

Eddie's face whitened. He caught the doctor's arm, his voice frantic. "Don't do it, Doc, please. Pa Hembre said he saved a horse that had hurt its leg. It couldn't do any heavy work, but Polly Jane could ride it. He said it could be done once in a while. What if this was that once? You wouldn't have any right to kill Apples without giving him a chance.

He's the most beautiful animal I ever saw. The most beautiful any of us ever saw. I never wanted any horse so bad." Eddie turned to Calico, pleading: "I promise I'll take care of him, Pop. You won't have to do a thing. I'll feed him and nurse him. I'll rig a bunk in the shed beside him. We won't bother you a smidgen. All we ask is just a chance. . . ."

"Hold on, Jigger, hold on," Calico said. He chuckled gruffly to hide the emotion in his voice. "If you want it that bad, who could refuse you? Give it a try, Doc. We can't lose anything."

Doc Purcell pursed his lips, then nodded slowly. "All right. But I think you're both in for a big disappointment."

The next few weeks were the hardest Eddie had ever spent. At first he was apprehensive that the sheriff or the schoolmarm would come to get him again. But it was summer and his only hope lay in the fact that they would have no reason to take him down into town until school opened in the fall. Even so, he ran and hid at any sign of a stranger approaching the cabin. More than anything in the world he wanted a chance to nurse Apples back to health.

He tended the stallion carefully from morning until night, staying alone with him when his father went out on another horse-running expedition. Calico let him sell one of the horses they had trapped for enough money to buy grain. Every day he went up into the high meadows to cut the sweet mountain grasses for Apples, finding patches of grama and alfalfa in the deep and shadowed coulées where the summer sun had not begun to cure it. And all the while he was looking forward with a mixture of eagerness and dread for the time when they would take the splint off.

Doc Purcell came out on purpose to do it, around noon one blistering hot day. Apples was still in the sling they had rigged up on pulleys with ropes and strips of an old blanket for the straps. The doctor removed the bandages and wooden slats that had held the leg immovable for so long.

They lowered the sling slightly, putting some of the animal's weight on the injured leg. But it would not hold him up and he almost fell. They hauled him a little higher in the sling, the leg hanging uselessly while he put all his weight on the other three.

The doctor shook his head. "I hate to say it, Eddie, but that horse isn't worth a plugged nickel."

Eddie refused to give up. Every day after that, with Calico's help, they lowered the sling a bit, encouraging a little more weight on the bad leg. Each morning before dawn, when the wind was still cold from the glaciers, Eddie spent long hours massaging the injured leg, rubbing hot tallow and neat's-foot oil in, wrapping it in heated blankets to restore the unused muscles. And each day he lowered the sling a little, forcing the horse, for a few minutes at a time, to put more and more weight on the leg. Then came the day when he lowered the sling completely.

It was a big defeat, because Apples stood there on three legs and would not put any weight on the fourth. Eddie led him into the corral, but still Apples would hobble about on only three legs. Finally Eddie got the idea of tying a Scotch hobble on the left hind leg. It was a hitch that ran over the horse's rump and allowed the boy to pull the hind hoof off the ground whenever he wished.

Then he started leading the stallion around the corral again. He pulled on the Scotch hobble every few feet. It jerked the hind hoof up for an instant, forcing Apples to put his weight on the weak front leg for just a touch. At that it almost buckled beneath him. But soon he learned how to put as little weight as possible against it, stepping gingerly onto the bad leg whenever Eddie pulled his rear leg up.

Working patiently, day after day, Eddie finally had the horse using his lame leg. Then he took off the Scotch hobble, and Apples limped around the corral on all four. It was a definite triumph for Eddie. He rewarded the stallion with an extra pint of corn that night.

Over dinner, Calico admitted what an advance it was. But he shook his head. "I wish you wouldn't get your hopes up too high, Eddie. Even if he is walking again, what good will it do you? A horse without any courage is like a sack without any bottom."

Eddie shook his head stubbornly. "I can't believe he's yellow. Something else made him keep from killing Devil when he had the chance."

"What?"

"I don't know," Eddie said. "But I was right before, wasn't I? I knew Apples wasn't a killer. I didn't know at the time that there were twins, but I just knew Apples couldn't be a killer."

Calico shook his head. "I admit you were right then. But this time we both saw it. Apples turned like a kicked dog. He had two chances to kill Devil and he let the horse scare him off."

"He isn't yellow," Eddie insisted stubbornly. "I know it."

Autumn came, with the dryness of August still making the air thin and brittle. The sky had a buttery color from the forest fires high in the Wind Rivers. A cottony silence lay over the land, with only the infrequent chatter of saucy magpies to break it. At last Eddie thought it was time to try mounting the horse.

With Calico watching, he led Apples to the fence, put a

bridle on him. Then he climbed to the top bar, so the jolt of swinging aboard would not unbalance the animal, and eased himself onto Apples' back.

At first the stallion refused to budge. But Eddie nudged him gently with moccasined heels, talking softly into his ear. "Come on now, Apples. You got this far. Nobody believed we could do it, but you got this far. You can walk alone. You can sure walk with me on top. I don't weigh so much. Just ease out on that leg and you won't have a bobble, you'll see. . . ."

The horse's ears began to twitch. He looked around at the boy, as if for reassurance. Eddie grinned and patted his neck, still talking. Finally, as if persuaded by the gentle voice, Apples took a tentative step. He almost stumbled, and quickly shifted his weight. But Eddie urged him on. The second time the step was stronger. In a moment they were moving slowly around the corral. The horse still limped heavily, but Eddie felt a triumph flush his face.

Calico shook his head wonderingly. "You sure don't ever know which way a dill pickle's going to squirt. I never thought I'd see this day. But you got a long way to go, Jigger. One quick turn could make him spill and break your neck. I couldn't ever trust a horse like that cantering over open country."

This did not dim Eddie's triumph. Day after day he walked the horse around the corral. The limp seemed to get better, and one day he decided to try riding into the meadows above the cabin. He took an easy trail, circling away and coming back toward the shack through the pines. He was so busy watching his horse that he had reached the edge of timber before he heard the voices. He pulled up so sharply Apples stumbled. It was Calico talking with June Weatherby outside the cabin.

Her bright hair flew like a battle flag in the wind and an angry flame burned in her blue eyes. "You owe a duty to Eddie's mother as well as to him," she said. "You know it was Cora's dearest wish that he should be educated. She even talked about the plans you'd made to have her live in town during the winter so he could go to school."

Calico's head was lowered and his face flushed. "We were doing better then, June. I thought I could afford to send them to town. It wouldn't have been like having him stay with strangers."

"The Hembres will treat him like their own son, Jim." She drew closer. "I saw how you looked at the Hembre house when Eddie broke his arm that time. You were comparing it with your shack here. You were thinking about the clean sheets and the home-cooked meals and the other children to play with."

Calico frowned. "I guess I was. But that isn't everything in life."

"Of course, it isn't. He needs the love and companionship you've given him. But there comes a time when he needs more. Do you want him to be a horse-runner all his life?"

"What's wrong with that? It's a good clean life. With breaks, a man can make of himself as he could in any other business."

"In other words, you aren't even giving Eddie a chance to make his own choice. You're going to keep him from seeing the outside world or learning anything, so that, even if he wanted to be something else, he couldn't because all he knows is how to chase wild horses."

That seemed to strike home. Calico's head came up and color dyed his cheeks. Eddie had a shaking feeling. June Weatherby stepped closer, her voice lowering.

"I can see it has been bothering you, Calico. You know you don't have any right to keep him from a chance like this. You've been thinking about it every night. You've been remembering what his mother wanted for him and what you promised her. I don't believe your conscience will let you keep him up here much longer."

XII

After June had left, Calico went back into the cabin and slammed the door. Eddie watched anxiously a moment, his heart that had been soaring so triumphantly dropping like a stone. Slowly he put Apples away and followed his father inside.

He found Calico, cooking dinner in moody silence. There were no queries as to how Eddie had come out with Apples or any easy small talk. First Calico burned the bread. Jerking it, smoking, from the oven, he muttered some disgusted comment about this food not being fit for a boy. Then, eating dinner, he stopped every third or fourth mouthful and stared at the table. Seeing him that way, knowing that he was thinking about what June Weatherby had said, Eddie finally blurted out that he had overheard the discussion. Calico banged his fork down. He got up and turned and walked across the room, facing the wall.

"You're thinking about what she said," Eddie muttered. "You're going to send me down there."

"No, I'm not," Calico said. He turned around, scowling at Eddie from under bushy red brows. "How do you feel about it?"

"You know how I feel," Eddie said. "As long as you want me, I'll stay here."

"As long as I want you," Calico echoed almost as if he were speaking to himself. "Yes," he said, "I guess that's it."

"What's it?"

Calico shook his head angrily. "Nothing. Let's not talk about it any more. It makes me mad to talk about it."

The time passed slowly for Eddie after that. He kept out of Calico's way as much as he could. He worked long hours with Apples, slowly, carefully, until he got the horse to the point where he could trot a little. The boy would have been perfectly happy, if only Calico had acted differently. The man's lean brown face was getting a tighter look day by day and his voice held a brittle edge. Eddie wondered if his father was remembering that it was nearly time for school to begin.

The days crawled by. The tension and the waiting began to weigh on Eddie until he almost wished something would happen. Frost yellowed the aspens. Snow fell on the lower ridges. Coyotes began to howl dismally about the cold winter ahead. The sound filled Eddie with a deep loneliness, sitting at supper with the silent stranger his father had become. For the first time the mountains seemed mysterious and frightening. He shivered, choking on a burned biscuit, wishing Calico would talk to him. But Calico, sitting moodily across the table, was always staring into his cup.

Is he thinking about what Miss Weatherby said? Eddie asked himself. *Is he thinking maybe he ought to send me down to the Hembres?* The boy didn't know. He only knew something was terribly wrong. Finally, unable to stay still any longer, he'd get up and clear the dishes away. Afterward, he'd lie awake for a long time in his bunk, staring out at the twinkling stars, half sick with worry.

Then one day something did happen. Eddie was out cutting hay in the high meadows behind the shack when he saw the sheriff pull up. Eddie stopped dead, terror seizing him. For a moment it was so still he could hear the rumbling voice of the sheriff talking to his father in front of the cabin. Anger swept over Eddie at the sound. He cinched up his belt, starting down to get Apples. He'd taken a couple of steps when he drew up short. No, he would be seen. Better just leg it out of here as fast as he could.

Hot blood pounding through his head, Eddie plunged into the brush behind the meadow. At first, he scrambled wildly through the brambles and dense thickets, regardless of the noise he made or the trail he was leaving. Then he made himself slow down. Fighting his panic, he moved more quietly, slipping across an open glade with the stealth of a lynx, using every tree and rock for cover.

Presently he struck a game trail and followed it to his favorite hiding place, the dead-end cañon known only to Calico and himself. No one could ever find him there unless he knew the place.

Panting, Eddie sank down on a boulder. Was he really safe? He had come on an impulse and out of habit. But now he began to wonder, dropping his head into his hands. He remembered how strangely his father had been acting and how much effect the schoolmarm's words seemed to have on him.

A rattle of brush brought Eddie to his feet. He listened, not wanting to believe it. But the sound came again. His father wouldn't make that much noise. He was a woodsman. The boy's eyes darted to the rock walls. They were too steep to climb. He was trapped!

Then Sheriff Kinsale pushed his way free of the clawing brush, wheezing like a walrus through his luxuriant handlebar mustache. He stopped, frowning uncomfortably at Eddie.

"Now, boy," he said, "I don't like this any more'n you do. You'll come peaceable, won't you?"

Eddie's shoulders sagged. He knew the sheriff wouldn't have found him unless Calico had told about this spot. He was right, then. His father had betrayed him.

"I'll come," he said huskily. "I haven't got any reason to stay around here any longer."

Later that afternoon, Apples stood peering dejectedly out of the pen, wondering why Eddie didn't come to see him. He felt lonesome and strangely uneasy. Where was the boy? He'd never been this late before.

Suddenly Eddie appeared from the brush at the edge of the meadow. Apples' heart leaped and he started forward, only to stop uncertainly. Why was Eddie walking like that, head all bent over until his dark hair hid his face? There was a big, heavy man walking behind the boy. They reached the wagon and stopped. Eddie looked over his shoulder at Apples. There were tears in his eyes. The heavy man glanced at Calico, who was standing stiffly beside the cabin. Then the man looked at Apples, and blew uncomfortably at his mustache and said in a wheezing voice: "Well, if you want to say good bye to him, Eddie, I guess I can wait five minutes."

Eddie turned to look at his father. Calico held out his hand, started to say something. Eddie's face grew tight and set.

"You don't need to say anything," he said. "You didn't have to send the sheriff after me, neither. If you wanted me to go, all you had to do was ask."

Without waiting to hear what his father would answer, Eddie went over to the horse. "I've got to go, Apples," he said, stroking the animal's neck with a shaking hand. "I'd like to take you with me, but I'm afraid your leg wouldn't stand up under that long trip. Maybe after a few weeks, when it's really healed up, I'll come back and get you."

Apples began to whinny and paw the ground as the boy finally turned away and walked back to the wagon, biting his lip to keep from crying.

Again Calico tried to speak. "Eddie," he finally managed, "you understand how it is. I just couldn't keep you here any longer. I had to give you a chance to be something better than a tramp horse-runner."

Eddie didn't answer. He just climbed stiffly into the wagon and sat stiffly waiting for the sheriff to follow. The latter looked helplessly at Calico, then clambered into the wagon.

Apples watched the wagon roll away. Where were they taking Eddie? Calico was watching, too, a bitter expression on his lean face. Then he turned and went inside. Apples heard him muttering, and then a great crash came, like some piece of furniture being hurled against the wall. After that everything was quiet.

For a long time Apples remained with his head hanging over the top bar of the corral. He felt a deep loneliness. But surely the boy would be back before nightfall. He had never left for long before.

Apples began to pace restlessly, looking off toward the mountains. The mare was up there somewhere. It turned his attention in another direction. He remembered the fight, and the other Appaloosa. Memory of the battle brought back a fragmentary feeling of the fear he'd known before Devil's flashing hoofs and sharp teeth.

It would be difficult to determine whether that was why Apples had been unable to kill the other animal when he had the chance. Was he really afraid? Or was it a sense of the kinship he had known when he had been reared beside the other horse that looked so much like him? In that moment of conquest, looking down at Devil, had he again been reminded of the time when they had run together in the green meadows, played together in the cool streams, eaten the tender bluegrass side by side. Was that what had stopped Apples, or was he really a coward?

The strange uncertainty was still stirring in the stallion when Calico appeared once more. The man shuffled moodily into the corral. He filled the grain fan, as if to pour it into the feed troughs. Then he set it down, forgetting it completely, staring off toward the mountains. The horses began to whinny. Calico looked up in surprise.

"Yeah," he said absently, "I guess you're thirsty."

He walked out the gate, letting it shut behind him, and shambled to the well. He pumped a half bucket of water. Then he stood there, hand on the pump handle, staring off down the road in the direction the wagon had taken.

Apparently forgetting the water, as he had the grain, he wandered back toward the cabin, stopping a couple of more times to stare off down the road. Finally, shaking his head, he shuffled inside.

Hungry and thirsty, the horses bunched up along the fence, whinnying, looking longingly at the water. A couple of them pushed Apples against the gate. His leg got pinched beneath the gate and the post. The gate swung open a little. Had Calico forgotten to latch it?

Apples poked his nose in the gap, pushing the gate wider. Then he forced himself through. Another horse followed him. As Apples realized he was free, all his wild instincts took over. Tossing his head, he whinnied shrilly and ran for timber.

He halted at the trees, looking back. The thought of Eddie had stopped him. In all the world, Eddie was the only human who had been kind to him. How lonely he would be without the boy. He remembered the long hours Eddie had spent with him while his leg was healing. It was as if he could hear the friendly voice again, making the pain so much easier to bear, as it talked on through the long nights—as if he could feel the gentle hands, rubbing the soothing oil into his leg. And the comradeship they had known during the long, hot days of fading summer, while Eddie was helping him to walk again. Loneliness for the boy struck through him, turned him back.

Just then Calico appeared at the door of his shack. When he saw the horses out of the pen, he shouted and began to run after Apples. It sent a streak of fear through the stallion. Again his wild instincts took possession, and he turned to flee.

He ran with the wind blowing his mane and the syrupy odor of heated pitch in his nostrils. He headed automatically for his old range, over in the Snakes. He headed for Paiute Cañon, where he had run as a colt, where he always headed when hounded by man. Would the bay mare be there? They had returned many times to the sanctuary, and she had probably gone there when she had escaped from the men.

He could not run long, for his leg began to ache. He slowed down to a trot, then a walk. The leg throbbed and hurt from the unaccustomed exercise. He had to stop and rest, grazing through the cured mountain grasses, drinking at creeks. When he started once more, his leg still hurt, and he was limping badly. He thought of the boy again. More than anything else, he wished Eddie was with him.

XIII

The rugged, snow-capped summits of the Tetons looked as if they had caught fire when Eddie woke the next morning.

For a moment he lay there, watching the mountains change color with the rising sun, drowsily enjoying the soft mattress and clean sheets. He had to admit that this was better than a bunk. And was he hungry? He smiled, sniffing the coffee and bacon on the air. There'd be fluffy biscuits, too, and eggs and stewed peaches like there had been when he was here the last time. Golly, would he dig into them!

Then Eddie stiffened. He remembered why he was here. Calico didn't want him around any more. Bitterness darkened his eyes. And there was that constant ache of longing for Apples. What good was a soft bed or a nice breakfast beside these? He had to go to school, too!

Eddie wondered desperately what school would be like. He'd never had a book of his own or been inside a schoolhouse. What he knew had been taught to him by his father. He thought about it all the time he was dressing in the new clothes Mrs. Hembre had brought him, the white shirt and wool pants, the clumsy brogans, heavy as buckets of coal, that squeaked when he walked. If only he could wear his old moccasins, he groaned to himself. What would he do if the kids laughed at him?

He had about made up his mind to duck out of the window when Mrs. Hembre called from the foot of the stairs that breakfast was ready. He heard Polly's clear voice answer from her room down the hall. Then she was running lightly past his door.

"Come on, Eddie," she said. "We'll be late for school."

With sudden shyness, he waited until he couldn't hear her footsteps any more. Then, reluctantly, he started out the door. He needed school, he thought, about like he needed two heads.

The kitchen was just as he remembered it, the bare floor white from lots of scrubbing, the red-checked tablecloth a bright spot of color in the room. His wind-burned face tightened under his long black hair and he dropped silently into his chair. They were all smiling at him but he couldn't bring himself to smile back. He saw Pa Hembre's eyes grow sober and Polly stir unhappily. He heard Ma Hembre's anxious sigh as she took the biscuits from the oven. Then she smiled, watching his eyes.

"It's a fine morning, Eddie," she said. "You being here makes it better yet. We want you to feel this is your home."

Eddie fidgeted with his spoon. He didn't know how to answer. He stared at her sweet, motherly face, touched with the morning sun, and his heart began to thud. It always did that when he looked at her. She brought back thoughts of his real mother.

"That's right," Pa Hembre said heartily. "And you'll feel more at home yet when you get to know the boys and girls at school."

"I'd rather not go to school," Eddie said thinly. "I won't fit in."

Pa Hembre stared. "Not fit in?"

Eddie caught his frowning glance at Ma. Stubbornly Eddie said: "I'm getting pretty old."

Ma Hembre came over and put her hand on his shoulder. "You're not too old. Any boy who can catch wild horses can do fine with spelling and arithmetic. Won't you do it to please me, son?"

A tremor ran across Eddie's bitter young face. Ma Hembre's hand on his shoulder almost broke down his resolve. He blinked hard. He was dimly aware of Polly, stepping on his toe and clearing her throat. From the head of the table he noticed Pa Hembre staring at him, genial face settling into stern lines. Grimly he wished they'd all let him alone but he knew they wouldn't. He muttered: "I . . . I don't need schooling."

"Eddie," Pa Hembre said sharply, "this stubbornness won't get you anywhere. You're going to school, and that's final. Eat your breakfast now so you can get started."

Eddie felt Ma's fingers tense. Polly's bright eyes pleaded with him across the table. Slowly he picked up his spoon, knowing he was licked.

"All right," he gulped. "I'd rather fight a grizzly, any day, but I'll go, if that's what you want."

The schoolhouse was a good ten minutes' walk from the Hembres'. Eddie started out with Polly, right after breakfast, the girl chattering and laughing and telling him all about the kids he would meet. A block down the street they came upon the same black-haired boy Eddie had seen from the window the first time he had come to the Hembres'.

"This is Dan Kinsale," Polly said. "He's the sheriff's boy."

Eddie knew he shouldn't dislike Dan Kinsale for being the sheriff's son. Or dislike the sheriff, either. After all, the man had only been doing his duty, bringing him in. But it wasn't any use. He found his fingers knotting into fists, felt a flush come to his face. He didn't even want to talk to this fellow.

Dan Kinsale seemed unaware of the anger seething inside Eddie. Swinging his books by a strap in one hand, he sent a sidelong grin at him. Casually he jumped to the rail fence and walked along, holding his hands out to balance himself. It was an obvious challenge and Eddie couldn't ignore it. He climbed up and started following Dan. But the brogans made him clumsy. He wasn't used to them. Suddenly he missed his footing and fell off. He hit the ground with a thud that shook his whole body. Dan Kinsale jumped off lightly, grinning at him.

Eddie got to his feet, face scarlet. He knew he was acting like a fool, a little kid, yet somehow he couldn't take such humiliation in front of Polly Jane. Despite himself he said: "Bet I can beat you to the corner."

Dan looked surprised. Then he grinned again and started to run. Eddie followed, catching up. For a moment he was in the lead and held it. Then his feet got to dragging in the heavy shoes. Try as he would, he couldn't get up any real speed. The curly-haired boy beat him to the corner easily and stood there, waiting for him.

"That wasn't very hard," Dan taunted. "What'll we do now?"

Helplessly Eddie glanced at Polly. More than anything he wanted her to be proud of him. But what could he do in these shoes?

At that moment June Weatherby appeared in the doorway of the schoolhouse and rang the bell. Polly started across the street toward the teacher but Eddie hesitated. The sight of the schoolmarm, looking untroubled and lovely in her pink, flowered dress, was like a blow to the stomach. If it hadn't been for her, he'd still be out with Calico. His heart thumped harder and he half turned to run. Then Polly called and he knew it was too late.

"Come on, Eddie," she said. "I'll go in with you."

Like a roped calf, he started after her, dragging back with every step. Then they were inside and all at once he found himself the target for dozens of inquisitive eyes. Coloring hotly, he glanced around the packed classroom.

A titter ran through the older children. He looked at the blackboard filled with nice, even writing and remembered his own careless scrawl. A few of the kids he knew, the rest he didn't. His glance returned to June Weatherby, who was standing behind the big desk up in front.

"Take that empty seat in the front row, Eddie," she said, smiling at him.

Again that titter ran through the back of the room. Eddie knew why. Only the littlest children were sitting in front. He felt a stab of anger at the schoolmarm.

"There'll be no more of that," she said, looking around at the tittering children. Her cheeks were pink and her eyes flashed. "As you can see, it is the only vacant seat left. Now if you'll come up here, Eddie, I'll give you your books."

Eddie clumped up the aisle, shoes squeaking at every step, and took the books she handed him, a geography, an arithmetic, and a history book. He had studied the same books in his father's cabin. But knowing the lessons wasn't everything. He'd never recited them to a roomful of unfriendly kids before. He turned around and slid into the empty front seat. It was far too small for him and his feet stuck away out. They looked big as a house. The scrubbed little boys and girls on either side looked soberly at his feet, then back at his face.

"Can't I switch with somebody?" Eddie looked around desperately. "It's too little."

"I'd like to let you," the teacher said ruefully, "but you'll have to stay there for now."

"All right, ma'am," Eddie mumbled. Vainly he tried to shove farther down in his seat. In the back of the room the titters grew to guffaws. June Weatherby rapped sharply for order, then picked up a piece of paper. "The first word on the spelling list for the eighth grade today is Mississippi. Eddie, will you spell it for us?"

Eddie stood up. He had learned that word a long time ago with his father. *This will be a cinch,* he thought. But when he opened his mouth to spell it, no sound came out. All these eyes on his back! It made him turn around and look. All he could see were faces, eyes, ears—grinning faces, watching eyes. Dan Kinsale was making some kind of signal to a boy across the room. Polly was frowning—or was she trying to keep from giggling? His long black hair swung into his eyes as he shifted from one foot to the other. His new shoes gave a loud squeak. One of the little girls beside him snickered.

"Try and think," the teacher said kindly. "I'm sure you know it."

He swallowed a big lump in his throat. He began: "M-i-s. . . ."

The lump came again, gagging him. Was there one S or two? He couldn't remember.

"Please, Eddie," June Weatherby pleaded. "I have to get on with the other classes."

He opened his mouth. Somebody giggled behind him. He looked around. One of the little girls was sticking out her tongue at him. Behind her a boy was grimacing and making some kind of signals with his hands. All those eyes! He knew they were just waiting for him to make a mistake. He would be the laughingstock of the whole school. One S or two? He swallowed again, moistened his lips. The kids were getting tired and restless; he was taking so long. He wanted to keep his eyes straight ahead but he couldn't help looking around. Their faces seemed to blur. How could he be so afraid? He'd topped Devil, hadn't he?

"Eddie, Eddie," the teacher said impatiently, regretting that she had ever made the mistake of starting this. But she must go through with it now.

He began again. "M-i. . . ." His voice cracked.

Laughter broke out behind him. He turned around, eyes

blazing angrily, fists clenched. Then he looked at June Weatherby. Why didn't she let him sit down? Couldn't she see how mixed up he was? If he were only home with his father, he could get it straightened out. This was worse than Indian torture.

June Weatherby rapped her ruler on her desk to silence the class. "I'll give you one more chance," she said.

Eddie cleared his throat. "M. . . ."

"Yeah," Dan Kinsale muttered under his breath. "M as in mule."

It wasn't loud enough for the teacher to hear but the class caught it and a wave of shrill laughter swept around the room.

The teacher clapped her hands together several times but they wouldn't stop. At last she turned to Eddie. He couldn't hear what she said, but he understood what she meant. Wooden-faced, he squeezed back into his seat.

The laughter ended in sudden silence and Eddie heard June Weatherby sigh unhappily. "Now who will volunteer to spell the word?" she asked quietly. The curly-haired boy's hand shot up and she nodded toward him. "Dan wants to try it."

Dan stood up and spelled it out in a loud, clear voice. "Correct!" June Weatherby said—but she did not smile.

Dan flashed Eddie a triumphant grin. Eddie stared back at him, a tight look coming over his face. He wondered grimly how Dan would look trying to top Devil.

After what seemed like a million years, June Weatherby rang the bell for recess. As the children slammed down their books and jumped up, she motioned for Eddie to wait. Stony-faced, he remained in his seat, looking past her when she started down the aisle.

She stopped beside him with a little rustle of her flowered skirts. He got a whiff of something that smelled like lilacs. "I'm sorry I had to seat you with the littlest children," she said. "But it *was* the only vacant seat. If I showed you any special privileges, and asked somebody else to take that place, it would only make things worse. Will you believe me, Eddie?"

The bitterness deepened in the boy's dark eyes. That sugary voice! She was trying hard to make him think she was his friend. But he knew better.

"I'm not going to stay with the babies," he muttered.

He saw her stiffen. "You won't be much of a man if you don't stick it out, Eddie," she said. Then her voice turned pleading again and she put her hand on his shoulder. "I'll have a seat built right away, Eddie, when you get over being so shy. Then you'll be accepted as one of them. I realize now that I never should have called on you right away like that, when you were feeling so strange. I thought it would make you feel as though you belonged. I'm sorry, Eddie. . . . Will we try again . . . together?"

Eddie looked up at her standing there, so pretty and pink-cheeked and earnest, and, in spite of his deep hurt, some strange impulse made him want to believe her.

"OK, ma'am," he said. "I'll try."

"Good," she said briskly. "Now maybe if you take this recess to study your lesson, you'll do better tomorrow."

He tried to do as she said but he couldn't concentrate. When she rang the bell and the other children trooped back in, he was still staring blankly at the first page of the geography. The rest of the day was a painful repetition of the morning, although the teacher did not again call on him to recite. It seemed like a lifetime before class was finally dismissed. Eddie saw the pupils stampede for the door, scooping up hats and gloves from where they'd heaped them at the rear of the room. Polly came to Eddie.

"We're choosing up sides for baseball, Eddie," she said. "Will you be on my team?"

He almost groaned. Baseball was something else he knew nothing about. But he realized she'd think he was afraid to face the kids if he refused. He went with her onto the field. She explained to him that there weren't enough boys the right age in town to make two full teams, so some of the girls and even the younger children were included. Already the boys and girls were taking their places.

Dan Kinsale had a ball in one hand and was swinging his arms in the center of the diamond. Polly explained to Eddie that he was on the pitcher's mound. Polly's team had won first up and they ranged themselves on the log that was used for a bench. A boy named Tom Brady took his place before the catcher and Dan began to pitch. Tom let the first one go by and Polly said it was a ball, low and outside. On the second pitch, Tom hit a grounder past the pitcher and beat the ball to first base.

As the game went on, Polly explained about flies and fouls, loaded bases and home runs. Eddie tried to follow, but it was a new language to him and he didn't understand half of what she was talking about. When Ray Sawyer hit a home run, the whole team leaped to their feet, shouting and yelling. But Eddie couldn't join in the excitement.

Then it was his turn at bat. The bat felt awkward in his hands and he didn't know how to stand. Polly tried to give him some advice but he still felt strange and out of place at the plate.

He saw Dan make the pitch and took a wild swing at the ball when it whizzed past. He missed it completely, heard it whack into the catcher's mitt behind.

"Wait'll they're strikes!" somebody shouted. "You

couldn't have reached that with a ten-foot pole."

Eddie settled himself flat-footed in the dirt, jaw clenched. The second pitch came and it looked wide. But just before the ball reached him it curved in, passing his waist three feet away. Too late he realized he should have swung.

"Strike two!" Dan Kinsale shouted. He laughed at Eddie. "Maybe you need some specs, new kid."

Eddie felt his face grow red. The kids were snickering and whispering behind him, just as they had in school. He wiped moist hands on the bat. This time he'd hit it or die trying. The ball came sizzling through the air. He started his swing. At the last moment it took that curve. He tried to duck but it was high and inside. It cracked him on the head. The world seemed to tip. He saw flashing lights and sky-rockets. He staggered backward and fell heavily.

Dazedly he heard the children running toward him. Dan Kinsale was first to reach him, catching him under the arms and helping him to his feet.

"Gee, Eddie, I didn't mean to hit you. . . ."

Eddie's eyes wouldn't focus as he tried to rise. It gave him a warped vision of Dan's face. It looked as though he was grinning. It brought rage boiling to the surface, all the frustration and bitterness that had been building up in Eddie through the day. He tried to tear free of Dan, shouting: "You did that on purpose!"

One of his flailing arms hit Dan in the chin, knocking him backward. Eddie saw anger rush into Dan's face and the boy lunged at him. One of his wildly swinging fists struck Eddie on the side of the head.

Eddie stumbled backward, trying to keep his feet. But his clumsy brogans tripped him and he fell. He rolled over and scrambled up. He rushed Dan and they grappled, hitting at each other, trying for a hold that would spill the other. Once more Eddie couldn't move his feet fast enough and a sudden shift of Dan's weight upset him. Lying there in the dust, he heard the kids yell encouragement and advice to Dan. "Sock him, Dan! Give him one for me . . . !" Then Polly's voice rose clear and high above the clamor.

"Eddie!" she cried. "It's your shoes stopping you."

Suddenly he knew she was right. His shoes had hindered him from the start. He rolled over and came to his feet. He saw Dan coming at him and dodged aside, running for the fence.

"Yellow!" the children screamed. "The new kid's yellow!"

But when he reached the fence, he turned around, tearing off his shoes. Dan had stopped halfway to the fence, thinking the fight was over. When he saw Eddie toss his shoes aside and straighten up, he paused, a look of surprise on his face. Then he started running toward Eddie again.

They met like a pair of wild horses, yelling and pounding each other. One of Dan's blows knocked Eddie backward but this time he didn't trip. He danced aside and ducked in under the flailing arm and hit Dan in the stomach. Then he grappled and hit his opponent in the stomach again. Then he hit him in the face. That knocked Dan down. Eddie stood above him, panting, his long hair falling down over his eyes.

"Get up and fight," he ordered.

Dan rolled over and Eddie let him get to his feet before rushing in. Dan caught the first blow on an upflung arm and ducked under, swinging for Eddie's stomach. But the brogans were not there to slow Eddie and trip him any more. He jumped away from the punch.

Then he rushed back in, striking his opponent's unprotected face and knocking him down again. Dan rolled over, dazed. His nose was bloody and he was blinking his eyes. He started to rise. He looked up at Eddie, standing over him to knock him down again, and sank back. The shouting children fell silent. Seeing the battle was over, Eddie turned and walked out of the schoolyard.

"Eddie!" Polly cried. "Come back."

He turned toward her, without stopping. "I'm going back to wild horses. They treat each other better'n you do." He ran down the street.

Polly started after him. "Wait!" she called. "Please, Eddie. . . ."

For a moment he paid no attention. On and on he ran, down the road that led out of town. Apples, at least, would be glad to see him. But Polly's footsteps kept following, her voice calling: "Eddie . . . wait . . . !"

He began to slow down, then he stopped. When she caught up with him, she was panting hard and could hardly speak. She grabbed his arm so he couldn't get away while she gasped out: "You've got to stay, Eddie. Beating Dan Kinsale isn't all there is to it. Your real fight is learning to live with people. If you run away from that, you're just as big a coward as if you'd run away from Dan."

He didn't look at her. He kept his head turned away and took his time answering. But he didn't miss the worried, disappointed look that had come over her face. He squirmed uneasily. He'd expected her to admire him for whipping Dan; now he realized his staying meant more to her than the fight. It sounded like the same thing his father had tried to tell him, only he hadn't quite understood it then and he didn't now.

"But the kids don't like me," he said tightly.

"How can they like you," she asked, with a sober little smile, "if you don't give them a chance to know you?"

Eddie swallowed hard. Somehow he wanted her to admire him. Suddenly his whipping Dan Kinsale didn't mean much to him, either. He scuffed his toes in the dirt. "All right," he said. "I'll stay."

XIV

Eddie didn't talk much, going to school with Polly the next morning. He held his shoulders straight under his clean, checked shirt, but his hands were cold with nervousness. At the first corner they met Dan Kinsale. The big boy looked at them sullenly, then stalked off. Set-faced, Eddie clumped on. His eyes never left the school up ahead that looked grim as a prison, even when other children appeared from houses along the way and joined Dan. He could hear them talking in low tones to each other and knew it was about him. He felt his face begin to get red.

"Don't pay any attention," Polly said softly. "They're just . . . well, sort of confused. They aren't sure how they feel about you yet."

Eddie started to say something, then shut his mouth hard.

"Besides," Polly continued eagerly, "if they aren't with you a hundred percent, they aren't against you, either, like they were yesterday. Just wait a few days, Eddie. They'll all be your friends. You'll see."

Eddie nodded. He didn't agree with Polly but a bargain was a bargain. He'd go through with this somehow.

The schoolmarm was standing in the door when they came up. She smiled at Eddie and motioned him inside. Once more he found himself the center of dozens of curious eyes as he walked to his seat in the front row. He felt a throbbing in his ears. Grimly he squeezed himself into the little seat.

The first lesson was in eighth-grade geography. June Weatherby rapped on the big globe of the world with her pencil and asked: "Dan Kinsale . . . what is the capital of Tennessee?"

Silence. Eddie looked around. His eyes met Dan's. The other boy frowned and turned his head. So Dan missed questions, too! Knowing that steadied Eddie. He squared around in his seat. Impulsively his hand shot up.

"Well, Eddie?" The teacher looked a little surprised.

Eddie flushed. Gosh, didn't she believe he knew anything? He was so put out at this reflection on his father's teaching that he hardly noticed how quiet the room had grown.

"The capital of Tennessee is Nashville," he said.

"Splendid." The teacher sounded very pleased. "Now the capital of Virginia . . . ?"

He could feel those eyes boring into his back and he wavered. Then he saw Polly smiling encouragement at him and suddenly remembered. "Richmond," he answered.

After that, it was easier. His confidence grew and he managed to answer all June Weatherby's questions, although they kept getting tougher. Finally she asked him to bound Algeria. Her face wore a kind of dazed, yet hopeful, look, as if she were giving him a chance to prove himself, although she didn't expect him to. The question upset Eddie momentarily, but again he rallied. He forgot the teacher, the staring children, even staunch Polly Jane. He only remembered his father, reading aloud to him by the light of a kerosene lamp. . . .

"Algeria's a French colony in North Africa," Eddie said

slowly. "The Mediterranean's on the north, Tunis is on the east, Morocco on the west, and the Sahara's on the south."

A buzz of whispers broke the silence of the room. The teacher held up her hand and the room grew still again. "Well," she said, smiling ruefully, "after that, maybe you'd better change seats with Dan."

Eddie felt a glow of triumph. It was the thing he'd like best of all, with Polly there to see. He started to get up. Then he saw Polly looking at him, and the expression on her face stopped him. She was watching him intently, as if waiting for something. But she wasn't smiling at all; she seemed to take no share in his triumph.

Somehow it made him remember what she had said the day before, about learning to live with people. He looked back at Dan. The boy's face was red and he was squirming in his seat and avoiding the eyes of the other kids. It made Eddie realize what a humiliation this would be to the boy.

Soberly Eddie settled back into the seat, shaking his head. "Maybe I know a little about geography, but my arithmetic's not much better than a first grader's. I'd better stay here till I brush up on that."

June Weatherby looked puzzled. But Eddie saw that Polly was smiling now. And then the schoolmarm smiled, too, as if she understood. "Maybe we can get that other seat built by tomorrow," she said.

As the children trooped out of the schoolhouse at recess, Dan came up to Eddie. His face was red and he had a funny, self-conscious expression. Eddie's heart began to thump. It looked as though Dan was going to make a friendly gesture—maybe thank him for not taking that seat in the back of the room.

But Dan didn't speak, after all. He just shifted from one

foot to the other, staring at the ground. Then he turned away.

A friend! Eddie thought bitterly. *He was probably going to jump me for answering all those questions when he couldn't. Then he lost his nerve.* He turned away, too, only in the other direction. He walked fast, just wanting to get away as far as he could, no matter where. Bleakly he decided there was no way to get along with these kids. What else had there been to do but answer those questions?

At the corner of the schoolhouse a couple of boys hailed him. They were lanky, sandy-haired Tom Brady and chunky, smiling Ray Sawyer. They had laughed loudest of all when Eddie was trying to spell Mississippi.

"Sorry, fellows," Eddie said grimly. "No more laughs. Try some place else."

Tom Brady cleared his throat and began slapping a baseball nervously into his catcher's mitt. "Gosh, Eddie," he said, "we didn't mean anything yesterday. We're always laughing at somebody. You'll find that out when you've been here longer."

Eddie didn't say anything. He just waited, staring at the two boys woodenly. At last Ray Sawyer blurted out: "Want to come over to the diamond and hit some flies for us? A good fighter like you is sure to be a whiz at baseball . . . with a little practice."

"Yeah, come on," Tom urged. "We thought we'd start you with batting."

"Nope," Eddie said shortly. "Not interested." He saw what they were up to. Just wanted him out there so they could poke more fun at him.

Tom Brady frowned. "OK," he said disgustedly. "Come on, Ray. We're just wasting time." He started off, drawing the chunky boy with him.

Just then Polly Jane ran over, curls bobbing. "I thought you kids were going to practice baseball," she said anxiously. "What's the matter?"

"Eddie's not interested," Tom said flatly.

Polly Jane studied Eddie for a moment. "Why not?" she asked. "Don't you feel up to it?"

Eddie looked at her a long time, realizing this was another test. Finally he nodded grimly. "Let's go."

Reluctantly Eddie followed the trio to the diamond. His ears burned at the memory of the other game. *I suppose they'll give me the works this time,* he told himself.

To his surprise, Tom spoke encouragingly. "You've got strong wrists," he said. "That's important to a hitter." Eddie felt a faint glow of pleasure. "Give him the bat, Ray. We'll let Polly catch and you pitch."

Eddie gingerly took the bat, as Tom trotted out into center field. At once a crowd began to gather. Painfully aware of their curious stares, Eddie took an awkward stance.

"You're standing wrong to begin with," Tom told him. "Point your left shoulder at the pitcher. Move your hands closer together. Relax."

Tom pulled the ball back to his chest, kicked out his leg, and hurled the ball like a regular veteran. Eddie swung. The ball plopped into Polly's mitt. Eddie stared blankly at her. She glanced back.

"Try again. And next time keep your eye on the ball. Don't watch the pitcher."

She returned the ball to Ray, and again he pitched. This time Eddie watched the ball. Again he swung. Again it plopped into Polly's mitt.

"You're still not relaxed," Tom said. "Swing with your whole body. Not just your arms."

Eddie was conscious of the other boys and girls watching him. Twice more Ray pitched the ball. Then on the third one, Eddie's bat connected. It popped feebly out toward first base and one of the boys ran in to make the catch. At the same time, however, a shout went up from the children. Polly jumped up and down, pounding Eddie on the shoulders. "You did it!" she cried. "You did it!"

Dan Kinsale was standing out near second base with three or four of the other boys. "Bob caught the ball!" he shouted. "The new kid's out. Let somebody else bat."

"We're not even playing!" Tom shouted at him. "What's the difference if he's out? He hit the ball, didn't he?"

Eddie just stood there, holding the bat, unable to believe he'd hit the ball at all. But as he heard Tom and Polly defend him, he realized how he'd misjudged them. They hadn't brought him out here to make fun of him—and he'd hit the ball. How could such a little thing seem like such a major achievement? He felt almost as proud as if he'd topped the worst bronco of them all!

Eddie's life fell quickly into a new pattern. Mornings he rose, had breakfast, walked to school with Polly. Here he did his lessons and played baseball during recess and after school. Saturdays he helped Pa Hembre at the livery stable and did chores about the yard.

Although they didn't fight again and Eddie tried his best to feel friendly toward Dan, there was still a gap between the two boys. Very soon Eddie had found out that baseball was Dan's obsession. The curly-haired boy would rather play the game than eat, and hoped to be a professional someday. Perhaps this was what made him work his ill-assorted squad of boys and girls so hard. It seemed to Eddie that Dan expected more out of the younger kids than they could give. Almost every day he heard grumbling and complaints from the boys on Dan's team. They were calling him the slave driver, and the tension was showing in their playing. Polly's team had always been the underdog. But now, with Eddie getting better and better, they were beginning to win games.

This seemed to make Dan grimmer than ever, and more than once he had hot arguments with his basemen or outfielders that ended with one of his boys walking off the field in anger.

Eddie talked to Polly about it on the way home one day.

"It's funny," he said. "When I first came, I didn't notice how Dan drove them."

"It wasn't so bad then," she told him. "He's changing."

"What's doing it?"

"Don't you know?" she asked. He glanced at her blankly, to see a wise smile on her face. When he didn't answer, she said quietly: "You."

His eyes widened. "Me?"

"Don't you remember the chip you had on your shoulder when you first came here? You thought everybody was against you . . . Dan most of all, because he was the sheriff's son."

He nodded. "I guess you're right. But he had a chip on his shoulder, too. He still has."

"That's the point. He's always been the leader among us kids. I think from the beginning he was afraid you'd take that away from him."

"But I'm just a green country kid. . . ."

"Who could break wild horses and bound Algeria," Polly said. "And now you're getting better than any of us at baseball. Dan isn't jealous or mean, Eddie. Not really. You just got off wrong with him from the start. Like when you thought he hit you on purpose with that curve ball. I'm sure he didn't."

"I know that now," he said. "But I've tried to change, Polly. I've tried to meet him halfway. I could have taken his seat and made him sit with the little kids that time."

"And he started to thank you for it, but he lost his nerve at the last minute," she said. "That proves he wants to be decent, Eddie."

He shook his head. "I wish I could straighten it out."

She smiled wisely "You'll find a way."

Next afternoon Eddie joined the others at baseball practice. Polly was first up and on Dan's second pitch she hit a pop fly between second and third. But Dolan, the shortstop, ran in to make the easy catch. At the last instant his foot struck a rough piece of ground and he stumbled and almost fell, missing the ball. He recovered quickly and scooped it up, making the throw to first. But Polly was already on the bag.

"I thought I told you to pick up your feet!" Dan shouted at Bud. "That's the third error in two days."

"I couldn't help it," Bud said. "I tripped. . . ."

"Then maybe you'd better go to the bench till you get some eyes in your toes," Dan said angrily.

A moan went up from the others on his team, and the second baseman called plaintively: "Dan, we're shorthanded as it is. We can't bench Bud, with Eddie coming up."

That seemed to make Dan even angrier. "Go on to the bench!" he shouted at Bud. "You won't have to worry about Eddie."

Eddie was already at the plate, and he watched Bud Dolan walk dejectedly off the field. But he knew it would only make Dan madder to say anything, and Dan would just take it out on the others in his team. Dan's face was red as he wound up. It looked like a strike, right across the plate. But Eddie knew Dan's wicked curve now, and waited until the last instant. The ball seemed to take a bounce in mid-air, five feet out from the plate. Only then did he swing at it.

The bat connected solidly with a loud crack. Dazedly Eddie watched the ball soar over Dan's head, over the whole yard, then clear the roof of the schoolhouse.

"It's a homer!" Ray Sawyer yelled. "Run, Eddie! Run!"

Eddie saw Polly darting excitedly for second. At a fast lope he followed her around the bags, while the center fielder circled the schoolhouse after the ball. When Eddie crossed home plate, his whole team was waiting there for him. He was the center of a shouting, yelling crowd, pounding him on the back. The ball had not been recovered yet and even some of Dan's team came in to congratulate Eddie. When the excitement had died down and the girls and boys began to drift back to their places, Tom Brady and Eddie were left alone for a moment. Tom was Dan's third baseman.

"That's the farthest any of us ever hit a ball, Eddie," he said. "Even Dan." He stared at his glove, thumping his fist into the pocket, looking uncomfortable. Then he glanced at Dan, and in a low voice said: "We've been talking about it quite a while now. This sort of decides it."

"Decides what?" Eddie asked.

"Dan's just been getting too hard on us lately. We've decided to elect a new captain. You're the best player of all. I know Polly'd let you go, if it meant being captain of the main team. . . ."

Captain! For a moment Eddie felt a surge of excitement.

This was what he had been working toward all the time, only half knowing it. The final recognition. The final proof that he was accepted by the kids. Nobody could say he didn't belong now.

He even wished his father were here to see. How proud he would be. How proud Polly would be. He wanted to go right over and tell her. Eddie Rivers, captain. . . . Then his whirl of excited thoughts stopped. He saw Dan, standing alone on the pitcher's mound. He was watching them closely, black brows twisted in a frown.

"Does Dan know about this?" Eddie asked.

"He overheard us talking about it yesterday," Tom said.

No wonder he's been so jumpy, Eddie thought. Somehow it reminded him of a stallion he had once seen after it had been defeated in battle over the right to rule the herd. He remembered how sorry he had been for the animal. It had been forced to leave the herd and go off alone while a younger, stronger stallion took over the leadership.

Somehow this was just like that. It would be the final blow to Dan's pride. Fear of losing the leadership was what had made him so ornery lately, what had made him drive his team so hard. Polly had said he wasn't like that at all, before Eddie came.

Eddie looked back at Tom Brady. He was confused now. He grinned uncomfortably. "Let's talk about it later, Tom. Your center fielder's got the ball."

"Sure, Eddie." Tom grinned. "But just remember. We're all for you."

Polly's team got another run before they were put out. As Eddie walked to his position at shortstop, he was still wrestling with his decision. Right now, he wanted to be captain more than anything else in the world. But he knew it would only widen the gap between him and Dan, would

200

probably ruin whatever chance he had left of befriending the boy.

What's the difference? he thought. *Dan sure hasn't gone out of his way to make friends with me. If he wanted to bury the hatchet, he could have done it a long time ago. I've got just as much right to be captain as he has.*

Tom Brady was first up. Polly's first pitch was a ball, low and outside. On the second one Tom connected—a pop fly floating right above shortstop, such an easy catch that even Tom slowed down in his run to first, thinking it was all over.

But as Eddie waited to make the catch, Dan's face seemed to come between him and the ball, lost, confused. When the ball hit Eddie's fingers, they were slack. It bounced out of his mitt onto the ground. He heard a dismal groan go up from his teammates and he looked at the ball, shaking his head in helpless anger at his mistake. Or had it been a mistake?

The second man up hit a hot grounder. It was the second baseman's ball and could have been a double play, with Tom Brady coming off first. But Eddie was still thinking about Dan and ran for the ball automatically. He collided with the second baseman and they both tumbled to the ground with the ball bounding between them. An outfielder got it but there was nobody on second to tag Tom. All the fielder could do was throw to third to keep Tom on second.

The second baseman got to his feet, brushing angrily at his dusty clothes, frowning. "You trying to be a grandstander, Eddie?" he demanded.

Eddie rose, shaking his head. "I'm sorry. Guess I was thinking about something else."

He limped back to his position. He could see Tom Brady

looking at him, a disappointed expression on his face. It tightened Polly up and she walked the next man. Dan was up then. With three men on, everybody was tense. Dan rubbed his foot on the ground, changed grips on the bat, glanced at Eddie. That same expression was on his face. He didn't look tough or mean at all. Just nervous and maybe a little scared. Maybe the same way Eddie had looked that first day at school—friendless, alone, wanting friends, yet going around with a chip on his shoulder because he didn't know how to make them.

The first pitch. A ball, high and outside.

Dan let it go, licked his lips, stared moodily at the plate. Eddie wiped the moisture off his hands.

The second pitch. Dan swung, connected. A grounder, past the pitcher and between second and third. Before he knew what he was doing, Eddie scooped it up. But in that last minute, with memory of Dan's face before him, he knew what he had to do.

Instead of throwing home, he turned and made an excited heave to first, throwing ten feet to the right of the bag. The baseman made a wild lunge to get the ball, but it whizzed past him and went out toward the road. With everybody howling and yelling Dan followed his teammates around the bases.

The first baseman didn't get to the ball until all three runners had crossed home ahead of Dan. And the throw to home didn't get there until Dan was over the plate and safe. Dan's whole team crowded around him, yelling and whooping and pounding him on the back. He was the hero of the hour and forgotten were all the tension and quarreling of earlier in the day. When it had died down, Dan grinned broadly and told Bud Dolan he could come off the bench and take his rightful turn at bat.

Through it all, Eddie stood dejectedly in the infield, pounding his mitt and looking at the ground. He wondered if he had done right. Would his own team hate him now? He saw Ray Sawyer coming over from third. And the second baseman was walking toward him. He was going to get it now.

Ray put his arm over Eddie's shoulder. "That's OK, Eddie. We all have our bad days."

"Sure," the second baseman said. "You just got excited."

Eddie felt a warmth run through him. "Thanks," he said huskily. "I guess I've got a lot to learn yet."

The game went on. But the play seemed to take the heart out of Polly's team. Dan's team got seven more runs before they struck out. As Dan's team walked out into the field Tom Brady halted a moment beside Eddie.

"What happened?" he asked. "I never saw anybody lose his head so bad."

Eddie nodded, looking at the ground. "I guess I'm just not sure of myself yet, Tom. Maybe you jumped the gun about making me captain. It looked like I was getting good, but it was just beginner's luck."

"Maybe you're right," Tom said awkwardly. "Maybe we better wait a while."

"Sure I'm right," Eddie said. "It'll be a long time before I'm as good as the captain you've got now."

Dan's team held the lead his play had given him, so that the game finished with a score of twenty to seven. In the dusk, the teams broke up and started home. Polly joined Eddie. She glanced at him in a troubled way. He didn't know exactly how to feel. Should he try to explain? Before he could speak he heard somebody behind them and turned to see Dan Kinsale.

The boy joined them hesitantly. He was red-faced, embarrassed-looking. It was the same expression he'd had when he'd seemed about to thank Eddie for not making him change seats. At the last instant, Eddie thought, he was going to lose his nerve again. But he didn't.

"Hi," he said awkwardly.

"Hi," Polly said. "It's been a long time since you walked home with us."

"I guess so." Dan walked by the fence, looking at the ground. He grimaced. "I guess I've been sort of rough on my kids, haven't I?"

"They know how you love the game," Polly said.

"It's more than that," Dan said. He sent a sidelong glance at Eddie. Then, with an embarrassed grin, he put his hand on Eddie's shoulder. "Don't feel bad about those fumbles, Eddie. Anybody could have made 'em. You just need a little more practice."

"I wish I could throw like you," Eddie said.

"That's one thing I can't teach him," Polly said.

Dan's grin broadened. "Why don't you come out early tomorrow. I'll give you some tips."

Eddie felt a glow come to his face in the dusk. "Thanks, Dan," he said. His voice sounded husky. "I sure need some help."

They were at Dan's house now. His grin grew embarrassed again. "Well," he said awkwardly, "be seeing you."

Polly and Eddie walked on through the growing darkness. At last she turned. Her eyes had a strange shine to them. "You had that pop fly right in your hands."

"Slippery fingers."

"You could have made that throw to first with your eyes closed."

"My eyes *have* been closed . . . until now."

"They wanted you to be captain, didn't they?" she asked.

"I guess so."

"It meant a lot to you."

"It meant more to Dan."

"You're right," she said. "He isn't so afraid of you, now that he's sure you won't take his place." She nodded knowingly. "I thought you'd find a way."

"You aren't mad at me?" he asked wonderingly.

"There are a lot of things more important than a baseball game, Eddie."

He smiled into the dusk. "I know that for sure now, Polly."

XV

The second Friday in November was Eddie's birthday. He hadn't told anybody, yet he thought about it, off and on, all day. Always before, there had been some little gift from his father on the breakfast table. Its absence this morning had left him with a queer, lonesome feeling.

Just before school was dismissed that afternoon, June Weatherby came over and put his copybook down on his desk. "Will you please stay and copy your history lesson over, Eddie?" she asked. "I couldn't read some of it." She smiled at him a little.

"All right, Miss Weatherby," Eddie said. Inside, he felt put out with himself for agreeing so readily. Lately he'd found himself doing this more and more. Was he getting to be a softy?

The schoolmarm rang the bell and the other children

jumped up with a cheerful banging of books and clattering of feet. Stifling a sigh, Eddie turned to a fresh page in his copybook and began to write. For half an hour he toiled, being careful to form clear, round letters. When he had finished, he took it up to the schoolmarm. She glanced at the first page and smiled approvingly.

"That's a big improvement, Eddie. You did it with good grace, too. You've changed a lot. Your father will be pleased."

Eddie tried to smile back, thinking how little she knew about things. His father didn't care about him much one way or another. Hadn't he forgotten his own son's birthday? And he didn't even have Apples to make a fuss over him any more. Eddie turned and left, walking slowly out the door and across the empty schoolyard. He wondered vaguely why everybody had gone home so early but the thought soon passed in the wave of homesickness he was feeling.

A wind had sprung up. There was a smell of winter in it, coming down off the mountains. It made him think harder than ever about his father. Bits of their life together flitted through his mind. Riding a mountain trail in the freshness of the early morning. Lying beside a campfire, watching the stars, while his father pointed them out and named them. June Weatherby coming with the sheriff while he hid in the haystack. He remembered his father jabbing the hay for him, pretending he couldn't find him. But most of all, he remembered the day his father sent him away, standing so tall and grim outside their cabin.

Eddie walked on slowly, staring at the ground. A tumbleweed rolled past him, driven by a sudden gust. He felt the wind's chill fingers rumpling his hair and tugging at his sweater, but he hardly noticed. He was thinking how miserable he'd been that day he left his father, how lonely since. And yet—he liked it here, too! In a sudden flash of understanding he had to admit it. There was something about having friends his own age, about going to school with them, and coming back to a well-ordered home that satisfied another part of him. Gradually, out of his confusion, one idea emerged. He needed them both. They were both a natural part of life. Yet how could that ever be? His father had to stay where he was to make a living. And anyhow, he didn't want his. . . .

Oh, forget it! he thought. *What's the good? I'd better get along home and see if there's something Ma Hembre wants me to do.*

But it looked as if neither Ma Hembre nor Polly was home when he finally turned in at the gate. The shades were drawn and everything was quiet. Dully he opened the front door and stepped inside. The darkness and stillness made him feel more lonesome than ever. Dejectedly he started toward the stairs. *I'll go and change into my old Levi's and get at that woodpile,* he thought. Then suddenly he heard a muffled giggle. The next instant the window shades snapped up. He wheeled, dazzled by the sudden light.

"Happy birthday, Eddie!" shouted a dozen voices.

In the wild hubbub of laughs and shouts that followed, Eddie stood there, staring around. Girls and boys were popping up from behind the sofa, the chairs, and the big old square upright piano in the corner. Eddie grinned sheepishly. He knew now why the schoolmarm had kept him after school and why the schoolyard had been emptied so early. To Eddie, who'd left things as usual when he went to school that morning and who had never attended a party, all this was pretty hard to take in. The room was decorated with gay streamers of colored paper and great boughs covered with yellow autumn leaves. What looked like borrowed chairs stood in a row. A donkey, cut out of black paper and minus a tail, was pinned to a sheet stretched along one wall. A kitchen broom stood beside it, evidently part of some game. Through the double doors opening into the dining room, Eddie saw June Weatherby and Ma Hembre putting food on the table. He blinked disbelievingly. Was all this for him?

"Welcome to your birthday party, Eddie!" Polly cried, eyes dancing with excitement.

Everybody whistled and cheered. Eddie felt his throat choke up. "G . . . gosh!" he stammered. "I didn't think anybody knew."

Suddenly a tall man rose from a chair in the corner. Pop! Eddie started to rush into his father's arms, speechless with happiness. Then he stopped dead. *I'm too big for that,* he thought, feeling like a fool. A battle began inside him. He wanted to forget the past, to know again the closeness and warmth he'd had with his father before—and he wasn't sure he ever could. For weeks now he'd been living with a sense of betrayal. It made him suspicious of his father. Was there something behind this visit here today? He stood there helplessly, not knowing what to do or say, a tall overgrown boy with a tense dark face and unhappy brown eyes. Then his father solved things by picking up something that leaned against his chair. It was a new bat.

"Happy birthday, Eddie!" He smiled, holding it out.

Eddie took the bat stiffly. "Thanks," he mumbled.

"That's all right, Eddie," Calico said. He waited as though expecting his son to say something more. Only Eddie couldn't think of anything. He heard the children moving impatiently behind him and for just a second he saw a tired, old look settle down over his father's smiling face.

I'm not showing up very well, he thought. *Guess Pop's not so pleased with me, after all.* Then it came to him what to say, and he wondered fiercely why he hadn't thought of it in the first place.

"How's Apples?" he blurted out. "Did you ride him down?"

Calico shook his head. "Apples is a little off his feed."

"What's the matter?" Eddie asked anxiously.

"Nothing much. His leg's fine. Don't you worry, Son."

Eddie had a sick feeling his father wasn't giving him a straight answer. Why? He could think of no reason. His doubt and suspicion flared up again. Yet why should his father deceive him about Apples? Sooner or later he would be bound to know, if anything serious was wrong. Standing there, seeing the smile on his father's face, it almost seemed that Calico was glad to see him. Why had he come to the party if he hadn't wanted to? Then there was the swell new bat. . . .

Someone nudged Eddie. He turned mechanically to see Jane Weatherby standing between the dining room doors. Her cheeks were pink, her lips smiling.

"All right, children," she said gaily. "The party has officially started. How about singing 'For He's a Jolly Good Fellow' to Eddie, then we'll eat and play games. Afterwards, you older ones might like to square dance. But we'd better start or Eddie's father won't be able to stay for it all."

Polly played the accompaniment on the old square piano with the schoolmarm's sweet soprano leading them, high and clear. The whole group joined in as if they meant every word. A lump rose in Eddie's throat. Was this really happening to him—Eddie Rivers—who'd hated school and had a fight the very first day? A warm sense of belonging filled him, a kind of happiness he'd never dreamed of feeling since leaving home.

As the song ended, everybody made a rush for the dining room. Eddie and his father were left alone in the middle of the parlor. Eddie studied Calico anxiously from the tail of his eye. He wanted to tell him all the things he had thought about on the way home but he didn't know how to start.

"Come on, Eddie!" Polly called.

"And hurry, for gosh sakes," Tom Brady groaned. "We're starving."

Eddie turned. He guessed he wouldn't try and explain, after all. It would sound kind of silly. His father was happy with things the way they were. You could tell by the big smile on his face. *He hasn't really missed me,* Eddie thought.

Blushing and stumbling, Eddie made his way to the head of the table. He sat down to a burst of whistling and cheering. After that, he didn't try to speak confidentially to his father, although Calico sat right next to him.

If Eddie hadn't been so unhappy, he would have gotten great pleasure out of the chicken sandwiches and potato salad piled high on his plate, and the steaming mug of hot chocolate standing beside it. But somehow he couldn't eat much. His eyes kept turning to his father, who was laughing and joking and having a wonderful time. Then he choked and couldn't swallow anything.

At last Ma Hembre went to the kitchen and brought back a big white cake with fourteen tiny lighted pink candles on it. She bustled forward and set it down in front of Eddie with a beaming smile.

"You're to cut it, Eddie," she said in her kindly way. "But first try and blow the candles out all at one time. If you do, you get your wish."

The room grew quiet. Eddie drew a deep breath, and

blew. As the last candle flickered out, he shut his eyes tightly. *Let everything come out right for Pop and me,* he thought. Deep in his heart he believed his wish was foolish. The lonesomeness and the belief that his father didn't want him had become part of him.

When the cake was cut and eaten, June Weatherby took charge. First they played a game especially for younger children called musical chairs. Eddie was bashful and hung back. But the others kept after him and before long he was taking part as happily as anybody. Yet, when he bumped into his father during the rush and scramble, his pleasure in the fun faded suddenly. For Calico said—"Excuse me."—in a polite voice as if Eddie were a stranger.

After playing Tin Tin, come in, another children's game that involved the broom, they pinned the tail on the donkey, then cleared the room for a square dance. June Weatherby asked Calico to do the calling and sat down at the piano. Soon her fingers were flying over the keyboard in a lively tune that made Eddie want to tap his feet. But he had never danced in his life before and lingered shyly in a corner. The others came and got him, though, and pulled him along into the dance. When he stepped on their toes and missed the calls, they just laughed. And pretty soon he got the hang of it. Caught up in the contagion of high spirits and comradeship, he stepped it off with the best of them.

"Swing your partners," Calico called, "gents to the left, ladies to the right . . . !"

Eddie's eyes turned to his father, standing on a kitchen chair, clapping his hands. In Eddie's confused mind it looked like his father had never been so full of fun.

Then the music stopped and everybody except Eddie crowded around Calico, joking and laughing. But Calico didn't seem to miss Eddie at all. He was too busy poking

Tom Brady playfully in the ribs and feeling the muscle on Ray Sawyer's arm. Blindly Eddie turned and slipped out into the hall.

Suddenly light footsteps came hurrying after him. Then he felt a gentle hand on his arm. "What's wrong, Eddie?" June Weatherby asked. "You don't seem to be having much fun. Is it because your father's acting as if nothing's wrong between you? He's just pretending, Eddie."

"I don't think so," Eddie said miserably. "He laughs and jokes and. . . ." His voice broke.

"He doesn't want to spoil the party," June Weatherby broke in earnestly. She drew the boy around toward her. "Look, Eddie. You really don't think your father betrayed you, do you? Don't you see it was the only way he could get you to come down here?"

He stood there, looking into her level eyes, not saying anything. All his worry and confusion seemed to leave him. *It's true,* he thought wonderingly. *I should have figured it out for myself.*

Maybe he had figured it out. Maybe an understanding of it all had been coming together piece by piece during these last weeks, but pride and humiliation and bitterness had kept him from seeing it clearly. It had taken this day to bring it all into focus.

June Weatherby smiled. "You do see, don't you, Eddie? Now go and tell Calico before he leaves." She gave the boy a little push.

Calico had found his hat and was saying good bye to Ma Hembre.

"I'll walk out front with you, Pop," Eddie said. "I've got something to tell you."

"Won't the others miss you?" his father said in that stiff, polite way. "The party isn't over yet."

"The schoolmarm will fix things," Eddie said.

Calico nodded, and led the way through the hall and out onto the front porch. Here the two stood for a moment in silence.

Then Eddie squared around, facing his father. There was nothing in the world but the tall lean man in the high-crowned hat. The mechanical smile was gone from his face now. It was lined and tired-looking, and there was a shine to his eyes, almost like tears.

Eddie suddenly realized how he'd misjudged his father. All that laughing and joking during the party had only been to cover up what was really inside. Calico had wanted to say so many things, too, just like Eddie, and had been unable to. They were both out of the same block. And this realization suddenly freed Eddie, breaking the dam of his pride. All the words he'd wanted to say poured out. He told his father how he thought he'd been betrayed, how lonely he'd been. How he'd hated school and fought the very first day.

"But now it's different," Eddie said. "You had to do it that way, and you were right. I'm willing to stay and finish, if that's what you want."

Calico put his hand on Eddie's shoulder, gripping it tightly. The haggard lines were gone from his face, but that brightness was still in his eyes. His voice seemed to tremble. "Aren't we a couple of fools? If you hadn't said that, I might have gone away without telling you how I feel. I thought you were still sore at me. I thought maybe I'd done the wrong thing, after all. But now it's going to work out, Eddie. You can stay here and have a dad, too. I got a bid for the horses from the Army that'll give me enough to buy the old Tolliver place on the edge of town. In a few months we'll be together again."

Eddie could hardly believe his ears. *My wish came true,*

he thought dazedly. He was all choked up again and he couldn't say what he wanted to. But this time he didn't have to. They understood each other. His father's grip on his shoulder relaxed. "I've got to go now," Calico said.

Eddie accompanied his father to the corral behind the house where Midnight was hitched. They said their good byes and Calico stepped reluctantly into the saddle. He smiled down at Eddie. But just before he turned the horse away, a troubled look came into his eyes.

As Eddie watched his father ride away, he felt his new-found happiness fade. Had Pop been thinking about the same thing he had in that last moment? What was really wrong with Apples?

XVI

Eddie had planned to wait until Christmas vacation to visit his father. But the question of Apples burned in his mind ceaselessly after his birthday. Finally he could stand it no longer. Thanksgiving was coming up and he would have four days off from school. Eddie told the Hembres he wanted to be with his father that week-end. Ma Hembre wanted him to stay with them for Thanksgiving, but Pa Hembre must have seen the ferment in Eddie, for he agreed to let the boy go.

They wanted to drive Eddie up in the wagon, but he wouldn't take them away from their Thanksgiving dinner. He had traveled the trail often and knew it well, and finally convinced them it would be safe for him to go alone. Pa let Eddie ride the big Hembre mare and early Thursday morning the boy bid them all good bye and started out on the long, familiar ride.

Ma Hembre had packed him a lunch and he was so eager to reach the cabin that he ate in the saddle. Early in the afternoon he topped a rise and saw the well-remembered building with its pattern of pole corrals and pens. Excitedly he thumped heels into the big mare and loped her down the road. But as he pulled up by the pens, he saw that Billygoat was not in sight. That meant his father was off running horses. And Apples. Where was Apples?

Frantically Eddie circled the pens, looking vainly in the black shadows of the sheds, the stalls. Finally, at the corner of the last corral, he stopped. He had to admit it. Apples was gone!

He understood now what had made his father answer him so strangely at his birthday party. The Appaloosa had been gone even then—had gotten away somehow—and Pop had not mentioned it, knowing what a blow it would be to Eddie, hoping to find Apples before Eddie came to the cabin. And that's where his father was now—out hunting the horse.

Moodily Eddie stared into the corrals, trying to decide what to do. Midnight was in the pen with another pair of horses. Eddie felt sorry that in his anxiety over Apples he had neglected his old pony. He went inside and Midnight trotted to him, nickering happily. He put an arm over the satiny neck, stroking it, while Midnight nuzzled him. He couldn't stay put here, waiting, while his father was out hunting Apples. He had to help somehow.

He tried to think where Pop would be hunting. At last he remembered the Indian he and his father had met in the Snakes, and what the man had said. The Appaloosa had been born in Paiute Cañon, always returned there when men chased him. The Indian had been talking about Devil, then. But if the horses were twins, that went for Apples, too. If he'd been born there, perhaps he, too, went back when he sought a real hideaway.

Eddie grew excited again with the possibility that he was right. It seemed the most natural thing in the world to start planning. Grimly he set about gathering all the portable food in the shack, extra clothes, blankets. He put the pack on one of the spare horses, then saddled Midnight. He turned the Hembre mare in with the one remaining horse, saw that they had enough feed and water for several days, closed up the cabin. Then he mounted and started into the mountains.

On every side the russet mantle of autumn lay across the shadowed cañons and stained the hillsides with vivid hues. The bright red and gold of frostbitten chokecherry made a crimson splash along the edges of the trail. The leaves of the mountain ash shimmered like silver in the last of the sunlight. But there was a hint of chill, of dampness in the air, that told Eddie there was snow somewhere ahead.

With night, the boy made camp, staked out Midnight and the pack horse, built his fire, cooked his meal. The darkness was full of strange, frightening sounds. Somewhere far off a wolf howled. Even with his exhaustion, it was hard to sleep.

He crossed south of Jackson Lake the next day and rose into the Snakes. The shaggy heads of the mountains were shrouded in haze. He knew that meant storm, up ahead of him, in the highest peaks. It grew colder as he crossed the river and rose through the passes. He sought familiar landmarks and was able to follow them pretty well. Toward afternoon, however, he reached the haze. It closed about him like a heavy mist. He kept riding but he couldn't see anything. Finally he stopped, unable to decide where he was.

The panic began to rise in him as he realized he was lost.

He got himself under control again. In the mountains, when you were lost, it was a good rule to keep going down. He turned his horse off on a steep slope and reached a valley and followed along it. The mist thinned, and he saw, stretched out ahead of him, the jackstraw pattern of corrals and a house. Maybe they could tell him where he was. He rode up to the door, dismounted, and knocked. In a moment it was opened. Haskins stood there.

Eddie gaped at him in surprise. He hadn't realized this was the man's ranch. Always before he had seen it from above, and it looked so different up close.

"I . . . I'm hunting Apples," Eddie gulped. "I figured you could tell me the way to Paiute Cañon."

Haskins scratched his bristly black beard, shaking his head in wonderment. "This is getting crazy. Calico was by here this morning. He was hunting Apples, too."

"Calico?" Eddie echoed.

"Yeah. He said Apples got loose that day they took you down to town. Calico wanted to find him before your birthday, so he could take him to you, but he couldn't do it. He's been through here half a dozen times, trying to pick up Apples' trail."

"Which way was he headed this time?" Eddie asked hurriedly.

"You can't go on in this weather, son. There's a storm brewing up above."

Eddie caught his arm. "I've got to go. Pop and Apples are all I've got in this world. If you won't tell me which way he went, I'll go on anyway."

Haskins frowned, finally shook his head. "You're a stubborn little cuss. I guess, if you got this far alone, you can take care of yourself all right. Calico thought that sooner or later Apples would drift back to Paiute Cañon, where he was born. This time Calico was on a fresh trail, and it was heading in that direction. He said he thought it was the wolves driving Apples back to his old stamping ground."

"Wolves?"

Haskins nodded. "A whole pack of 'em, according to the tracks Calico was following. They'd tail Apples till this storm busts. When he's beaten by the wind and the snow till he's too tired to run, they'll pull him down."

Eddie tugged his arm. "Which way? Which way?"

"You follow this valley north to Jackson Creek. Stay with the creek till you reach headwaters. That's Loon Lake. Paiute Cañon begins on its north side."

The boy wheeled back to his horse.

"Hold it a minute." Haskins's voice stopped him. The man turned back inside, came out a moment later with a shaggy bearskin coat. He handed it to Eddie. "You better put this on. That denim jacket ain't fit for the weather you'll meet."

Eddie slipped into the warm coat, grinning at the man. "Gee, you're sure different from last time."

Haskins grinned sheepishly. "I guess I have acted pretty mean. But Calico told me them Appaloosas are twins. When I realized I'd been blaming Apples for what Devil did, I felt like a fool. If it hadn't been for you, I would have killed Apples a couple of times. I wish I could help you now. But if I left my ranch, Devil might come in and take what studs are left."

"You've helped me enough," Eddie said. "I won't forget it."

He mounted again. Haskins looked at the ominous haze shrouding the peaks, held out his hand, as if about to protest once more. Then he saw the stubborn, set line of

Eddie's face, and dropped his hand wordlessly. The boy gigged Midnight forward, pulling the reluctant pack horse behind.

Eddie followed the valley upward until it became a pass, filled with the lonely howl of the wind. Already that wind was beginning to carry feathery flakes of snow against him. The fir and pine gave way to the tamarack and twisted juniper of higher altitudes. A mountain sheep appeared on a ledge far above, its curving horns outlined against the sky. In a darkening day, Eddie found Jackson Creek. The trail following its bank became a ledge, slippery with ice. The chill wind buffeted the boy, eating through the thick coat until he was shivering constantly. It made him think of Apples, somewhere ahead, hounded by those wolves.

Eddie had lost all track of time when he reached the lake. The wind was a gale now, whipping snow against him in a smothering curtain. Eyes squinted against it, he followed the shore of the lake until he reached the mouth of a cañon lying between two steep ridges of the mountain.

He drove Midnight into the cañon, hoping against hope that he would sight Apples ahead before the storm closed down completely. The howl of the wind deafened him; snow whipped against him in gusts so strong it almost tore him from the saddle. He could not see ten feet ahead. He felt the trail rise beneath him again, another ledge. Then Midnight stumbled.

Eddie tried to pull him up. But the horse had slipped on the icy edge of the shelving trail. He fought to stay erect for an instant. Then Eddie felt the horse toppling over, felt himself pitched from the saddle.

He struck the cushiony snow, sank deeply. Choking, gasping, he began to fight like a wolf in a trap. Panic knotted his stomach. His heart beat a fierce tattoo against his ribs. Then his feet struck something solid. It was bare rock, beneath the snow. He followed the spine of it out of the drift and stood up, sleeving snow from his eyes. He could not see Midnight anywhere.

Slowly, painfully, Eddie made his way back through the drifts to the trail. He was sopping wet and shivering from the cold. But still he could not see the horse. He called. There was no answering whinny. The storm blotted out everything. Eddie's heart sank, and he remembered something his father had told him. The surest way a man can kill himself is to get lost in a blizzard without his horse.

XVII

When Calico Jim reached the bottom of Paiute Cañon, he halted Billygoat and his pack horse. The storm buffeted at him, howling like a hundred devils. If he hadn't lost the wolf trail, he would have reached here yesterday.

The wolves had chased Apples into a spur cañon on the other side of the lake. Following their trail late in the afternoon before, Calico had lost the tracks in the hard rock slopes of the cañon. It had taken him until night to find it again. Unable to follow it by dark, he had been forced to camp. In the morning, the tracks had led him up the steep side of the spur cañon, across a mesa, and down into Paiute Cañon. Already the storm had been building. Before the snow blotted out everything, Calico had been able to see that the wolves were still hanging on, driving Apples, waiting to pull him down.

But now the snow was falling so thickly that Calico couldn't see ten feet ahead, much less find any tracks on the ground. The best he could do was push blindly on into the cañon, hoping that Apples would stay on the bottom. If the stallion took another trail up to the ridges or the mesa tops, he would lose him completely. But even that was a faint hope, for he was already more than a day behind the Appaloosa. Those wolves might have already pulled him down.

Calico knew what a blow the loss of the horse would be to Eddie. He felt a deep sense of betraying the boy by letting Apples in for this. It was what drove him on into the cañon, against his own better judgment. A man was a fool not to seek shelter in this storm. But he knew he wouldn't be able to face Eddie again if Apples were killed.

The wind fought Calico savagely. It shifted back and forth. It dealt him quick blows from the flank, like a cougar teasing his prey. Then it howled about his head like a wolf pack. Then it ripped at his coat like a grizzly trying to tear him to ribbons.

Suddenly he seemed to see movement ahead. He pulled Billygoat up sharply, blinking his eyes. Had he imagined it? He wiped snow from his eyes with a soggy sleeve. There it was again. He put his heels into Billygoat's flanks. The mule grunted disgustedly and plunged on through a deep drift.

Then Calico could see that the movement was an animal—a horse! He pushed Billygoat harder, the pack horse coming heavily behind. The animal ahead took shape and color.

"Apples!" Calico shouted. "Apples!"

Then he stopped, for he could see the animal clearly now. It wasn't Apples. It was the Appaloosa's mate, the bay mare, floundering toward him in the drifts.

"Sulphur and molasses!" Calico exclaimed. "How did you get here?"

★ ★ ★ ★ ★

A mile up Paiute Cañon, Devil was throwing a fit. It was back in a sheltered cut-off, where he had driven his band to escape the main force of the storm. He was circling them, kicking up snow like a plow, as he sought the bay mare. A young stallion tried to drift away, and Devil nipped at his heels. The young horse jumped back with a whinny of pain. Devil ran on around the band, snorting in rage.

Where was that mare? She had been with the band a few minutes ago. She had been with them for two days now. Devil had brought her across Jackson Hole with the two mares he had stolen from Haskins, and had joined his main band here in Paiute Cañon. They had been on a high meadow yesterday, when they heard the wolves. They had seen Apples go by, in the cañon below, stumbling and limping, followed by the sinister shadows of the wolves.

The bay mare had tried to escape then, apparently wanting to help Apples. But Devil had prevented it, herding her back into the band on every attempt. He had kept close watch on her all that night and this morning, until the storm had blown up. Then he had driven his band for the shelter of this cut-off. He stopped circling them, realizing at last that she was not among the band. What would draw her away? Apples again? Could the other Appaloosa have evaded the wolves and come back into Paiute Cañon? Had the mare caught his scent on the wind, or heard his whinny during a lull in the storm?

It angered Devil beyond caution. He had gone through too much getting that mare to lose her now. She could not have gotten far away. Knowing fear of the storm would keep the rest of his band here, he turned out of the cut-off into the main cañon.

As soon as he left the sheltering jaws of the cut-off, the

fury of the storm caught him up. The howl of the wind deafened him. The blown snow blinded him. He sank belly deep in some of the drifts. He sought the shelter of an overhanging cliff and stood quietly, snorting, blinking his eyes. Getting his directions again, he plowed once more into the snow. Then, plunging through a drift, he came into a sheltered spot where the dense timber had guarded the ground from the snow. It was powdered across the rock faces here only inches deep. He stopped short. On the other side of the shelter, huddled in a crevice of rocks, was a human! Devil strained to see more clearly. It was the black-haired boy, Eddie.

Apples was in Paiute Cañon, too. The day before, the wolves had chased him through the cañon and out into the rugged mountains beyond. But he had returned, for even then he had been failing. The constant flight had worn him down. He knew that he could not go much farther. It was the age-old instinct of self-preservation that had caused him to make a great circle through the mountains and come back to the cañon where he had been born, because he had known his first safety here. His mother and father had protected him from just such menaces as these wolves. It was natural that he should wish to make his last stand here.

It had not all been running. Many times he stopped with his back against a cliff or a great rock, snorting in defiance. Sometimes the wolves had tried to attack. But he had sent more than one of them back with a deep wound from his sharp teeth or a broken leg from his deadly hoofs. Now, he knew, he would soon make his last stand. They saw how beaten down he was by the storm. Struggling through the deep drifts had sapped the last of his strength. He was numb with cold and stumbling with exhaustion, and their next attack would be the final one.

Without knowing it, Apples passed the cut-off where Devil had left his band. He floundered on through knee-deep snow. With half-blind eyes he made out the dim, fluttering shapes of the wolves on his flanks. There was a lull in the wind, and a long howl took its place. He saw a rocky slope rising from the fog of wind-blown snow ahead of him. That was as good a place as any to make his last stand. There was a big rock he could stand against to protect his rear. They would have to come at him from the front, and he could go down fighting.

But as Apples neared the rock, he stopped. Was that a wolf? That big shape ahead of him? It couldn't be. He stumbled on for a couple more steps. It was a horse. An Appaloosa! Devil!

Apples stopped short in surprise. There was a human approaching the horse. It was the black-haired Eddie! Too exhausted to understand the situation right away, Apples watched as Eddie staggered up to Devil, talking to him in a low voice.

"Apples," Eddie said, "it's me. Can't you see? It's Eddie. I've come to help you." He was approaching Devil, hand outstretched. "I've come to take you back."

Devil stood rigidly, pink nostrils flared, a crazy look in his eyes. As Apples finally realized what Eddie meant to do, he let out a shrill whinny and started stumbling toward the boy. But the storm sounds blotted out his warning. Eddie walked right up to Devil, grinning confidently now, reaching out to pat his neck.

"I knew you'd remember me, Apples. We're going to be together now, you and me. I. . . ."

As the boy touched him, Devil let out a wild scream and reared up. One of his flailing hoofs struck Eddie's chest, knocking him to the ground. Devil reared above the prostrate figure, eyes rolling crazily in his head, that killer scream rising above the howl of the wind again. Floundering toward them, Apples saw that Eddie was too dazed by the first blow to move. In another instant the boy would be trampled to death.

Forgotten were the wolves. Forgotten was Apples' exhaustion. He lunged forward with a challenging whinny. His bad leg buckled and he almost fell, but he gave a vast lunge with his powerful haunches. It threw him against Devil just as the other Appaloosa came down. The blow knocked Devil aside. His lashing forehoofs missed Eddie's head by inches. He recovered himself and wheeled, with a raging squeal, to charge at this added foe.

Apples dodged aside clumsily, snapping at Devil's throat as the horse went by. He missed and his teeth popped like a gunshot. Devil wheeled again, and for an instant the battle stopped. The two animals faced each other like statues, in that utter stillness which always precedes a fight to the death between two stallions. Eddie groaned and rolled over. Apparently he was remembering the other fight, for he came to one knee, shaking his head, crying out:

"Apples, don't . . . he'll kill you . . . !"

Ignoring him, the two horses rose up on their hind legs and went at each other with bloodcurdling bugles. They met in mid-air, hoofs flailing, teeth popping. One of Devil's sharp hoofs struck Apples' head, almost knocking him off his hind hoofs. Dazed, Apples felt Devil's teeth sink deeply into his shoulder. The pain ran like fire through him and he twisted away in a frantic effort to escape.

He flailed wildly at Devil's head. He felt one of his hoofs strike the Appaloosa's brow, saw Devil reel back under the blow. He came down on all fours and charged into the un-

225

balanced horse, knocking him off his feet. Devil rolled away beneath him, but Apples lunged after him, rearing up above his twisting body.

"You've got him!" Eddie yelled. "Finish it now, Apples, finish it . . . !"

But something held Apples back. He knew he was in a position for the kill. But he could not bring himself to trample the horse beneath him. It was those vague memories again—memories of the two of them in this cañon, frolicking together through the green meadows, rolling together in the cool waters, sleeping together at the feet of the same mother and father.

Devil took advantage of that momentary hesitancy, rolling from beneath the deadly hoofs and scrambling to his feet. Then he came back at Apples with a rush. All his weight rammed into the other horse, knocking him off balance. Apples tried to wheel away, but his long run was telling on him. Exhaustion seemed to hobble his feet. They would not move as quickly as they should. They tripped him up, and Devil lunged against him once more.

Those teeth gnashed at Apple's throat. He whirled, trying to avoid them. Devil reared up, striking for his shoulders, his head. A blow dazed Apples. Devil rammed against him once more, knocking him to the ground.

Apples looked up at the killer reared above him, too dazed to move. He saw the crazy, savage look in Devil's eyes and knew he was through. In that instant, Eddie cried out and ran for Devil. He threw himself against the horse, knocking him off balance.

Devil staggered backward, then whirled on the boy. Again those hoofs flailed. Again Eddie went down. And again Devil reared above him, that crazy killer look making his eyes cold and vicious.

In that fearful instant, Apples stumbled to his feet. He saw he would have to make his choice now. If he didn't kill Devil, the horse would kill Eddie. Those memories of his colthood with the other Appaloosa were blotted out. They were blotted out by other memories—memories of soft hands and a gentle voice. Of the long nights in the shed back at Calico's, with a black-haired boy sitting up with him, rubbing his leg, patting his neck, pleading with him to get well.

As Devil started to come down, Apples lunged at him again. His teeth caught at the other horse's unprotected throat, hung on. Screaming in pain, Devil twisted away. He tore loose and tried to wheel into position. Apples followed with a lunge. His bad leg gave way beneath him and he almost fell. He stumbled erect to see Devil coming at him. His eyes were filmed with exhaustion. It was like lifting a great weight to rear up and meet the other horse, but he knew this was his last chance. He had to finish it now, or both he and Eddie would die.

Eddie lay on the ground, too dazed from the second blow of Devil's hoofs to rise. Snow was blowing like a thickening scarf across the dim outlines of the battling horses. The boy could barely see the wolves, hanging back, sitting in a circle on their haunches. They were licking their slavering jowls and waiting for the end of the battle, when they could rush in and pull down the weakened victor.

The battle was carrying the twin Appaloosas farther and farther away from Eddie. During a lull in the howling wind, he could hear the sodden impact of flesh on flesh, bone on bone, could hear the gunshot pop of teeth coming together, the squeals of pain, the screams of rage. Then he saw one horse go down. The other reared up, brought his forehoofs down heavily on the fallen animal's head. The downed

Appaloosa gave a spasmodic lunge, fell back, lying still.

The other horse reeled away and stopped, swaying, almost falling. Eddie forced himself erect, stumbling toward the animal. Desperately he sent his plea through the uproar of the storm. "Apples?"

XVIII

Calico Jim had first heard the furious sounds of the battle during a lull in the storm. He had been a half mile down the cañon from the fight, but the insane screams had been carried clearly to him. The little bay mare had snapped her head up, fighting savagely to free herself of the lead rope he had put on her neck. Calico urged Billygoat ahead, but even the mule could not keep up with the impatient mare. Finally she was pulling both the mule and the pack horse along in her wake as she floundered through the deep drifts toward the sounds of battle.

Calico thought it was Apples, fighting off the wolves. He already had his gun out, keeping one hand over the muzzle so it wouldn't clog with snow. Before he reached the scene of battle, however, the sounds stopped. There was only the battering of the wind again.

Then, dead ahead, he heard the dismal howl of a wolf. He straightened in the saddle, then booted Billygoat so hard that the mule jumped ahead with a disgusted grunt. They charged through the last of the snow and came upon the scene of battle.

There was one Appaloosa down, and one standing. Beside the horse still on its feet stood Eddie. He had hold of its mane and was looking fearfully at the wolves, now slinking in a circle around him. When he saw Calico, he cried out.

"Pop, it's Apples! Get those wolves out of here. They've been chasing him for two days and they aren't going to get him now. Get them out . . . !"

Calico swung off Billygoat, leaving him ground-hitched. He snapped the lever on his Winchester and took a shot at the nearest wolf. The beast leaped in mid-air, howling in pain. It was only stung, but it ran off with its tail between its legs. Calico fired at the next one, saw him cringe from the bullet whining over his head, and turn to dart away. The others faded into the storm. They were man-wise and knew a healthy fear of a barking gun. Seeing that they were driven away, Eddie called to Calico again.

"It's Apples, Pop! He saved my life. He isn't yellow! I told you he wasn't yellow! He didn't want to kill Devil that last time because Devil's his brother. Some folks might say horses aren't that smart, but I know they are. He couldn't kill Devil 'cause Devil was his brother. But when he saw Devil would kill me, he knew he had to kill him. It was the only reason he did it, the only reason he did it, Pop, to save my life . . . !"

There was hysteria in Eddie's voice, and Calico realized it was the babbling of a boy near the point of collapse. "Sure, Jigger, sure," he said quietly. He went close and put an arm around Eddie's shoulders, warming him. "We'll just find a tight spot where we can sit this storm out and then we'll take Apples back. He'll be all yours again. You came a long way to get him, and he's yours for good now."

Eddie gulped, unable to believe his ears. "But I thought you wanted to make a show horse out of him and sell him."

"That was before I realized how bad you wanted to make him your own. If you'd go through all this for him, how could I take him away from you?"

"You mean we can take him back to town with us and keep him there while I go to school next year?"

"If that's what you want."

"It sure is," Eddie said. He turned to the horse. "How about you, Apples?"

The Appaloosa threw up his head and whinnied. It was feeble but it sounded happy.

"Looks like we got the OK from the boss," Calico said. "Everything's all right now."

Eddie leaned over and put both arms around Apples' neck. "It sure is," he said. "Sulphur and molasses, it sure is!"

About the Author

Les Savage, Jr. was born in Alhambra, California and grew up in Los Angeles. His first published story was "Bullets and Bullwhips" accepted by the prestigious magazine, Street & Smith's *Western Story*. Almost ninety more magazine stories followed, all set on the American frontier, many of them published in Fiction House magazines such as *Frontier Stories* and *Lariat Story Magazine* where Savage became a superstar with his name on many covers. His first novel, *Treasure of the Brasada*, appeared from Simon & Schuster in 1947. Due to his preference for historical accuracy, Savage often ran into problems with book editors in the 1950s who were concerned about marriages between his protagonists and women of different races—a commonplace on the real frontier but not in much Western fiction in that decade. Savage died young, at thirty-five, from complications arising out of hereditary diabetes and elevated cholesterol. However, as a result of the censorship imposed on many of his works, only now are they being fully restored by returning to the author's original manuscripts. Among Savage's finest Western stories are *Fire Dance at Spider Rock* (Five Star Westerns, 1995), *Medicine Wheel* (Five Star Westerns, 1996), *Coffin Gap* (Five Star Westerns, 1997), *Phantoms in the Night* (Five Star Westerns, 1998), *The Bloody Quarter* (Five Star Westerns, 1999), *In the Land of Little Sticks* (Five Star Westerns, 2000), and *The Cavan Breed* (Five Star Westerns, 2001). Much as Stephen Crane before him, while he wrote, the shadow of his imminent

231

death grew longer and longer across his young life, and he knew that, if he was going to do it at all, he would have to do it quickly. He did it well, and, now that his novels and stories are being restored to what he had intended them to be, his achievement irradiated by his powerful and profoundly sensitive imagination will be with us always, as he had wanted it to be, as he had so rushed against time and mortality that it might be. *Trail of the Silver Saddle* will be his next Five Star Western.